A Guilty Mind

A Guilty Mind

A Detective Cancini Mystery

K. L. MURPHY

WITNESS
IMPULSE
An Imprint of HarperCollinsPublishers

EPub Edition JUNE 2016 ISBN: 9780062491626
Print Edition ISBN: 9780062491671

10 9 8 7 6 5 4 3 2 1

*For David—who makes me laugh every day,
and for Cameron, Thomas, Luke, and Meredith—with all my love*

Chapter One

"I DIDN'T MEAN to kill her," the man said, his voice on the tape muffled. "It was an accident. I swear."

Straining to make out the words, the therapist leaned forward and listened for his own response. "Tell me about it," he prompted. "What happened?"

Alone in the office, the hour late, the doctor settled back in his chair, stroking his trim brown mustache. In the few moments of silence that followed, the only sound was the faint whirring of the tape player. When the patient spoke, he described the violent death of the girl. Twice, he stopped, his words stilted and sentences fragmented. Brows furrowed in concentration, the therapist made occasional notes in the book lying open on his desk. Clicking off the tape, he replaced it with a cassette from a more recent session. On the new tape, the doctor spoke first. "Why were you afraid of her?"

The patient snorted. "Humph. You'd know if you'd ever met her."

"But I haven't."

The man's drawl was slow and precise. "And you never will. That's for sure."

"Why not?"

The man sighed. "You know why not." The doctor recalled the patient had waved a well-manicured hand in the air, his lips turned down in a pout. "I don't want to talk about her today. Let's talk about something else."

He stopped the tape. With each session, Dr. Michael pushed harder and dug deeper. If the patient could open up a little more and face the painful memories head-on, they might find some answers. For both of them, he was eager to make this happen sooner rather than later. He chewed on the end of his pen and restarted the tape. "I think we need to clear the air about this, George. Perhaps it would help you to move forward."

"I can't," George insisted, his voice cracking. "Don't you understand that I can't?"

Dr. Michael stopped the tape a second time. He adjusted the glasses on his nose and wrote one word in the notebook: *Afraid.* He tapped the pen against the page. Over the last several weeks and months, Dr. Michael had grown increasingly concerned for this patient. Early on, he'd been horrified by what he'd learned, but later, as George's story unfolded, his feelings had changed. Yes, George's actions were reprehensible, but weren't there mitigating circumstances? Was his pain and suffering justified? The doctor frowned and hit the play button again.

"Okay, but what about the other thing we talked about?"

George had eyed him warily. "What other thing?"

The patient's response surprised the therapist. George had expressed fear and reticence before, but also a deep desire to be free of the past. The idea of confession, of doing the right thing, had once attracted him. "You know what I'm talking about, George. It's time to come forward."

The man had shaken his head, hot anger erasing all traces of his Southern accent. "No, I can't now."

"Maybe not now, but in time."

"No." A redness had risen from his neck to his cheeks.

"Don't give up, George. You're ready. You're—"

"Would you get off it?" The patient had jumped to his feet, his voice thundering. "Just leave it alone. Please."

The doctor flinched, the patient's recorded voice exploded in the empty office. Once again, he paused the tape and stared unseeing at the walls of his office. Maybe he wasn't the best therapist for George. In his profession, he heard secrets every day. Dr. Michael was required to keep those confidences, but this time it bordered on criminal. He ran his hands through his thinning hair. Even with all the progress they'd made, George had begun to fight his advice to come forward and speak the truth. The therapist was convinced something—or someone—was working against him. Even more disturbing, however, were his patient's moods, increasingly erratic, and at times even violent. Maybe he wasn't helping George after all.

The old air conditioner rumbled to life, chugging and blasting puffs of frigid air. As the cooling system drained the power, the lights flickered and died, plunging the doctor into darkness. "Damn." He shivered, cursing the old building's faulty wiring. When the lights came on again, he blinked and rubbed the goose bumps on his arms. As he rifled through the box of tapes, his thoughts returned to George. Dr. Michael suspected the man's guilt, like a virus, had infected every aspect of the patient's life. He believed the only medicine came in the form of a full confession. If George remained silent, he might never recover.

A creaking noise made him look up. He waited, cocking his ear toward the door. "Sandy?" He called his secretary's name and glanced at his watch. He couldn't imagine why she would return to the office at this hour. "Sandy?"

Silence. Several minutes passed and his shoulders loosened. He inserted another tape into the machine. The ancient air conditioner rattled and sputtered a second time. "Ah," he said out loud. Cold gusts of air blew across the back of his neck, and he blinked in the darkness until the shadows disappeared in the light. He shook his head, and pressed play.

"Tell me again about the accident," he heard himself say. "Tell me exactly how it happened and everything you remember."

"What's the point? I wish I never had to think about it or be reminded of it—ever again!"

"I know, but let's do it anyway, okay?"

"Sure. Okay." George had cleared his throat. "When I first went to the boathouse that day, I wanted to take my mind off things, off her. I was cleaning the boat, and she surprised me, showing up without any warning. She started in on me, wanting to end things. I couldn't let her do that, you know, considering the situation. I tried to talk to her but she just wouldn't listen." George had paused. When he'd spoken again, his voice sounded far away, lost in the past. "It was so hot that day, and I remember her skin was sweaty, her face kinda red. I was worried about her, but when I tried to tell her, she just got mad again. I tried to be patient, I did, but then I started to get mad, too."

Listening with his ear turned toward the machine, the doctor returned to making notes. A bang followed by a soft thump made him sit up straight and put down his pen. He froze, hands pressed against the wood of the desk. He waited, but the air conditioner did not rumble to life. Again, he called his secretary's name, and again, there was only silence. As the minutes ticked by and he heard nothing, he felt silly. George and the stories of death must be getting under his skin. With his reading glasses in his right hand, he walked around his desk and stepped through the doorway. The office door remained closed. Eyes scanning the outer office, he spied a fallen picture frame. He exhaled and picked up the frame. The image of Sandy and her husband smiled at him. He glanced around again, shrugged, and placed the silver frame back on Sandy's desk.

Footsteps approached from behind. The doctor's head shot up in the second before the knife ripped into the flesh of his back. Dr. Michael screamed and his knees buckled. The gold-rimmed reading glasses slipped from his fingers and landed softly on the carpet. Dr. Michael fell forward. He clawed at the desk, struggling to keep himself upright. Blood poured out of the ugly gash, staining the cream-colored rug. Disoriented, he reached out for the phone on the desk. As he picked up the receiver, the knife slashed a second time and then a third. The phone slipped from his grasp and hit the desk with a clatter. He could feel the life draining from his body, hear the hollow sound of his own breath. He inhaled through his mouth, pushed up from the desk, and turned his head. Eyes wide, he fell backward. He knew his killer.

"Why? Why?" the doctor gasped.

His assailant said nothing. The killer stepped around the man and replaced the phone, silencing the hum of the dial tone. Dr. Michael slumped to the floor. Blood thumped in his ears. He could hear the raw, ragged sounds coming from his chest. His killer's feet came into view and he saw the knife drop onto the carpet near his glasses. The doctor struggled to crawl away, his hand outstretched.

The gold of his wedding band glittered under the office's soft lighting. The killer reached down with a black-gloved hand and pocketed the wire-rimmed glasses. Paralyzed, the doctor heard the office door open, then click shut.

The doctor's eyes glazed and blurred. He gasped one last breath. Down the hall, the cassette tape played on and the droning voice of his patient drifted across the quiet of the small office.

"I wanted to confess then, but I didn't. Then later, when I had the chance, I still didn't come forward. And then, of course, it was too late."

Chapter Two

Detective Michael Cancini stood over the victim. "Who discovered the body?"

A short, squat, uniformed policeman stepped forward. "I believe it was the guy's secretary." He glanced at a notebook in his right hand. "Her name is Sandy Watson. She came in at eight-thirty this morning, her usual time according to her, and found the victim lying on the floor." Jerking a thumb, he indicated the private office behind him. "She's in there with Smitty. Pretty upset, too. Apparently she's been with the guy for years."

Scanning the outer office, the detective noted a single hallway leading to a coffee room and bathroom. An alcove to his right contained two well-worn leather chairs. A short stack of magazines sat neatly on a wooden table tucked between the chairs. Dozens of medical journals and books filled a walnut bookcase along the wall behind the secretary's desk. A crack ran along the top of the plaster wall from the door to the corner, just below the heavy molding. The building was old, but it was neat and clean.

The office occupied the second floor of a converted rowhouse on a quiet street in D.C. The neighborhood was just far enough from downtown that daytime traffic was light and the street was empty at night and on weekends. Cancini sighed. The murder rate in this section of town was low, almost nonexistent.

"What do ya think, boss?" asked a third officer. "Some psycho patient?"

Cancini didn't answer. He snapped on a pair of plastic gloves and crouched next to the body, careful to avoid the bloodstained carpet around the victim. The doctor lay on his stomach, face turned in profile. The detective shifted his weight, moving a little closer. A white dress shirt, shredded by long tears, clung to the man's back. The deep wounds, covered by blood and fabric, made it difficult to guess how many times the victim had been stabbed. Maybe three, possibly four. Either way, Cancini knew those details would be determined by the coroner. Picking up each of the victim's hands, he inspected them for skin under the nails or any signs of a struggle but saw nothing. Instinct told him the therapist lying on the floor had never seen the attack coming.

The presumed murder weapon lay only inches from the body, blood already hard and crusty on its surface. Bending closer to examine the knife, he dared not move it before the precinct photographer had taken all the requisite shots. A stickler for procedure, Cancini knew from experience how the little things, seemingly insignificant facts like the placement of the murder weapon, could tie the evidence together into a solid and seamless case. He studied the knife from end to tip. Ordinary wooden handle. Large, shiny blade. Very much like the kitchen knife he had in his own home. He made a mental note to have someone check out the brand of knife and where in the city it was sold.

He stood, his glance raking the young officer who'd spoken

moments earlier. "Did you just ask me to speculate on this case, Wilder, after I'd been here all of, what, two minutes?"

Wilder flushed. "Uh, no, sir, I didn't mean anything. I was only—"

"Good. Glad to hear it." His eyes swept the room again, and he peeled the plastic gloves from his hands. He stepped around the front of the desk, circling it slowly. Most of the items on the desk had been pushed forward, leaving the edge closest to the victim clear. He shifted his gaze to Wilder. "It's too early to theorize," he said. "Without any evidence, that is. This isn't an episode of *Law & Order*, you know. It won't be over in an hour."

The two young officers exchanged looks. Wilder stared at the floor. "Sorry."

Cancini said nothing. He knew his own reputation. He didn't tolerate mistakes, laziness, or anything short of his expectations. He wasn't unfriendly, but he wasn't friendly, either. Partners didn't stick around. His last one transferred to Vice after only six months. Smithson—Smitty to the guys in the department—was his latest and hadn't been around long enough to quit. Still, hard-headed and stubbornly ambitious, Wilder often volunteered to be a part of Cancini's team. The detective decided the man was either brave or stupid.

Standing up straighter, Wilder took a breath. "What do you want me to do? Knock on a few doors? See what's what in this place?"

Coming back around the desk, the older detective held up one hand. He crouched again, his bony butt resting on his heels. Turning his face in profile, he looked into the ashen face of the victim. Up close, Cancini saw a slight indentation on the bridge of the man's nose. He rocked forward, his eyes never leaving the man's face. After a moment, he stood, his bones creaking as he uncurled from the floor. "Does he look surprised to you?" he asked.

Both officers took one step closer. "Well, his eyes do look kinda open, don't they?" Wilder said. "But it could be the shock of having someone knife you in the back, you know."

"Possibly," Cancini said. He shoved the rubber gloves into his jacket pocket.

The squat officer bent forward at the waist. "I don't know. Maybe it was the killer himself that surprised the vic. Maybe he knew the guy."

"Maybe." Cancini kept his tone noncommittal. He waved a hand and both officers stepped away, their backs ramrod straight. "It looks like he might have worn glasses. He's got a mark on his nose. Has anyone seen a pair?" Both officers shrugged. Cancini made a note to check with his partner, then nodded toward the door. "Any sign of a break-in? Forced entry?"

Wilder shook his head. "No. I heard the secretary say the door was closed when she got here, but not locked."

"I don't suppose we'd be lucky enough to have any videotape, maybe at the front door of the building?"

"That would be nice, but no," Wilder said. "The security in this building is pretty poor."

"Figures." He brushed his hand over his spiky hair. "How many keys to the place?"

"According to the dead guy's secretary, only three. The doctor had two—kept a spare at home—and she had the third," answered Smitty. The tall, lanky detective stepped out of the dead man's private office.

"How's the secretary doing?" Cancini asked.

"Not great," Smitty said. "I think she's pretty torn up. Blames herself for letting him work late."

Cancini arched one dark eyebrow. "Why would that be her fault?"

Smitty shrugged his thin shoulders. "She's sort of the mother-hen type, I think. The lady says the doc only worked late when his wife was out of town. Otherwise, he left at six like clockwork. Last night he worked late."

Each of the men let that sink in. The time of death would be pinned down by the medical examiner, but if the secretary was telling the truth, the doctor was murdered sometime between six the previous night and eight-thirty that morning.

"Has anyone located the wife yet?"

"The secretary says the wife was speaking at some convention in Chicago. I tracked down her hotel room, but no one answered," Smitty said. "I've got a contact up there who's gonna try and find her at the convention and have her give me a call. Then we'll get her back here as soon as possible."

"When did the wife leave for Chicago?"

"Yesterday morning."

"Okay." He nodded, facing Smitty. "Let's confirm the time she departed and find out if she was seen by someone, anyone, last night."

White-blond hair fell over the slender detective's face. He seemed about to say something, thought better of it, and grunted in agreement. "Anything else?"

Cancini considered the dead man sprawled on the floor. He guessed late forties or early fifties. Plenty of time to make enemies. "Yeah, go ahead and start a check on the guy's family. Find out if there were any kids, ex-wives, bitter siblings. Also, find out what kind of relationship the doctor and his wife had."

"You suspect the wife, boss?" Wilder asked, flinching under the detective's dark gaze.

"Jesus, Wilder. You're giving me a headache," he said. "I have no evidence, remember? I'm just following procedure."

"Sorry."

"Stop saying you're sorry." Cancini rolled his eyes. "Sometimes the insurance money looks good or someone's playing around. Who knows? Let's check on both of those. Still, considering what this guy did for a living, listening to people pour out their personal problems . . . like I said, who knows?" Wilder's head bobbed up and down. "It's wide open right now."

Smitty spoke up. "The secretary keeps the appointment book, knows all the patients by name. She might be able to tell you a few things."

"Good." Cancini scanned the outer office again. His eyes came to rest on the jumble of items pushed to one edge of the secretary's desk. He wanted the crime scene preserved as quickly as possible. "Where's the photographer?"

"On his way," said the uniformed officer with the tree-trunk body. He checked his watch. "He should be here any minute."

"Good. Can you wait for him and make sure he gets everything in this office?" The man nodded. "I want the coffee room, office door, and every angle around this desk and the body."

"Sure, no problem."

"Wilder, I need you to wait for the coroner. And stay with the print guys, too. I don't want anything missed this time," Cancini said. Wilder sucked in his breath but said nothing, nodding.

Cancini looked toward the doctor's private office. He had

a lot of questions for the secretary, but he didn't relish the task. She could be in shock, fragile. She'd had no time to grieve and was about to be bombarded by a pushy homicide detective. Yet it had to be done. She would be at her most revealing without intending to be. Later, when she had time to think about things, she would most likely clam up and hide behind a lawyer, even if she was guilty of nothing. Or worse, she would invoke all the doctor-patient privacy rights that so often stymied a homicide investigation. Such was the way of the modern world. After more than twenty years on the force, the investigations had not gotten easier, even with all the forensic advances. Cancini believed that for every step forward achieved by science, the legal system itself took two steps back. Even a guilty man, a man who had confessed every detail of a horrific crime, could find himself free on a technicality. He squared his shoulders and stepped through the door.

A small woman sat perched on the edge of the couch. Bent forward, she held her head in her hands. Her hair, medium brown and streaked with gray, hung in a short ponytail at the base of her neck. A few stray pieces had fallen loose, partially obscuring her pale, tear-streaked face. He cleared his throat once. Stifling a sob, she lifted her head and blinked. In an instant, Cancini understood Smitty's snap judgment of Mrs. Watson. Her face, kind and compassionate, reminded him of someone's mother or grandmother. Light brown eyes shimmered with tears. The interview would not be easy.

He stepped forward. "Mrs. Watson, my name is Detective Cancini." He gestured at the sofa. "May I?" Her lips quivered. After a moment, she nodded once. He sat and took both her hands, wrapping them in his. "I'm sorry for your loss."

Chapter Three

GEORGE SAT ON the steps of the small bungalow, knees jutting up toward his chest, and breathed in the crisp night air. A nearly empty bottle of Jack Black, swiped from his dad's liquor cabinet, sat next to him. Eyes bleary, he turned toward the drive and the approaching headlights. She was late. He grabbed the neck of the bottle and drank deeply, coughing at the strong taste of the alcohol. Hand holding tight to the railing, he staggered to his feet. Watching the car, he waited.

The battered yellow Toyota rolled to a stop on the gravel drive. He watched her alight from the car and walk toward him, hips swaying with each step. Wavy chestnut hair fell past her shoulders, accentuating almond eyes and an olive complexion. Tall and lean, she brushed at the hair, pushing it off her face. The black stretch pants and white shirt she wore for work at the Red Raider Tavern could not hide the curves of her lithe body. Drawing in his breath, he felt a rush in his stomach at the sight of her.

"Where've you been?" he asked. He heard the slur in his voice and concentrated as he spoke. "You were s'posed to be here an hour ago."

Facing him, she brushed it off. "Bob made me work late because Susie didn't show up."

"You could have called."

She squatted and picked up the bottle, tipping it slightly. Her dark eyes slid back and forth between him and the liquor. "You're drunk."

George started to deny it, then thought better of it. "Yeah, maybe I am." Sinking to the steps again, he ran his fingers through his longish hair. Stubble had erupted across his chin. Sitting next to him, she reached over and touched it, lightly rubbing her fingers across the rough skin. Reaching up, he took her hand in his. "I was afraid you wouldn't come."

"I almost didn't," she said, eyes weary.

The single light on the porch cast shadows across their faces. They sat together for several minutes, holding hands, staring out at the river that ran along the edge of the property. A full moon hung in the cloudless sky, perfectly reflected in the calm waters. Glancing at her, he saw the wisps of glossy hair that caressed her high-boned cheeks in the warm breeze. Closing his eyes, he took deep breaths to counteract the woozy effect of the Jack Daniel's. "I'm glad you're here," he whispered.

She pulled her hand away. "I haven't changed my mind, George."

"But I have." He leaned closer. "Let's get married." Her eyes narrowed. "I mean it," he said. "I'll graduate next month and we can have the wedding right after that if you want."

She looked away. "What about your girlfriend? What about her?"

"I told you I was through with Mary Helen."

"Yeah, right." Sarah stood and took a few steps toward the river, her back to him. "I saw you, remember?"

"That wasn't my idea. It was my father's. He invited her to dinner, not me."

Her back stiffened and she whirled, eyes flashing. "You know, George, I may not be part of your la-di-da society or born with money or anything else for that matter, but that doesn't make me stupid. Even if your father did invite Mary Helen, it's because he thought you were still with her." Hands on hips, her top lip curled into a sneer. "That's what you want, isn't it, George?"

"No," he said, and lurched to his feet.

She yanked her arm away. "Don't touch me."

Hand outstretched, he froze. The young man understood her anger, knowing in his heart it was well deserved. When she'd told him about the baby, he'd been scared, behaving in the immature way many college boys would. But later, after she'd walked out on him, he'd been ashamed. Worse, he realized his affair with the townie girl had turned into something real, something that mattered. Hiding out from his family, his friends, and Mary Helen, he'd spent the last couple of days thinking, making a decision on his own. It wouldn't be easy, but he knew it was right.

"I don't want your pity," she said, eyes boring into his.

Swaying, he made a promise. "It's not pity, Sarah. I want to marry you and raise this baby. I really do." She was quiet, but he saw the doubt in her eyes. He reached out for her again, and this time, she didn't stop him. "I know you don't trust me and you have every reason not to, but I mean it. I've been thinking about it all weekend and I'm sure. Please believe me."

"I don't know." Tears slipped over her cheeks and she brushed them away. "I don't even know what I want."

He pulled her close and stroked her silky hair. She reached up and circled his neck, fingers brushing the hair skirting the collar of his shirt. Kissing her forehead and her cheeks, he moaned. She arched closer to him, quietly sobbing. Without words, he took her hand and led her inside. Together they slowly climbed the stairs to the bedroom, the one he thought of as theirs.

The jarring sound of the telephone interrupted the dream, yanking him back from the past and into the present. The hazy images, both beautiful and heartbreaking, vanished. He lay still, savoring the memory. The phone rang a second time, insistent and loud. Head aching, he stirred. Bright sunlight streamed through the windows and stung his eyes. He glared at the digital clock and swallowed, fighting the rising nausea. The phone rang again. He threw back the covers.

"Hello?" George's throat hurt and his mouth tasted like ash.

"Mr. Vandenberg? It's Sandy Watson from Dr. Michael's office." The woman's voice was little more than a whisper.

He flopped back down and squeezed his eyes shut. "Yes?"

"I was calling to let you know your appointment with Dr. Michael this afternoon will have to be canceled."

"Oh." He sat up again. The extra session had been Dr. Michael's idea. After the way their appointment the day before had ended, George had readily agreed. Had something changed? "Can I reschedule?" He wanted to tell his therapist that the dream was back, more detailed and vivid than ever. "I need to see him."

"I'm sorry, Mr. Vandenberg, that won't be possible." He thought he heard a muffled sound, a cough or a cry, before she spoke again. "If you have an emergency or would like me to refer another doctor, please give me a call at the office."

"But why?" Swinging his legs around, he stood up. "Have I done something to offend Dr. Michael? Did I do something wrong?"

"I'm sorry."

"But—" He held the receiver away from his ear. Mrs. Watson had hung up on him, the loud buzz of the broken connection ringing in his ear.

With a start, George realized he was buck-naked. His slacks, coat, and tie were strewn around the room, apparently flung from his body in a drunken stagger. A pair of leather shoes had been dropped in the hallway leading to the bedroom. White silk boxer shorts were crumpled on the bathroom floor. His wife would not have approved. The quick thought as he spotted his shirt dangling from a lamp brought a smile to his lips. Then, remembering the previous day's session with his therapist, the smile faded. Everything had not gone as he'd hoped and now the dream was coming almost every night. George needed that appointment. Snapping up the phone again, he dialed Dr. Michael's office. Three times he tried, but after repeatedly getting a busy signal, he slammed down the phone.

It took three cups of black coffee and another hour before George felt human again. He drove to his therapist's office. Grumbling, he parked a couple of blocks from the building when he encountered a small traffic snarl. Baffled by the unexplained delay, he walked the remaining distance. The sun, a fireball in the sky, beat down on him, and sweat trickled down his back. Half a block from the office, he stopped short. Four police cars blocked the street and a handful of uniformed officers kept onlookers behind a makeshift barricade. A shiver ran up his spine and sweat broke out on his forehead.

George's steps slowed. A small crowd filled the sidewalk in front of Dr. Michael's building. He shaded his eyes, unsure. Inching forward, he pushed his way through until he was standing in the front of the semicircle of gawkers. Next to him, a young woman wearing a press card scribbled in a memo pad. Every few minutes, she glanced up at the doors, watching for anything new. Straining his ears, George tried to hear the conversation between some of the policemen but caught only snatches of meaningless chitchat.

An uncomfortable, tingly sensation formed in the pit of his stomach. Taking deep breaths as Dr. Michael had taught him, he closed his eyes and concentrated on relaxation. The panic attacks, mild but disorienting, were relatively new for George. He'd never had them before he began seeing Dr. Michael, but lately, like the dreams, they were coming more frequently. He was not a stupid man. The subject matter of their sessions was having an unsettling effect on him, often putting him on edge, making his moods unpredictable. Still, he didn't know why he should be having one now. After several minutes, his breathing slowed to normal. Opening his eyes, he found the young woman staring at him. With a sheepish grin, he shrugged his shoulders.

"Hey," he asked the reporter, "what's going on here?"

Pursing her lips, the woman gave an answer that was short and chilling. "Homicide."

A hum rose in the crowd and she lost interest in him, her attention focused on a dark-haired man who'd just exited the building. A badge hung around his neck. The uniformed officers spread out, clearing a path for the detective. A man of medium stature and size, he was nevertheless a commanding presence at the scene. His eyes, intelligent and world-weary, were deep-set next to an aquiline nose that dominated a hawkish face. He moved with surefootedness, and George watched, mouth hanging open. After a few moments, Mrs. Watson followed. The detective leaned down and spoke in her ear. He gave her shoulder a slight squeeze and steered her toward an unmarked vehicle. George stepped back to make room for the group and trounced on the reporter's foot. She yelped, drawing Mrs. Watson's attention. The secretary's head shot up, her red-rimmed eyes locking on his. He raised his hand in a half wave. She broke into a sob and his hand dropped back to his side. George watched the car pull away, staring long after she was gone and out of sight. As the crowd dispersed, the realization hit him like a punch to his gut. Dr. Michael was dead.

Chapter Four

Coffee. Cancini needed it, craved it like a junkie needed heroin or meth. A few years earlier, he'd given up cigarettes, resulting in a caffeine addiction in overdrive. After the long morning at the Michael crime scene, he made a beeline for the office pot, pouring some of the vile black liquid that passed for coffee into a flimsy paper cup. He gulped as much as he could without scalding the roof of his mouth and considered the questioning ahead of him. Mrs. Watson, the victim's secretary, waited in a room down the hall. She hadn't yet thought to call a lawyer but had insisted on phoning her husband for support. Cancini, sympathetic to the woman's grief and shock at discovering the dead body of her boss, had agreed. At the therapist's office, the secretary's eyes had flooded with tears and her words had been difficult to understand through the sobs. Believing the murder scene itself was making it harder on the woman, he'd suggested she accompany him to the station. He needed the lady coherent.

Cup in hand, Cancini watched Mrs. Watson through a large pane of one-way glass. How much did she know and how much would she be willing to tell? Her pale face, wiped clean of smeared mascara, wore the blank, disoriented expression of a woman who'd unexpectedly lost someone close to her. Was she acting? The detective couldn't say, but he doubted it. Her grief appeared genuine.

He tossed the empty cup in the trash and shoved his hands in his pockets. Watching her blink back the tears, he knew he couldn't walk in blazing with questions. If he came off like a bully, he would never get any answers. However, he had other concerns. How versed was she in patients' rights and privacy issues? Did the doctor confide in her about his patients? What about his wife? His family? How much did she know? Considering the woman's emotional state, the interview would not be easy. Still, his only focus had to be the body sent to the morgue, the body turning colder with each passing minute.

Smitty appeared by his side. "The husband is here. You want me to send him in?"

Cancini shook his head. "No. Let me talk to her first, see if I can get anywhere. Tell him she's in the middle of giving a statement and to wait."

The young detective agreed. "By the way, I confirmed the wife's alibi. She was in Chi-town last night, having dinner with some of the other speakers. About six or seven witnesses can account for her whereabouts."

Cancini glanced at Smitty. "Did you notice there were no pictures of the wife in the doctor's office?"

"Yeah. You think it means something?"

"Don't know, but let's look into the nature of their relationship, interview neighbors, friends, coworkers. Do it kinda quiet, though. If the lady has anything to hide, we don't want her trying to hush anyone up. It's too soon to rule anyone out."

His white-blond hair flopped over his eyes. "I'll get right on it. Anything else?"

Cancini's eyes slid back to the glass. Cancini liked the young man's temperament, his smarts. He hoped it lasted. "I want you to watch the interview, let me know if you have any observations."

"Sure."

He grabbed two fresh cups of coffee. "Mrs. Watson, I'd like to offer my sympathies again for the loss of your boss." He passed her a cup and laid his notebook on the table. Her lips quivered and she blinked, fresh tears threatening to fall. He reached out and took her hands again, just as he'd done at Dr. Michael's office. Her mouth moved, but there was no sound. He held her gaze and squeezed her hands gently. "It's okay. I know how hard this day has been. Losing someone you care about is one of the hardest things there is." This time, she made no attempt to talk, just nodded.

Cancini had insisted on speaking with Mrs. Watson alone. Using compassion wasn't a popular or recommended technique, and he knew the irony of his approach drew snide comments from some of the other men. Most explained it away as good acting, the ultimate bait-and-switch. First gain their trust, then pounce. Cancini, for his part, did nothing to dissuade them or offer any explanation. He suspected Smitty had his own theory about Cancini's soft-spoken manner with witnesses, particularly the families and friends of the victims.

Cancini's eyes never left Mrs. Watson's face. "Let's take a deep breath together," he said. She nodded slowly, and they did. "I'm going to ask you some questions and it's important you answer them in the best way you can." He paused. "This won't be pleasant, but anything you know, any information you have, even without realizing it, could help us find Dr. Michael's murderer." She squeezed her eyes shut, and he waited a moment until she opened them again. "Can you do it? Can you help me?"

"I'll try," she said. "I'll do my best." He relaxed and let go of her hands. "Is my husband here yet?"

"I haven't seen him," the detective said, evading the truth. He didn't want her distracted during the questioning, or worse, given advice that might impede the investigation. "I'm sure you'll be with him soon." He pushed the coffee and a box of tissues across the table. "Mrs. Watson, I'm sorry, but we'll need to start at the beginning again, when you found Dr. Michael." She dropped her gaze. "I understand if you need to take your time."

With an apology, she took a handful of tissues and dabbed at her eyes and wiped her nose.

"It's okay, Mrs. Watson. Whenever you're ready."

"I'm ready," she whispered, taking another deep breath. "I came in at eight-thirty. I come in at the same time every day." Her voice trembled, but she stayed focused on her story, the words slow and deliberate. Lines of concentration deepened on her forehead. "The door wasn't locked. I didn't think much of it, though. Sometimes Dr. Michael comes in a little early to prepare for the day's appointments." She paused and bit her trembling lip. "When I got inside, I saw him right away. He was just lying there on the floor."

"Go on," he said, his voice soft.

"I think I screamed. I'm not sure though. It seems like I would have. There was so much blood, you know. Then I called 911." She stopped again. "That's all there is to tell. I'm sorry."

"It's okay, Mrs. Watson. You're doing fine." He reached across the table and patted her hand. "Did you see anyone else when you arrived at the office? Anyone on the elevator? Anyone or anything unusual?"

She rubbed her forehead. "The only person I saw was Mr. Tebow. He has an accounting office on the first floor. I always stick my head in and say hi in the mornings."

Cancini wrote the name in his notebook. "Did you see or speak to anyone else?"

"No."

"Okay. What time did you leave the office last night?"

"Around six I guess."

"Did you see anyone when you left?"

"No. The travel agency on the top floor closes at five and Mr. Tebow was still there I think, but his door was closed."

He made a note to have all the tenants in the building interviewed before the day was out. "Do you always leave at six?"

"Oh yes, every night. Dr. Michael and I usually walk out together, but Mrs. Michael was out of town, so he wanted to work late."

"Did he do that often?"

"No," she said. "Only when Mrs. Michael wasn't in town. They were very close." She frowned, eyes welling again. "Has anyone contacted her yet? She's going to be heartbroken."

"Yes, ma'am. I believe she's arriving at Ronald Reagan shortly." Making a couple of quick notes, Detective Cancini changed the subject. "How many appointments did the doctor have yesterday?"

"Seven," she said, twisting her wedding ring. "He always sees seven a day."

"Did anything strange happen in those appointments?" Her head came up. "You know, like did anything unusual go on yesterday with any of his patients?"

"No," Mrs. Watson said. "Not that I know of."

"Was he having any trouble with any of his patients?" It wasn't privileged information, he reasoned, if the doctor had already confided it to his secretary. "Maybe any confrontations or anything he might have told you about?"

"You don't think . . ." She hesitated, her eyes wide. "Maybe one of his patients killed him?"

"I don't think anything yet, Mrs. Watson. I'm only trying to find out about the doctor's day. I may need to question anyone who had contact with the doctor yesterday." When she was silent, he probed again. "Had he said anything about any patient giving him trouble or difficulty? Maybe someone was threatening him?"

"Well, no, he didn't say anything in particular. I mean, I noticed things sometimes, about certain patients, but Dr. Michael would never confide in me about his cases. He's a real stickler for privacy and—" She slapped her hand over her mouth, stifling another sob. The detective waited, nudging the tissue box once more. "Oh my God," she whispered, "I'm so sorry. I just can't believe he's gone. It doesn't seem real."

He waited a few minutes, then asked, "Did Dr. Michael wear glasses?"

"He had prescription reading glasses. They were gold."

"Did he need them to work?"

Her brows drew together. "I think so. He wore them quite a bit."

"Okay." Cancini made a note to follow up on the glasses, then asked, "Did he go out for lunch yesterday?"

"He picked up a sandwich and brought it back to the office."

"Okay. Did he go out for any reason later in the day?"

Smitty interrupted then. He bent close to Cancini, keeping his voice low. "The wife's on the phone, calling from the plane. She insists she needs to talk to the lead detective right away, won't talk to anyone else."

Cancini rose. "Smitty, can you bring Mrs. Watson some more coffee?" To her, he said, "I need you to stay a little longer, okay? I won't be long."

Cancini followed Smitty to the phone. "She may know something about a patient. See what you can find out."

"Sure." Smitty hesitated, then said, "By the way, the captain wants to see you as soon as you're done."

Cancini's eyes rolled. A dull pain thudded in his head. "Perfect."

"Sorry."

"It's not your fault." He picked up the blinking line. "Cancini here."

"Detective Cancini." She spoke fast, her voice husky. "This is Nora Michael. Are you the lead detective on my husband's case?"

"Yes, ma'am. I'm sorry about your husband." He wrote her name in his notebook.

"Thank you, Detective, but that's not why I called. Well, it is, but not exactly."

He'd expected to hear sorrow, anguish, and even anger. Instead, he found it difficult to reconcile the confident, throaty voice on the phone with what he expected from a woman whose husband had been fatally knifed in the back. "I'm listening."

"It's about my brother."

"Your brother?"

"Yes. He's dead, too."

Chapter Five

George gripped the heavy glass in his large hands and took a long drink. He tasted the icy vodka on his tongue and felt the cool liquid slide down his throat. He shouldn't be drinking, but why the hell not? At least his heartbeat and breathing had returned to normal. It was that reporter, the one who used the word "homicide." He didn't want to believe it, but there was no other explanation. Surely that look of devastation on Sandy Watson's face could mean only one thing. Dr. Michael was gone—murdered! How? Why? Tossing back the rest of his drink, he ordered a second. The bartender brought a fresh vodka tonic and moved down the polished oak bar.

A large hand clapped him on the back. "Georgie, I didn't expect to see you here after last night, ol' buddy." Wincing at the childish nickname, he shook hands with Fred Trenton, his boyhood friend. The burly man, wearing a collared shirt with powder-blue slacks, plopped onto the barstool next to him. "Man, if I was you, it would have taken me two days to sleep that one off." Nodding at the vodka tonic, he said, "Guess you're a better man than me."

George raised the drink in a halfhearted gesture of cheers. It occurred to George he barely remembered seeing his friend the previous evening.

With his bulk perched precariously on the stool, Fred rested his thick forearms on the bar. Turning to face his old chum, he asked, "Why'd you run out in such a hurry last night anyway? The party was just getting going."

George had only a vague memory of leaving the club. "It was getting late."

"Late?" Fred repeated. "It was only ten o'clock."

George shrugged, sucking on the vodka tonic. "Well, like you said, I guess I'd had enough."

"I'll second that." Preston Cain sat next to Fred. "You must have started into the scotch pretty early, Vandenberg. I tried to call you a cab, but you're such a stubborn asshole, you were gone before I could stop you."

"Sorry," George said. It was true he'd begun drinking early. His session with Dr. Michael that afternoon had been rough and ended badly. Angry and disappointed in himself, George had driven to the club to drown his worries in the best bottle of scotch the place had to offer.

"Doesn't matter to me," Preston said. "It was the manager who thought maybe you shouldn't drive. I'm not your babysitter."

Raising a hand to get the bartender back, George wished they would both go away. He couldn't stop thinking about Dr. Michael. Why would someone kill him? Dr. Michael was a good man. Even in their most painful sessions, the man had always been kind and compassionate. Yet, George had to admit their most recent sessions had been difficult. The doctor pushed harder and with more urgency, and their relationship had become strained. Now, none of that mattered. Everything they'd worked toward, everything George had hoped for, was gone. There would be no more possibility of confession, no more hard decisions to make. George expected to feel some relief. Instead, he was overwhelmed with sadness. For nearly a year, George had allowed Dr. Michael to lighten his burdens. In fact, he'd welcomed the dream of confession until outside forces made the reality nearly impossible. Without Dr. Michael, those same burdens seemed heavier than ever.

"George, how do you see your future?" Dr. Michael had asked in their final session.

Averting his eyes, George remained silent, afraid to give an answer, afraid to speak at all.

When no response was forthcoming, Dr. Michael said, "Correct me if I'm wrong, but I thought that's why you started coming to me. To change how things are, to make things better, to have a chance at a happy life."

He frowned. "I don't deserve a happy life."

"That's not you talking, George. What's happened these last few weeks? You said things have changed. What things? Why have you changed your mind about coming forward?"

"Nothing's different. It's for the best."

"I don't believe that. Something happened. What is it?"

"Nothing," George said. He rubbed his hands across his thighs. "Just let it go, for God's sake."

The therapist sat back in his chair, stroking his mustache, watching his patient. George couldn't meet the doctor's eyes. He folded his arms and clamped his lips into a thin, hard line. A tiny vein pulsed in his temple. "You're afraid of something, or someone." Dr. Michael uncrossed his legs and shifted toward him. "Who is it, George? Who are you afraid of?"

"No one. Goddammit, I'm not afraid of anyone." He jumped to his feet and stabbed the air in front of the doctor. "Why can't you just believe that I've changed my mind?"

"I think you want to confess, George, so something or someone is causing this," he said, his eyes never leaving George's face.

"Well, you're wrong. You don't' know everything, okay?" He gestured wildly, his face reddening. "Why can't you accept that I don't want to play your pointless cleansing-of-the-soul game anymore? Why can't you leave me alone?" George stepped forward, towering over the therapist. Dr. Michael shrank in his chair.

"You need to calm down, George."

"Jesus! Don't tell me what to do! For God's sake, don't I get enough of that at home? I sure as hell don't need it from you." Fists curled tightly, his eyes were dark with fury. Dr. Michael paled but remained in the chair, motionless and silent. George turned away, sweeping a ceramic lamp to the floor, the smashed bits scattering across the floor. Staring at the broken lamp, he felt his anger evaporate. He fell onto the sofa, limp and devastated.

"I'm sorry," he said, words like a moan. "I'm sorry."

"It's okay, George," Dr. Michael said softly, still gripping the arms of his chair.

George raised his eyes. "No. It's not okay and we both know it."

"It's only a lamp," the doctor said. "But this anger of yours goes back to what I'm saying. This is not an easy thing I'm suggesting, George, and I can't make you do it, nor do I want to. I'm sorry if you feel pushed by me. I want the decision to be yours. You're so close. Without this step, it may be difficult for you to overcome your . . ." The doctor seemed to hesitate, as though searching for a word that wouldn't offend his patient. "Your guilt."

George stood awkwardly, a tear slipping from his eye. "I can never be free, Dr. Michael. It's out of my hands," he said, his voice empty of the passion it had held only moments earlier. "I'm tired. Time's up for today, Doc."

He'd walked out, nearly knocking into Mrs. Watson. Brushing by her without a word, he'd gone straight to the club and a fifth of the best scotch he could get his hands on. It was not the kind of day or night that made a man proud.

Less than twenty-four hours later, seated at the bar between two of his oldest friends, men who'd known him most of his life—through college, marriage, and children—he felt painfully alone. They didn't really know him. Dr. Michael did, though. George wished he could have the day back, do the session again and thank his therapist for listening when no one else could. He wiped at his eyes. Now, it was too late.

"Mr. Vandenberg?" George's head jerked up. The bartender stood in front of him. "Your wife's on the phone. Said she hasn't been able to get you on your cell."

"Oh."

"You can take the call over there." He pointed to a small table and phone in the corner of the bar.

Excusing himself, he went to the table and picked up the receiver. "Mary Helen?"

"George! I've been so worried. Where have you been?" his wife asked, her Southern lilt more pronounced than usual.

He took a breath. "Here mostly. Sorry my phone wasn't on."

"You're all right then?"

"Yes. I'm fine."

"You missed your conference call with Daddy this morning." She didn't disguise the scorn in her voice. "Again. I had to explain you called me to cancel for you and I forgot. You know I hate it when you do this to me, George. What's your excuse this time?"

Falling into the leather chair, he decided he was too exhausted to fight with his wife. "I don't have one."

"That's so like you, George. God, you make me so mad."

"Sorry."

"You must think I'm stupid. Why don't you admit that you were out drinking all night, and were too hungover to remember the conference call?" Without waiting for a response, she said, "I'm right, aren't I? And knowing you, when you weren't drunk, you were probably spilling your guts to that quack doctor again. Is that where you were, George? Please tell me the truth for a change."

"Shut up!" Fred and Preston looked over, and he lowered his voice. "Dr. Michael's not a quack and it's not what you think."

For a moment, neither of them spoke. During the brief silence, George closed his eyes and waited, knowing she would demand an explanation. "Okay, George, if it's not what I think," she drawled icily, "then what is it?"

He slumped down in the chair. His heart pounded in his chest. "Dr. Michael is dead. The police were outside his building today."

"What? Oh my God. Are you sure?"

"I'm sure. It's awful. I was in the crowd outside his office and I saw his secretary. She was crying and everything. Some reporter told me it was a homicide."

"Oh my God," she said again.

"I still can't believe it. He's dead, Mary Helen, dead."

"Jesus, George," she said, her voice dropping to a whisper. "What have you done?"

Chapter Six

Mrs. Michael sat across from Cancini, dry-eyed, her back ramrod straight.

"I'd like to offer my condolences again, Mrs. Michael," he said. She nodded once. "I also wanted to thank you for flying home so quickly."

"Of course. I came straight from the airport," she said.

Cancini sat back and studied the widow. She was tall, possibly taller than he. She wore a well-fitted ivory linen business suit and large pearl earrings. No trace of tears stained her smooth skin or mussed her lightly applied mascara. Her manner, icy and distant, contrasted with the sensual curve of her mouth and cheeks. On her ring finger, he spied a plain gold ring. Her fingers, long and shapely, were marred by short, stubby nails.

She pulled a creased piece of paper from her purse and placed it on the table. "I've never believed my brother's death was an accident."

"I'm not sure I understand," Cancini said. He wrote *Brother?* in his notebook.

Nora Michael unfolded the page. "I'm sorry. I'm not making any sense, am I? My brother was killed a year ago in a hit-and-run accident, run down in the street. The police never found the driver or the car. They ruled it an accident. But I never believed that and I still don't." She paused, her tone a little quieter. "Neither did my Edmund."

Her husband had just been murdered, brutally stabbed, and she was babbling on about her brother being killed in a car accident a year earlier. Cancini was baffled. She sounded sane, but so did a lot of people who were stark raving mad. "Mrs. Michael, you do understand that I've been assigned to the murder investigation of your husband, right? I'm afraid I can't help you with your brother's accident."

"No! No, you're not listening," she said, her voice rising an octave. "This is about my husband. That's why I've brought you this." She slid the paper across the table. "It's why I'm more convinced than ever my brother was murdered, too."

Cancini took the page, holding it between his thumb and index fingers. He read the words twice. After a few moments, he raised his eyes to meet her gaze. "If I've got this right, you're telling me you think the deaths are related?"

"Yes, Detective, I do."

He sat back, studying Mrs. Michael. "Okay," he said, "I think I see what you mean."

Her shoulders slumped and she let out a long sigh. "I knew it. They were both murdered then. It's connected."

"I didn't say that exactly." Cancini glanced from the paper to the woman. "It could be important. But I don't know that yet."

Her eyes narrowed. "Could be?" She reached for the paper to snatch it back. "That's all you have to say? It could be important?"

Cancini pulled the page out of reach, leaving the lady's long fingers grabbing at air. "It's evidence, Mrs. Michael, and as such will need to be checked out. The deaths being connected is possible, but until I know more, that's all I can say."

"But the threat is clear!"

"Maybe, but your husband was a head doctor, a shrink."

"That's an offensive expression, Detective."

"Sorry. It could just be a crank note from one of his more colorful patients or former patients."

"Or one of my brother's."

The detective frowned. "Your brother was a shr— psychiatrist, too?"

"Yes. They went to medical school together. After my brother died, some of his patients started seeing my husband. Not all of them, but some." She paused, her dark eyes wandering to the glass. She plucked absently at her skirt. "That's why when the letter came I got so upset. Edmund though, he didn't give it a thought. Said I was making too much of it."

"But you didn't think so?"

"Yes. No. I don't know what I thought."

He looked at the note again. "When was the letter sent?"

She shook her head. "It wasn't sent. It was pushed through the mail slot in our front door. We went to bed one night and in the morning, it was just there, lying on the floor."

"How long ago was that?"

Tiny lines appeared between her arched brows. "A few days ago maybe. I'm not sure the exact day."

"But you didn't go to the police?"

"My husband didn't want to. As I said, he thought I was overreacting, but I knew I wasn't. Sean's death was not an accident." She paused, taking a deep breath.

"Sean was your brother?"

"Yes. Dr. Sean Burns. They could never locate the car that ran him over and it had dark windows and none of the witnesses could give a good description. But I talked to one of the witnesses myself and—"

"What?" Cancini interrupted. "You talked to a witness? On your own?"

She brushed aside his question. "That's not the point. The woman I spoke with said the car sped up when my brother came out of the building. She knows because she works at the magazine stand on the corner and she'd noticed the car circling the block a few times before my brother came out. Then she said the car sped up and practically flattened him to the ground!" The widow paused and rubbed her arms "The detective—Harrison, I think was his name—he wouldn't listen and said he had no proof of anything suspicious."

Cancini examined the slip of paper he held between his fingers. "Did your brother have any enemies? Had there been any threats?"

"No," the lady said, eyes flashing. "And I know what you're going to ask next, but he wasn't in any kind of trouble or anything like that. I had my own suspicions. When Edmund took over some of my brother's patients, I told him I didn't like it."

"Why's that?"

"My brother liked a challenge. No neurosis or paranoia was too much for him. Edmund thought I was being silly. He actually thought it was cute." She waved a hand at the memory. "I don't know how many of my brother's patients he was seeing, but some."

"You suspected a patient then?"

"Yes, but the police couldn't question the patients much because of privilege. Edmund, of course, agreed." She clucked her tongue. "Just like him, too."

"The investigation stalled," Cancini said.

"I guess you could put it that way, but from my vantage point, it never got started. They swept it under the rug and slapped the word 'accident' on it." Her chin tilted up, her full mouth set in a hard line.

"You think the note proves a connection?"

"I do. Like I said, after my brother died, some of his patients began seeing Edmund. I had a bad feeling about it." Mrs. Michael hesitated, cocked her head to one side. "There was one he seemed determined to take. I wouldn't be surprised if—" She stopped mid-sentence when the door slammed against the wall.

"Don't say anything, Nora." A tall man in a gray suit rushed to the woman's side. He placed a hand on her shoulder and glared at Cancini. "Detective, you should know better than to question Mrs. Michael without an attorney present."

Smitty, a why-am-I-not-surprised expression pasted on his face, followed the man into the room and closed the door behind him.

Gesturing for Smitty to approach, the dark-haired detective said, "I wasn't aware she needed a lawyer." Cancini folded the note, careful to touch the edges only. He handed it to his young partner, then whispered instructions to have it placed in evidence and dusted for prints. Aloud, he said, "As far as I know, she isn't being charged with anything."

The attorney looked from the letter to his client. "Nora, is that what I think it is?"

They all watched Smitty leave the room, the note dangling from his fingertips. She touched her lawyer's arm. "Yes, Gerard, and don't get yourself in a tizzy about it."

"I thought we agreed I needed to see that first," the man said, thin lips pursed.

"No, Gerard, you agreed."

He sucked in his cheeks. "Nevertheless," he said, "you shouldn't have turned it over to the police, nor should you have spoken to them without me present. I told you that on the phone."

Cancini leaned back on the hard wooden chair. "Are you suggesting the lady has something to hide?"

"Of course not!" The lawyer wagged a long, bony finger in Cancini's direction. "Everyone has the right to the presence of an attorney, you imbecile, and you know it."

Sitting forward, his face darkening, the detective said, "For your information, Mrs. Michael came to me with this letter. She phoned me and insisted on coming in right away. This investigation is barely under way and I'm happy to take any leads I can get. I think you're getting a little ahead of yourself, Gerard." He allowed a trace of sarcasm to creep into his tone. "But if you think she needs a lawyer, maybe there's something I need to know about." Cancini's eyes lit on the widow. "How about it, Mrs. Michael?"

"How dare you?" The lawyer's pale skin turned a blustery red. "I am merely pointing out that it's in her best interest to have the advice of counsel when she is being interrogated by the police. And don't give me that crap about her coming to you. We both know you'll take advantage of her goodwill given the opportunity. It's my job to protect my client and I don't think there's a respectable attorney in this town who wouldn't do the same."

"Stop it!" Mrs. Michael jumped to her feet. "Gerard, please stop treating me like a child. I know what I'm doing. I may not practice criminal law, but I'm still a lawyer, too." She faced Cancini, one hand on her hip. "Detective, as absurd as this question is, am I a suspect in the murder of my own husband?"

Rising to his feet, Cancini found he had to look up at the widow. In three-inch heels, she stood two inches taller than he. "It's too early for us to have any suspects, ma'am," he said. "I meant it when I said we're just getting started. So for now, the answer is no, but I can't tell you for sure where the investigation might lead."

She stared at him for several minutes, then nodded. Her hand dropped to her side. "Fair enough."

"Detective," the lawyer asked, "is it true that the secretary discovered the body?"

"She did."

"Well, assuming you've had the chance to question her, is there anything you can share with Mrs. Michael? Anything that might shed some light on the reason for this terrible tragedy?"

Smitty reentered the room. "No," Cancini said.

Holding the detective's gaze, the attorney seemed to consider the brief answer. "I see." Leaning toward his client, he whispered in her ear.

With a nod, she hooked her purse on her shoulder and smoothed her skirt. "You'll let me know what leads you get from the letter?"

"We'll look into it." Gerard took Nora Michael's elbow, steering her toward the door. "Oh, by the way, Mrs. Michael, there was a patient you started to tell me about?"

Squeezing the lady's elbow, the lawyer answered for her. "The next time Mrs. Michael speaks to the police will be under the advice of counsel and I think she's said enough for today. She needs time to grieve. This has all been very shocking for her."

Cancini sat down again, watching the pair leave. "Shocking, huh? How could he tell?"

"Yeah, she doesn't seem too broken up, does she?"

"No, she doesn't." Cancini's eyes crinkled. "Kinda reminds me of my ex on the day of our divorce."

Smitty pulled out a chair and flipped it around. He sat with his long legs splayed out in front of him. "What's your read on the lady then?"

Cancini's smile faded. His ex had kept her emotions close and at arm's length. Mrs. Michael appeared to be cut from the same cloth. Still, the nails of her long and elegant fingers were chewed and broken. In spite of her outward calm, she'd swung one leg nervously for the duration of the interview. "I don't know. People deal with bad news in all different ways, I guess. What I do know is that asshole lawyer isn't doing her any favors. It's just all the more reason for you to do a thorough background check on her. You know the drill."

"And the note?"

"A death threat. Allegedly," Cancini said. "Dropped through the mail slot in their door a few days ago."

"Do you think it's for real?"

"Who knows?" Cancini said. "The thing was written in block letters on a plain piece of notebook paper, like the kind kids use at school. So even if it is legit, if there aren't any prints, it'll be impossible to trace."

"But if she is telling the truth, the two deaths could be connected."

"That's a pretty big if." Cancini stood again and slid his notebook into his pocket. "I need some coffee. Want some?"

"Sure. What did the letter say anyway?"

"Just this . . ." Cancini recited the short message, having memorized the words after only one reading.

"Stop pushing or you'll end up in a body bag like your brother-in-law."

Chapter Seven

"Please don't go." George sat up on one elbow, his eyes drinking in the lush curves of her body. A light sheen of sweat glistened on her olive skin. "Stay."

She pulled the white shirt across her breasts. "I can't." She moved to the edge of the bed, her back to him, and pulled on her shoes.

"Sarah, I love you," he said. "I want to make this work." Raising her head, she said nothing. "What can I say to make you believe me?"

She rose, her almond eyes wet with tears. "I think I need to be alone right now, George."

"But—"

"No, I mean it." Shaking her long dark hair, she tipped her chin in the air. "I'm not asking you to marry me, George. I don't even know if that's what I want. I need time. Don't you get it? I don't know what I want yet. This baby . . ." She sighed. "I don't know what's best for us yet." Her dark eyes softened. "Try to understand I need a little more time to make up my mind. Okay?"

He forced a smile, swallowing back the doubts pricking at his brain. "Sure, I guess. How long?"

"I don't know," she said with a shrug. "A couple of days maybe."

"Can I call you?"

"No, and don't come by, either. Wait for me to call you. Please." She made him promise.

An hour later, he still lay on the bed, his hand absently reaching over to the opposite side, long grown cold. A light from the hall cast a soft glow about the room and shadows danced across the floor and walls. A warm breeze blew the cotton curtains aside, bringing in the heady aroma of wildflowers mixed with the scent of the James River. The thought of a future without Sarah made him tremble. Still, he fought the desire to go after her. He'd promised, and blinded by the kind of idealistic love that is bestowed only on the young, he remained convinced that everything would turn out all right.

More than two decades later, George wished desperately he could do it all again, rewrite history, make her stay with him that night. But he couldn't and she hadn't. A car horn sounded behind him and forced him to pay attention to the heavy traffic and let go of the daydream. He turned the radio up. The drive to Richmond was slow and arduous, and for once, he was grateful for the delay. What would he face when he arrived home? Mary Helen had never been the easiest of wives, and from the tone of her voice during their last conversation, he doubted it would be any different on this particular day.

She hadn't always been like that, of course. Once they'd been young and in love. Their relationship had seemed so natural. Their families had known each other for decades. A wedding was just assumed. Then he'd met Sarah.

It wasn't supposed to affect Mary Helen. It was supposed to be a fling, just a townie girl working in a bar, someone to spend time with before he settled down into the life planned for him. Then a funny thing happened. Sarah had made him laugh. She'd made him act silly. With her, he'd relaxed. And he'd liked it. A lot. She was bright, unrefined but gentle, and gracious in all the ways that counted. He'd felt drawn to her, wanting to spend more and more time with her. Pulling away from Mary Helen, he'd told neither girl about the other. In retrospect, however, he realized that Mary Helen had probably known all along. Far more sophisticated than George, she'd simply decided to wait things out, assuming the affair would take its natural course and he would return to her more devoted than ever, ready to begin their lives as Mr. and Mrs. Vandenberg. The baby had taken her by surprise.

"Well," she'd said, after she slapped him, "you just tell her to get rid of it."

Rubbing his cheek with his hand, George had flinched. "She wants to keep it, Mary Helen."

Both of the sorority girl's hands were on her hips. "She can't. We have our future to think of and I don't think we need her interfering."

Stunned, George wasn't sure he'd heard her correctly. "What do you mean?"

"It will ruin everything." Her eyes had welled up. "My father told me he's already booked the club for a September wedding. She's got to get rid of it before then."

He'd stopped rubbing his cheek, staring. Her father was planning their wedding? "But I haven't even proposed!"

With a wave of her hand, she'd ignored the obvious. "Well, not yet, but we've talked about it. These things have to be done in advance. You know that. I wish you hadn't complicated things with this . . . this person. You can't tell anyone, you know. You haven't, have you?"

Shaking his head dumbly, he hadn't been able to comprehend what she was talking about, understand why she was still standing there, or why she would still want to marry him. "Mary Helen, have you been listening to me at all? It's my baby, too."

"Yes, honey. I heard you." She'd reached up and pushed a stray lock of hair off his forehead. "You made a mistake, that's all. It's natural to need a final fling before you make a big commitment like marriage. It's too bad she got pregnant, but with her kind, I shouldn't be surprised." The soft lilt of her voice had acquired an edge he'd never noticed before, a brittleness that hardened her delicate features, pulling the skin tightly into a mask. "Never mind about that—what's done is done. We'll get through this, George, I promise." Standing on tiptoe, she'd reached up and pecked him on his red cheek. "Call me tonight." And with those words, she'd spun away, leaving him to gape after her, awed by her sheer bravado and will.

Pulling into the circular drive, George sat in the car and leaned back against the calfskin leather seat. The memories were as close as yesterday. Head pounding, he concentrated on breathing in and out, focusing on the act itself. Nothing had gone the way he'd planned. Not getting married, not the twenty-odd years since then, not today. A familiar lethargy washed over him. When he'd first started seeing Dr. Michael, he was depressed and apathetic, but hopeful. Each session had been important, sometimes providing breakthroughs, sometimes sad, sometimes encouraging. The therapist had been steady in his mission, directing George to be truthful with himself as well as his doctor. The process of laying his life out on the table proved cathartic. Forced to face his sins, he'd come to the realization that he could change his life, give it meaning and correct past mistakes. His wife had not agreed.

"It's all well and good for you," she'd said one evening, arranging flowers, "to pour your heart out to some stranger, but please don't publicize it. Lord knows what our friends would think, and then there would be the children. They'd be devastated."

Arguing was pointless. "But Mary Helen, it helps me. Getting it out, being able tell someone. It's the best I've felt in years."

Mary Helen dropped the flowers in her hands. Her eyes narrowed. "Confession may be good for the soul," she'd said through clenched teeth, "but it is not good for this family. Do you understand me?"

After that, his sessions with Dr. Michael changed. Hope fell by the wayside, replaced by a growing fury. Dr. Michael may have sensed Mary Helen's influence but he couldn't understand the extent of her ability to control George, to crush his spirit when the need arose. George despised this weakness in himself, but most of the time he simply accepted his miserable life as his penance, his punishment for the things he'd done.

He sat in the car and gazed at the large, traditional brick house in front of him, his house. The lush lawn, landscaped with bright flowers and evergreens, rolled past the drive. Giant pots filled with pink and purple blooms flanked the wide steps. The sun and color blinded him and he blinked. The front door opened. Mary Helen stepped out, ageless, as pretty as she'd been in college. Her blond hair, cut in a perfect bob, framed her delicate features and lithe figure. She skipped down the steps, her red lips turned down in a frown.

"George, what in God's name are you doing sitting here in the driveway? I heard you pull in ten minutes ago."

He stared at his hands on the steering wheel. "Sorry. I'm just tired from the drive, I guess." Pulling up the door handle, he got out and stood over her.

"C'mon, George, you've kept Larry waiting long enough."

He stopped. "Why is Larry here?"

"Because I called him," she said. "After we spoke and you told me about that doctor of yours, I thought maybe we should speak to someone, you know, be prepared."

His square jaw dropped. "Prepared for what?"

"I'm sure I don't know for what," she said, waving a polished hand in the air. "When it comes to you, George, I think it's best we consider all the possibilities." His mouth closed into a thin line, the drumming at his skull gathering strength. "After all, George, cleaning up your messes has always seemed to fall on my shoulders."

"Mary Helen, that isn't necessary."

"Not necessary?" His wife's words cut through the sweet spring air. "Which part? Not to remind you of your mistakes? Not to fix things so our lives and our children's lives aren't ruined? Or not to figure out what kind of a mess you've gotten us into this time?"

"I didn't do anything, Mary Helen."

Cerulean eyes raked over him and he flinched under her penetrating gaze. With only a trace of contempt in her tone, she said, "I think we should talk to Larry now."

Chapter Eight

Cancini shivered. Morgues with their stainless steel and white interiors gave him the creeps. Memories from long ago, distant but still so vivid, came bubbling up, leaving him with a dry mouth and stinging eyes. He blinked, but not before the image of his young mother, ashen and lifeless, flashed before him. Swallowing, he cleared his throat, eager to get on with it and get the hell out of the only place that succeeded in making him feel like a lost twelve-year-old boy. He drummed his fingers on the arm of the chair and took deep breaths, the medicinal air nearly choking him.

The coroner read from a chart, a phone to her ear. She looked over her glasses and mouthed an apology.

The chilly office made him regret leaving his leather blazer in the car. He tapped his foot in time with his fingers.

"Detective Cancini." Dr. Kate Stevenson spoke in a singsong tone that matched the cheery smile on her face. "How are you today?"

"Fine," he said, stone-faced. "I'm fine. What did you find out?"

She picked up a file, and her smile faded. "Three separate stab wounds. They were deep wounds, each made with a large blade, all roughly in the center of the back. The primary cause of death here was the loss of blood combined with severe organ damage."

Nodding, Cancini said, "We found a knife at the scene. Looked like a regular butcher knife. Does that sound about right?"

"Absolutely. Actually, Detective, this was a straightforward autopsy. Not all of the tox reports are back, but so far, nothing unusual in the victim's bloodstream—no drugs, no alcohol."

"Anything under the nails? Scratches? Any sign of a struggle?" Cancini rattled off his usual trio of questions. He'd seen nothing at the scene, but he understood forensic evidence was not always visible with the naked eye.

"Nothing like that. It wouldn't be crazy to assume the victim didn't see the attack coming," she said. "There are no wounds other than in the back and there's no indication that he fought it off at all."

"I didn't see anything at the crime scene, either. Nothing was out of place, only a few items knocked off the secretary's desk. I'm figuring that happened after the stabbing." Standing, the detective paced, hands thrust deep in his pockets, thinking aloud. "The perp could have cleaned up, but it looks like a surprise to me. And the way the vic's eyes were open . . . it's another indication of surprise. He was working late. He was alone. The secretary said she locked the door at six when she left." He glanced up to see Kate watching him, hands folded across her desk. "But the perp either had a key or the doc let him in. Either way, I'm guessing he wasn't expecting the knife in the back." He paused and she remained quiet, waiting. Cancini stopped pacing. "So far, we don't have much to go on. Is there anything you can tell me about our murderer? Any clue at all?"

"It appears likely the killer was right-handed."

He'd been hoping for more. That detail covered the majority of the population. "Anything else?"

She picked up a pencil and rolled it back and forth between her hands. "Maybe, but it could be nothing."

"Go on."

"The placement of the stab wounds might be significant."

"Significant how?"

Kate put the pencil down. "There were three wounds, two close together at relatively the same spot on the victim's back. The third wound, though, was higher by three to four inches. The angle of two cuts appears to be similar, but the other one is slightly different, as though it were made when the victim was in a different position." She paused. He felt her watching him, trying to read his expression. "My best guess is the victim was standing for the first stab wound and had fallen forward, most likely onto the desk you mentioned, for the other two."

It made some sense to him, but he was curious. "Why do you think that?"

"For one thing, I saw the pattern of blood on the rug and spatters on the desk. Second, a lot of force was necessary to inflict wounds that deep. That's easier if the murderer is standing over their victim. All that combined with the placement and angle of the wounds I already mentioned—well, it supports my theory."

"Like this?" He bent forward in a quick motion, his body parallel to her desk. His face came close to hers.

"Yes." Kate held his gaze and he stood up again. "If we assume the single wound was first, the victim was most likely standing. That wound is higher on the back and might have killed him eventually. But the other two sped up the process. The internal bleeding after the organ damage was fatal."

Staring at her, his fingers twitched. "Where are you going with this, Kate?"

She smiled. "Direct as ever, aren't you, Detective?" She came around the desk and stood directly behind him. She touched the middle of his back, her tone authoritative. "Here's where the solitary wound was located." Then, raising her arm slowly, a pen clutched in her hand, she paused for a split second before she finished with a quick stabbing motion. She touched his back again. "Is this the same spot, the one where the victim was stabbed?"

Intrigued, he shook his head. "No, that one was higher."

"Right. Now bend forward like before." Again she pointed out the placement of the stab wounds on the therapist, then pretended to knife him twice more before asking him to compare the simulated locations. "Do you see the difference?"

He straightened and faced the medical examiner. "All the wounds on the victim were higher than yours on me."

"Do you know why?"

A man of only average height, he stood several inches over the small woman. "I think I do."

"How tall are you, Detective?"

"Five-ten."

"I'm only five-two," she said. "You've got a lot of inches on me."

Cancini followed her logic. "But our victim had no such height advantage on his killer."

"That's right. Maybe an inch or two. No more. Dr. Michael was six feet and one-half inch. I think your perp was approximately the same, maybe slightly shorter. It's possible, of course, that the killer might have made a conscious effort to change their height, so it's not conclusive. But if they didn't, based on the angle and placement of the wounds, I'm guessing your killer is in the range of five-ten to six feet, between your height and the victim's." Walking back around the desk, the medical examiner sat and leaned back in her chair. "That's all I have."

He had an approximate height. He knew the perp was right-handed and used an ordinary butcher knife. It was circumstantial but could prove useful later. "Thanks, Kate. It's more than I had when I came in here."

"Sure. That's my job."

Cancini, hand on the doorknob, turned back to the woman behind the desk. "Could there be any significance to the number of stab wounds?"

Twin lines appeared between her brows. "What do you mean?"

"Could the attacker have been angry or crazy maybe?"

"Oh." He watched her face as she made the connection between the idea of an unbalanced act or momentary insanity in the murder of the therapist. "I don't know, Detective. I'm not an expert at motive."

"But you are an expert at forensics. You've seen cases where the attacker went a little crazy before. Is this like that?"

She hesitated. "It's hard to say. Usually in cases of extreme psychosis or emotion, the killer will stab over and over, long after the person is dead."

"Dr. Michael was only stabbed three times."

"It doesn't fit the norm of extreme psychosis, but that doesn't mean it isn't. There is one other thing though." She pushed her glasses up on her nose. "The victim didn't suffer long. He died in a matter of minutes. I'd have to say the murderer was quite efficient."

"Efficient? That doesn't sound like extreme psychosis at all."

"Probably not the kind you mean," she said. "But that doesn't mean the killer wasn't angry at the victim or that they weren't unbalanced. It only means they weren't swept up by emotion. There was some rational thought going on at the time of the murder. Still, I can't speak with any authority here. It's only a snap judgment. You should talk to a psychologist if you want a better picture of your murderer."

"I will." He cocked his head, thinking about her use of the word "efficient" to describe the victim's death. *Efficient.* This was not a word that evoked images of uncontrollable rage or anger or any other strong emotion. To him, it sounded premeditated. He hesitated at the door. "I don't know. There's something."

"What are you thinking?"

"It's more of a feeling. I think whoever we're dealing with is pretty smart. Really smart. And cold." The office had been mostly undisturbed, nothing but the victim's glasses missing. There could be no doubt Dr. Michael had been targeted. A crime of passion? Maybe, but also very, very personal. "I just hope, for all our sakes, he's made a mistake."

Chapter Nine

GEORGE SQUINTED AT his watch and sipped the icy beer. Sarah wasn't due for another half hour. Beads of perspiration on his brow congealed to a single trickle down his cheek. He turned on the fans, avoiding running the air conditioner. He didn't need prying questions from his father. Checking the time again, he sighed.

Outside, he watched the sunlight reflected on the water. Dancing sparkles like diamonds popped up and disappeared in the ripples before reappearing again. A pair of boats cruised into view, their wake disturbing the crystal beauty of the water. He grabbed a lawn chair and another beer. Moving closer to the river, he sat under a large oak tree. He took a long swig of beer and wiped his mouth. George had avoided his friends and Mary Helen for days. He'd kept to the library during the day and escaped to the cottage each evening. The separation from Sarah, although less than a week, felt like an eternity. In the heat, his T-shirt clung to his skin. He stretched his legs and shut his eyes to the glare of the sun. His mind drifted.

"George?" a woman's voice called his name, the lilting tone

tinged with irritation. "George, are you listening to me?" His eyes popped open. "Good God, are you asleep?"

"No. No." He raised his head and sat up straight. "I'm awake."

Mary Helen glared at him. "We were saying how important it is to establish where you were last night—the whole night." She emphasized the final three words.

"That's right," Larry said. He held a memo pad in his hands. "So, George, what time did you arrive at the club?"

"I don't know exactly. Before six, I guess."

"Can't you be more specific?" his wife asked.

George bowed his head and let out a breath. He stood and walked to the great window overlooking the front yard. Condensation in the windows crept from the corners to the middle. He reached up and traced the lines in the windows with his finger. "Five forty-five."

"That's fine, George," Larry said, making notes. "Can you tell me who saw you, what you ate, how long you were there?"

The pain in his head throbbed and the muscles in his neck and shoulders tightened. "Jesus," he said, and wheeled around, "is this necessary? I haven't done anything." No one spoke. Larry shifted in his chair and looked down at his notes. Mary Helen stiffened, her tiny hands gripping the arms of the settee. He rubbed his temples and sank onto the sofa. "I'm sorry," he said, avoiding Mary Helen's piercing gaze. "I just have this terrible headache and I don't know why we're doing this."

An awkward quiet settled over the room. Knowing he'd been rude, knowing he'd been uncooperative, George was still more perturbed than sorry. With each passing minute, he grew more agitated. Why was Mary Helen putting him through this torture? Why did she always think she knew what was best?

"I need a drink." At the bar, he poured a vodka, splashed in a smidge of tonic, and added a lime for good measure.

"Feeling better now, darling?"

George tensed at her sarcastic tone. "Yes, yes I am," he said, and lifted his glass to them both. He guzzled the drink and reached for the bottle. "In fact, I think I'll have another."

Mary Helen's eyes, hard as blue marbles, followed him to the sofa. "If you're quite through?"

George took another sip. He did feel better. "What do you want to know?"

Clearing his throat, Larry rattled off one question after another. He wrote down each answer, gradually taking George through the events of the previous evening. "Where did you go when you left the club?"

"Home. To my apartment."

"You're sure? You didn't stop anywhere? Get gas? Buy cigarettes? Anything like that?"

Frowning, George didn't answer. He thought maybe he had stopped for cigarettes, but he couldn't remember.

"Well?" Mary Helen pursed her lips.

"I don't remember." He wanted a cigarette at that moment, but his wife didn't allow them in the house. "I might have stopped, but it could have been the night before. I might be mixed up."

Larry put down his pen, eyes questioning. "You don't know whether you stopped anywhere?"

"No," he said. "I had a lot to drink at the club."

His wife snorted. "Imagine that."

Ignoring Mrs. Vandenberg's sarcasm, the attorney focused on George. "Fine. You think you went straight home. We'll go with that for now. Did you go straight to bed? Watch TV?"

George remembered the clothes strewn across the bedroom and bathroom. "I think I went straight to bed."

"He probably passed out," Mary Helen said. "I tried calling him about eleven or so and no one answered. I wanted to remind him about his conference call with Daddy, although I don't know why I bothered." George cradled the empty glass and belched. She shot him a look. "Perfect."

Larry pressed his lips together. "Well, it's good that a lot of people saw you at the club." He picked up his notepad, stood, and addressed Mary Helen. "I'm sorry I have to go. Lucy and I are going to the ballet tonight, and she'll kill me if I'm late."

"Thank you for coming on such short notice, Larry." Mary Helen followed him to the door, her smile strained. "You'll let me know if you find out anything?"

"Of course." The lawyer shook their hands.

"Find out what?" George asked after the attorney was gone.

"What do you think? For God's sake, George, sometimes you are so dense. Dr. Michael's murder! I'd like to know what happened to Dr. Michael. Wouldn't you?" Averting his eyes, he made no comment. Trailing him back to the bar, Mary Helen kept at him. "The police will probably find out who all his patients were and start asking questions, and who knows what they'll dig up. What if they find out about you, George?" Unresponsive, he flopped on the sofa, a fresh drink balanced on his chest. "You don't even care, do you? Even if you didn't have anything to do with whatever happened to that doctor of yours, what about us? What if they find out about you and what you did before?"

"I didn't kill Dr. Michael."

"How would you know?" She threw her hands up in the air.

"You can't even remember if you stopped for cigarettes. How do you know what you did?"

"I didn't kill Dr. Michael," he repeated, the denial a little less definite, the words a little quieter.

"What if you had one of your episodes? Maybe that's why you don't remember," she said, eyes narrowed.

The blood rushed to his head, pounding again. "Don't."

"And sometimes you can't control your temper, George. Don't forget that."

"How could I when you're constantly reminding me?" He jumped to his feet and pushed past her. "I'm going up for a shower."

"George," she said, her voice bordering on shrill, "we are not finished."

"Oh yes, we are." He took the steps two at a time. In the bathroom, he slammed and locked the door behind him.

"Damn you!" He heard the shout from the stairs as he turned the shower on full blast, drowning out the sound, drowning out everything. The water hit his face and pelted his skin, the heat loosening some of the strain in his neck and shoulders. He stood like that for several minutes, allowing the water to wash over him. Just for a moment, he felt clean and new. Then it was gone. The meeting with Larry and the fight with Mary Helen, it all made him so tired. All he wanted to do was forget.

Later, clean and changed, he snuck back downstairs and shut himself in the library, a nightcap in his hand. Almost welcoming the dream now, he closed his eyes, letting the past rush forward and fill his mind, erasing the misery of the present.

Down by the river, he waited for Sarah and dozed under the hot sun. The sound of her car on the gravel drive startled him. He watched as she parked in front of the guest cottage. He held his breath, resisting the urge to turn and drink in every step she took.

"George? Is that you down there?"

"Here." She came to him, long legs flashing, sinewy arms swinging at her sides. The halter top and shorts she wore clung to her body and her tan skin glowed in the afternoon light.

George sucked in his breath. "God, you're beautiful," he whispered. "So beautiful."

Chapter Ten

"Is this it?" Cancini asked. He tapped the black book lying on the desk.

Smitty nodded. "Mrs. Watson said it lists all of Michael's appointments in and out of the office. I've got Wilder checking out her computer, but she says she hardly used it. She swears this is all we should need."

Cancini pulled his head to the right, his ear close to his shoulder. He repeated the stretch to the left.

"You okay?"

"Headache." He opened the appointment book. "How far back does it go?"

"Five months. To January. I think the ones from previous years are in the files."

He turned the pages until he came to the day of the murder. The appointments were written neatly in the book, first initial followed by a last name, each marked in one-hour blocks of time. Two periods were left blank, the first hour of the morning and lunch. "Do we have the full names of the patients?" Smitty handed him a folded piece of paper. Cancini copied the list in his note-book. Then flipping back, he added the names of the patients who had come in the day before, too. "Mrs. Watson said he went out to pick up a sandwich for lunch."

"Yep. There's a deli on the corner he went to every day. Brought it back to the office and ate at his desk," Smitty said. "Real creature of habit, this guy."

"So, no change in routine this week?"

"Nope. Mrs. Watson said he used lunch to catch up on his notes." Cancini glanced at his young partner. "I know what you're going to say, but she wouldn't give me those. The warrant was pretty narrow. Notes and files weren't covered. Sorry."

Cancini wasn't surprised. "Doesn't matter. If we need them, we'll take a run at getting another subpoena later. What did you find out about the wife?"

Smitty sat down at his desk. "Some, but not a lot. No kids and no close family. Only marriage for both. She's a lawyer with Harkin & Fenner, works in tax litigation, high-priced clients. Nobody in her office had much to say about her. Professional, always polite, good at her job, that kinda stuff."

"How long has she been there?"

"Five years. One odd thing though. I didn't get to talk to everyone but it doesn't seem she socialized with her coworkers. She didn't do the office Christmas party or the summer cookout. Ate lunch alone in her office. Apparently, the lady is business-friendly, but, and I quote, 'snotty.' "

"Snotty?"

"Yeah, as in stuck-up."

"Anyone ever met Dr. Michael?"

"Nope."

Cancini leaned back, eyes on his partner's face. He thought briefly of the woman who'd sat before him only hours earlier. The description didn't seem all that far off. Smart and classy but no kids and no close friends. Other than her husband, the woman liked to be alone. This last part, at least, he understood. "Okay. Where was she before Harkin & Fenner?"

"Boston. That's where they're from. She stayed even after her husband had set up practice here. According to the personnel lady at the firm, she moved to Washington because Dr. Michael was complaining about the weekend commuting."

The pain at the base of his neck radiated up the back of his head. "How long had the Michaels been married?"

"About fifteen years."

"And they never had kids? No other family?"

"Just the dead brother for her. Dr. Michael's folks died when he was in his twenties. No siblings."

"Odd," he said. It appeared both their family trees were dying out. Was no children a conscious choice? He ran his hand over his short hair. If it was, he wondered if it was significant. "Interesting."

"What's interesting?" Smitty asked.

Cancini reached in his drawer for a bottle of aspirin. "I'm wondering why Mrs. Michael had to be convinced to move to the same town to be with her husband. I want to know why Mrs. Watson made it out as though Mr. and Mrs. Michael were lovebirds, him always so anxious to get home to her." He swallowed two pills with cold coffee. "There's something about this relationship I find curious. I need to know more."

"I'll see what I can find out. I have a friend in Boston."

"Anything he can get. Work history, friends, neighbors." He

tapped on the desk. "Could be a reason, a local reason, she wasn't in any hurry to move closer to dear old hubby."

Smitty arched one eyebrow. "You think she had a little something on the side?"

"I have no idea." Cancini shrugged. "She's attractive, smart, has money. No kids to weigh her down. Could've been one of those modern marriages." In his mind, he pictured her again. "You never know."

"I guess. She's still a looker, that's for sure."

"Still? Are you implying she's old?"

Smitty's face flushed. "No. That's not what I meant, but she's older than me. That's all."

"So's most of the population." Standing, the detective picked up his notebook and slipped it in his jacket pocket. "I'm going to track down some of these names and check out some alibis."

"Sure. I'll call my buddy in Boston now. Might take another run at Mrs. Watson, too," Smitty said. He started to pick up the phone, then turned back to Cancini. "By the way, did you get the report from the print guys?"

Cancini picked through the files on his desk and tossed a manila folder to his partner. "The knife was clean but the door and the knob weren't. Prints were all over the office, most of them smudges or partials. So far, no matches with FBI files or any other files. My guess is they belong to patients, Mrs. Watson, and the doctor himself. Speaking of prints, what about the cleaning service?"

"Commercial company. A crew of two came in at six-thirty according to their records. Emptied trash cans, cleaned the floors and bathroom. Gone by seven and on to the next office. Said the door was locked when they came in; they used their company passkey and locked it again when they left."

"Anyone see Dr. Michael?"

"Yep, both of 'em. He was working at his desk. Both are immigrants and don't speak much English."

"That's convenient. How can we be sure they didn't knife him, intend to rob him, but something went wrong?"

"We don't. Seems unlikely, though, since a call was made from the doctor's desk phone around nine and our cleaning service was working in another building by then. There are witnesses."

"What about the call? Have we traced it yet?"

"Still working on it."

"Let me know." Cancini mind turned over the little evidence they had. "Let's assume all we've been told is true. That means Dr. Michael was still alive in his office after seven P.M., after the cleaning service had left. Let's also assume the door is locked as they claim. After that, someone, either the victim or possibly our perp, used the phone at approximately nine P.M." He paused, hands shoved deep in his pockets. "For now, based on the fact that no blood was found on or near the doctor's desk, I'm going to assume the doctor himself used the phone. With me so far?"

Smitty nodded.

"He's alive at nine. Is the perp already there? We don't know." Cancini paused and stretched his neck again. "Damn, that hurts."

"You're old."

"Tell me about it. All right, I think we can safely assume the murder took place at the secretary's desk and not in Dr. Michael's office. Since we have no evidence to place the perp in the office where the call was made, let's assume the perp hadn't yet arrived. Sometime after the call, Dr. Michael is knifed in the back."

"Makes sense, but how did he get in?"

Cancini's eyes came to rest on the younger man. "That's the

question, isn't it? Did the perp come in with a key or was he let in by Dr. Michael himself?"

"According to Mrs. Watson, only she and Dr. Michael had keys," Smitty reminded him. "He must have let his killer in."

"Maybe," Cancini said. "Let's look at it a different way. The murder weapon was clean and the doorknob wasn't. Based on that, I think it's safe to assume the perp was wearing gloves."

"Or wiped the knife clean."

"I don't think so. First, if you take the time to wipe the knife clean, you're going to wipe everything you touched. The print guys didn't find any other surfaces that had been wiped. Second, although the knife handle was clean of prints, there were blood spatters that weren't wiped away. He must have been wearing gloves."

Smitty considered this information. "Okay, I'll buy it. He was wearing gloves, but that also implies the murder—or some other crime that led to the murder—was planned, at least to some degree."

"Exactly. So, until we get something that disproves our theory, the murder was at least partially premeditated. Our perp is either someone who knew the victim and was let in or had access to his office through one of the keys we know about. If we assume premeditation, our perp knew enough to know the victim would work late that night."

"Like one of his patients?"

"Could be."

"The wife? Someone he worked with?"

"Any"—he pulled on his faded leather sport coat—"or all of the above."

A desk officer approached the two detectives. "Cancini, a Sandy Watson is on the phone for you. Line four."

"Speak of the devil." He sat down again. "Cancini here."

"Detective," she said. "It's Sandy Watson. I . . . I don't know if I'm doing the right thing." Near tears, her words were barely audible. "But if it helps you to find out whoever killed Dr. Michael . . ." A choked sob came across the phone line.

He pressed the phone to his ear, kept his voice low and soothing. "Mrs. Watson, anything you can tell me may be helpful. I know you cared a great deal for the doctor, so if you know anything . . ."

Her crying slowed then. "It's about Dr. Michael, but I don't know if it means anything. He'd been preoccupied, anxious about something this week. I think he was worried."

Cancini jotted down the time, the lady's name, and a line about the doctor's worries. "What makes you think something was bothering him, Mrs. Watson?"

"Well, when something was on his mind, he would become distant, give one-word answers. All week he never asked about how I was doing, didn't thank me like he did each day, barely touched his sandwich. It just wasn't like him. The doctor was the kindest man." Her words broke off. A minute went by before she spoke again. "I'm sorry. I still just can't believe it."

"It's fine, Mrs. Watson. You were saying about the doctor?"

"Oh. Right. Well, like I said, he always took an interest in people and how they were doing. This week he was different, not rude or anything, just, you know, preoccupied."

"Okay. Was he worried about a patient maybe?"

"I honestly don't know. He didn't talk to me about his cases."

"But you knew something was wrong," the detective asked, pressing. "Did you ask him if everything was all right?"

"Oh no, Detective, not this time. I assumed whatever was bothering him was none of my business."

"This time? Has he been like this before?"

"Only once." She spoke haltingly, the words hanging in the air. "I—I don't know if I should say anything more."

He took a deep breath. "Mrs. Watson, it could be important to the case."

"We-ell, I guess it would be all right. It was right around when Mrs. Michael's brother died. The doctor was not himself at all. He was short, even with Mrs. Michael. She even went—" The woman hesitated, breaking off. "Well, things were, I don't know how to put this, but I guess they were awkward."

"That was about a year ago, right?"

"Yes, Detective."

He put down his pen. He already knew about the brother's hit-and-run death. "Well, Mrs. Watson, I think it's understandable they would both be upset after the death of Mrs. Michael's brother. I'm sure it was a difficult time for everyone."

"Oh no, Detective, it wasn't after the accident," she said, then stopped.

Cancini leaned forward, picking up his pen once again. "Yes?"

"You might not understand," she whispered. "Dr. Michael loved her so much. He was devoted."

He heard the protective, maternal tone in her voice. "If there's something I need to know, Mrs. Watson, now is the time."

There was silence, followed by a ragged sigh. "The doctor, he was upset, worried, for quite a while. He seemed, well, kind of unhappy." A moment passed while he waited. "Not after the accident, Detective. Before."

Chapter Eleven

"I'M NOT GOING to stay," she said. Dark circles rimmed her eyes. "So don't ask me." Sarah sat on the ground, knees pulled up to her chest and head turned away from him. She plucked at the grass, avoiding his gaze.

Sipping on the warm beer, he stared out at the river. A small boat motored past. He watched the ripples atop the water grow wider until they reached the shore, disappearing.

"I only came because I knew you needed to hear something, but . . ." She paused, her ponytail dipping and bobbing with her words. "I haven't decided anything yet."

"Sarah," he started, "you know I—"

"Stop." She glared at him, her brown eyes dark under the shade of the tree. "Just let me finish." Silenced, George sat back, mouth shut. "I'm having a hard time figuring this out, and pressure from you is not going to help." Her slender arms loosened and she stretched her legs. Her tawny skin glistened in the bright sunlight of the afternoon. "This isn't about you, you know. It's about my life and the baby's, our future."

Desperately wanting to interrupt and declare it their future—not just hers—he bit his tongue. He didn't want to anger her or scare her away.

"I don't know if I want to get married because of the baby and I don't know if I want to marry you." Swallowing hard, he glimpsed the tears on her long lashes. "It's not that I don't love you. I do. But I just can't see what kind of future we'd have. I'm a waitress and you're . . ." Lines appeared across her forehead. "You're from a family that doesn't want someone like me as your wife." She blinked away the unspilled tears. "I'm not stupid, George, and I know you would never have proposed to me if I wasn't pregnant. That's no way to start a life, a family." She curled her legs under her again.

He reached out and touched the rounded curve of her shoulder. She stiffened but remained silent. Gathering courage when she didn't brush his hand away, he squeezed. "Can I talk now?"

Wiping at her face, she didn't look at him. "Sure. I guess."

Knowing everything mattered in that moment, he chose honesty, something he believed she deserved, especially since he'd already deceived her about Mary Helen early in their relationship. Mouth dry, he told her she was right about the proposal. He wouldn't have been thinking about marriage, but now he was grateful, even happy. "Sarah, this baby has forced me to look at what I want to do with my life. When we first started, I just wanted to have fun. I had a girlfriend and I needed a break from her. You were that break." Sarah shook his hand from her shoulder, but he kept talking. "And then I started to like you, really like you. I probably would have just kept things as they were, but everything changed. You found out about Mary Helen and then, well, this. The old me, the one who just wanted to have fun, would have run away."

"You did run away," she said. "You hurt me, George." Hearing her words felt like having the wind knocked out of him, leaving him momentarily speechless. "But that doesn't matter now," she said, her voice firm, "and I don't want to talk about it."

Hesitating, he took her at her word and bit back the apologies. "When I started thinking about not being with you, not talking with you and holding your hand, not watching you brush your hair, not seeing you . . . I realized I loved you." She snorted. His heart pounded, but he plowed on. "When I came out here by myself, without anyone, I was surprised how calm I felt, how sure of what I wanted. You don't know what that's like. No one tells you what you're supposed to be, which school to go to, who you should date. You always say what you think. You do what you think is right. That's the kind of life I want to live, too—with you."

Wide-eyed, she leaned away from him. "And you think being married to me will magically change your life?"

"Yes. No." George hung his head. "That's not what I meant."

"Then what did you mean?"

"I meant that I like the person I am when I'm with you. I like me better when I'm with you than when I'm with anyone else. I think—no, I'm sure—you bring out the best in me." Her mouth opened, the pink lips parting. "It sounds crazy, but what I think I'm trying to say is that you being pregnant has only made me realize that I'd want to marry you even if there was no baby."

Her pretty mouth shut and her dark eyes searched his. Holding her gaze, he wanted to cover her in kisses and hold her tight, but he forced himself to wait. He gripped the beer bottle in his hand as though it were a life raft and he was adrift at sea.

The minutes dragged on until she spoke again. "What would our life be like, George?"

Hope flooded his mind and his voice shook. "Wh-what do you mean?"

She turned away from the river, her voice faraway. "How would it start? What would our wedding be like? What would your parents say? Where would we live?"

"I don't know," he said. "I haven't thought about that yet."

"Well, I have." Sarah rose and brushed the dirt from her shorts. "I'm going home now. I've got some more thinking to do."

"Can I call?" he asked, afraid to push, afraid not to.

"No, I don't think so."

He felt the energy seep from him. His arms slipped to his sides and his eyes stung. Had she already made up her mind then?

"George, whatever happens, whatever I decide, I do love you. Not the man you think you're expected to be, but the man I saw, the man I knew these last few months." She leaned over and kissed the top of his head, her soft lips momentarily brushing his skin. "I'll call you soon. I promise."

Just as he had then, he reached up, his fingers feeling for the memory of her kiss. As always, the past fell away and the dream faded, and he felt only the lines that had deepened across his forehead. His nightcap, empty now, sat balanced in his lap. Who was the man she knew? Where was he now? When had he lost himself? Was it right after the accident? Right after she was gone? Or was it after years of marriage to a woman he didn't love?

He let out a long breath, wishing for Dr. Michael. At least with the therapist, he'd been honest—most of the time, anyway. But now, with Dr. Michael apparently murdered, his wife had brought in a lawyer to protect George from himself. Was Mary Helen right? Did he need a lawyer? He rubbed his temples. The hammering in his skull refused to go away, pounding and pounding.

He leaned back and rolled the cool glass across his head. Without Dr. Michael, he was back where he started, on his own. He could find a new therapist, but in his heart, he knew the problems wouldn't go away until he grew a backbone. The past, the dreams that haunted him day in and day out, were his and Mary Helen's and Sarah's. No amount of therapy could erase what had already been done. Yet the future, that was another matter. If he followed the advice of Dr. Michael, the future was not lost.

He blinked in the darkness. Who would want to kill Dr. Michael? He groaned, frustrated. He couldn't even remember the events of the previous night. Had he blacked out again? Dr. Michael had repeatedly expressed concern about the drinking, the blackouts, all of it. But George hadn't wanted to hear it. Cursing the headache, he went over the day again; trying to remember. First the business lunch, then the appointment with Dr. Michael and the outburst during the session. Later, he'd drowned his sorrows in a bottle of scotch. That was it. After driving away from the club, swerving across the parking lot, he couldn't remember. Not driving home to his apartment. Not tossing his clothes across the floor. Not falling naked into the sheets. No matter how hard he tried, his memory remained a blank slate. There in the darkness, he again heard the accusation in his wife's words—*What have you done?*

Chapter Twelve

He could have conducted the interviews over the phone, but Cancini preferred to ask questions in person. Studying each individual's face and their mannerisms, he could better gauge their reactions. He'd spoken to about half of Dr. Michael's final appointments, driving all over the city and suburbs to look into each patient's eyes at the precise moment he informed them their therapist was dead. A few burst into tears while others had to sit down, the shock causing their legs to give out. Two, however, did not seem to care—expression slack, shoulders shrugging as though he were telling them nothing more significant than the latest weather report.

"Well, I wasn't getting all that much out of therapy anyway," said one young woman without looking up from the menu in her hands. "I just thought it was a cool thing to do." Cancini had caught Lauren Temple on her break at the restaurant where she served as a hostess. When a waitress approached to take the young woman's order, she unfolded her napkin and spread it across her lap. "What happened to him, anyway?"

"That's what we're trying to find out," Cancini said. Tables around them filled and the noise level in the restaurant swelled. He squirmed in his seat. Too many people and too much commotion. His stomach growled at the good smells emanating from the kitchen, but he left his menu untouched. "We're asking everyone who had an appointment with the doctor yesterday where they were last evening."

"Oh." She didn't hide the tiny smile playing across her lips. "Dr. Michael was murdered then?"

Goose bumps rose on his forearms. Who was this girl? "I didn't say that, Miss Temple. We're still investigating the cause of—"

"I know what you said, Detective, and I know what you didn't say. I can figure it out for myself. Therapist turns up dead and police start asking his patients where they were on such and such a night." The waitress brought a glass of iced tea and set it in front of the girl. "Do you think I'm dumb? Come on."

Cancini didn't know what he thought of the young woman seated across from him, but he didn't think she was dumb. She was brighter than most and self-assured. The death of her therapist seemed inconsequential to her and she did not hide her apathy. Her delight at the idea of murder got under his skin. "You don't seem terribly surprised."

She squeezed the lemon into the glass, her tone casual. "Not much surprises me."

"That's pretty cynical," he said.

"Whatever." A plate of pasta with garlic bread arrived. She dug in, twisting the pasta around her fork. "Sorry. I've gotta eat so I can get back to work."

"You never answered my question, Miss Temple. Where were you last night, say after six or so?"

"Ah, now we're getting down to it." She wiped the sauce from her lips. "I was at my boyfriend's place. We ordered Chinese, watched a movie, stayed in for the night . . ." She winked. "You know."

Cancini wrote it down in his notebook, ignoring her insinuation. "The boyfriend's name?"

The girl put her fork down, the metal clinking against the china plate. "For real?"

"Yes, for real. I want to know his name, address, phone, when you got there, how long you were there. Okay?" He ripped a piece of paper from his notebook and pushed it across the table.

"Whatever," she said again, tearing apart the crust of her garlic bread. "Jake Melbourne. Right around six. Spent the whole night." She wrote an address and phone number on the paper and handed it back.

"He'll verify that?"

She frowned. "Of course. Why wouldn't he?"

"No reason, Miss Temple." The detective slid from the chair and stood over the girl. "Thank you for your time."

The interviews were brief, no more than basic information, questions limited by that annoying code of medical ethics—the patient's right to privacy. Knowing he needed to be careful, Cancini held back, frustrated by the law. Any of the doctor's patients could be a viable suspect, but according to the judge who allowed the detectives to use the appointment book, he could only ask where they were at the time of the victim's death. It wasn't enough. He needed more.

"By the book," he said, and slammed the door to his ten-year-old Chevrolet. "Goddamn rules." The captain had issued the same warning to the entire department so many times, he could recite the speech word for word. Too many cases had been overturned and too many trials stopped midway. Too many guilty men had been set free to steal again, rape again, and murder again. Cancini himself had been burned by a technicality when a search was ruled illegal and all the subsequent evidence was thrown out before a jury could even hear a word. The smug look on the murderer's face had brought the detective to his feet. His desire to leap over the railing and smack the smirk from the lowlife's lips almost got the better of him. Now, everything he and the rest of the squad did had to be beyond reproach. By the book. It made his ulcers burn.

Patients' rights, subpoenas, legal mumbo-jumbo; it all made his head spin until he wondered if he was too old for the job, a relic trying to hang on in a world going way too fast. Still, he couldn't quit, couldn't retire. He didn't know how to do anything else, and it was too late for him to learn. Besides, even if he was a dinosaur in a modern society, the department needed him. They counted on his bloodhound instinct and depended on his unnatural persistence. At least that's what he told himself. So, here he was again, with another brutal murder case, no clear-cut motive, and his hands tied right from the outset. Surely the nature of the crime, the cold-blooded manner in which Dr. Michael was slain, should tell him something. Definitely not a case of highly charged emotions but still, there was an element of hatred. He felt it. Nothing was taken and no one was sexually assaulted. It was no accident. He believed what he'd told Kate. The killer was smart and cold as ice.

Honing in on a suspect, however, was another matter. He already had questions about the doctor's marriage, but considering what the guy did for a living, he couldn't rule out anything. So, in interrogating each patient, he listened to his gut, all the while keeping it "by the book." Still, if the department lawyers and the district attorney were to give the go-ahead, loosening the noose and getting him subpoenas for patient files, he would be back, nose to the ground. He grunted. For now, he had to be satisfied with names, faces, and a list of alibis.

Hungry and thirsty, Cancini sauntered into his favorite watering hole, a place that could only be described kindly as a dive. Long and narrow, the bar was just wide enough for a few wobbly tables, a battered jukebox playing oldies from the sixties, and a heavily scarred wooden bar. Solitary figures sat on rickety stools, nursing draft beer and Jack Daniel's. The air smelled of onions and old Christmas tree–shaped fresheners.

Smitty sat at the end of the bar with his back to the door and a cell phone to his ear. Sliding onto the stool next to his partner, Cancini reached for the picked-over nuts in the wooden bowl.

"Can you verify the dates for me?" the younger detective asked as he wrote in his notepad. "Can you tell me how the tickets were paid for?" Cancini munched on a stale cashew, listening. "Yeah, I got it. Any trips since then? . . . Okay. Thanks." Smitty set the phone on the bar and picked up his beer. "I might have something."

"Yeah?"

"Remember how Mrs. Watson indicated the Michaels weren't getting along right before her brother was run down? Well, I had a little talk with the housekeeper this afternoon. Seems that about a year ago, Mrs. Michael made several trips back to Boston, one time gone for two weeks straight. Miss Angelo, that's the housekeeper, didn't want to say much, but she admitted she heard the Michaels fighting about it."

Cancini brushed the salt from his fingers and licked his lips. "Business trips?"

"Nope." Smitty handed over a report. "Talked to HR at her office. The lady took a leave of absence for that time. That was the airline on the phone. I've got the dates for all six trips. All paid for in cash. The last trip was about a week before the brother's accident."

"Did the fighting stop when the trips did?"

"Yeah, at least she thought so."

"We still don't know what she was doing in Boston?"

"Not yet."

"Okay. Get me a copy of those dates and see if we can find out where she stayed. Even if they had marriage problems a year ago, it doesn't prove anything now."

"No," Smitty said, "but the secretary did say something was bothering Dr. Michael this week—same as before."

"Agreed. It might not hurt to ask the widow a few questions."

An icy mug landed on the bar. "Can I get a cheeseburger?" Cancini asked, getting a quick nod in return. "Loaded and don't overcook it this time, Monty."

The bartender walked away, raising his right hand and middle finger. "It'll be burned, just like you like it," Monty said over his shoulder.

Smitty laughed out loud. "Is this your regular place?"

"Yeah." He gave his partner a sideways glance. "And I wanna keep it that way. Understand?" Not a large-group kind of guy, he rarely socialized with any of the other detectives in the department. It wasn't that he didn't get along with the guys well enough—he did—but he preferred to keep his private life private. And truthfully, he didn't mind his loner reputation, finding it kept most of the nosier bunch as well as the kiss-ups away. At this stage in his life, he didn't have the energy or the patience. Fleetingly, it occurred to him perhaps he and Mrs. Michael had something in common. Cancini polished off his mug in less than a minute and wiped the foam from his lips.

"It's your place." Smitty was quiet a moment, then said, "Not a great place to meet women though."

Cancini snorted. "Who says I'm looking?"

"No one," Smitty said. "But it wouldn't hurt you to go on a date or something . . . sometime."

The detective liked the younger man, found him an easy partner who possessed good instincts, but he didn't like the turn this conversation was taking. Everyone knew about his divorce and where his ex-wife now spent her nights, but Cancini knew it wasn't her he missed. Was he lonely? Maybe. But that was his business. He grunted. "What for?"

"No reason." Smitty swallowed the rest of his beer. He stared at the mirrored bar in front of him, then picked up his notebook. "Listen, there is one other thing. It's about the knife."

"Yeah? What about it?"

"I don't know how much help it is, but it's sold at one of those chain stores that carries kitchen stuff."

"Which one?"

"Williams-Sonoma. Heard of it?"

Monty returned with a burger, silverware, and napkins. Melted cheese dripped down the bun and ketchup pooled on the plate. A mound of fries completed the meal. Cancini's mouth watered and he chomped down on the burger right away. Grease dripped from his lips to his chin. He wiped it away with a wad of cocktail napkins. A second round of drinks arrived with the food. Devouring most of the burger and two large handfuls of fries, the detective washed the burger down with a second icy beer. "I've seen it. Expensive, right?"

"Uh-huh. You can get that knife—that specific brand and type used to murder Dr. Michael—at the store, through the catalog, or order it off the Web site. It's usually part of a set, but you can special order it by itself as a replacement courtesy. The blade itself measures eight inches with a solid wooden handle."

"Three different ways to buy the knife, huh? That could make it hard."

"Not to mention that with some customers paying in cash, you would never get a complete list. It's a needle in a haystack."

Cancini whistled under his breath. "That isn't much help." He drummed his fingers on the bar, his short nails skipping over the deep nicks and scars in the wood. "Still, you can't buy it at your local Kmart, so that might tell us a little something about the killer."

"There is another thing that might help. This particular knife was only introduced in the last two years, so at least the information, if we have to get it, is fairly recent."

Cancini pushed his plate away. "This case is starting to get on my nerves. Everything is like a taste of pie, never the whole piece, not even as much as a whole bite. It's not getting us anywhere. We got nothin'."

Smitty said nothing, neither agreeing nor disagreeing.

With his fingers, Cancini wiped at the condensation on the mug. Every hour that passed, the killer would be harder to track. They needed something solid. Conjecture and speculation was getting them nowhere. He touched his head to his temples, tired of the pain. Monty brought a glass of water and wiped away his mess. Cancini stared down into his glass. Why did he keep doing it? He figured a doctor like Michael would have a theory or two, but he had a guess of his own. He needed the job, needed the cases. They filled the long hours and helped him forget. It was true he hadn't been on a date since his wife had left, but he didn't need to be fixed up, didn't want to be fixed up. He was better alone.

He chugged the rest of his beer, shaking off the melancholy. Dr. Michael and his murder required his focus. He looked over at Smitty. "Some cops say there's no such thing as the perfect crime, but that's not the way I see it. I say there's no such thing as the perfect killer. They're only human like you and me. Even if the crime scene yields nothing and you can't find a lick of evidence anywhere, the killer will still mess up somehow, sometime. It might even happen years later." His eyes burned. "The crime itself might be perfect, but the killer isn't. Nobody is."

Chapter Thirteen

"It's for you." Mary Helen handed him the phone, lips turned down in disapproval. "A detective from the Washington police," she said, her delicate hand cupped over the phone.

He rose from the kitchen table. The scrambled eggs and sausage he'd eaten rumbled in his belly. "This is George Vandenberg." He turned his back on his wife.

The voice on the other end of the line was deep and gruff, but not harsh. "Mr. Vandenberg, my name is Detective Mike Cancini and I'm sorry to have to track you down at your home in Richmond, but I have a couple of questions for you."

George gripped the kitchen counter with his left hand. "What is this about, Detective?"

"Well, I don't like doing this over the phone, but since you're not in Washington, there's no other way. Dr. Edmund Michael, I believe you're a patient of his, is that right?"

"Yes, I am."

"I'm afraid I have some bad news for you." Five seconds ticked by. "He's been killed."

Hearing it out loud made him shiver. "That's terrible."

"Dr. Michael died two nights ago and we're asking all his patients with appointments that day to verify their whereabouts that day and evening." George could feel his wife's eyes boring into his back. He wiped his left hand on his pants. "Mr. Vandenberg? Are you there?"

"Yes, Detective, I'm here," he said. "That was Thursday, right? I did have an appointment with Dr. Michael that day, as you said. After I left his office, I went to my country club for drinks. There was a members' party." Larry had advised George to be honest and keep it simple. With his attorney's advice in mind, he briefly outlined the evening, concluding with his departure from the club and his return to his apartment.

"Fine," Cancini said. "I assume you can give me some names of people who saw you at the club."

"Yes, sir." George heard a pen scratching as he rattled off half a dozen names of members he knew had been at the party.

"What time did you say you left the club and what time did you get home?"

Holding the phone, George hesitated. "I think I left around ten or so and went straight home, so that would put me back at my apartment around ten-fifteen, maybe a little after." He forced a laugh. "I'm not sure the exact time. Like I told you before, I did have a few drinks."

"Okay, got it."

A wave of relief washed over him. "Anything else I can do, let me know."

"One more thing," Cancini said. "Was anyone with you in your apartment that night? Can anyone verify you were there from, let's say, ten-thirty on?"

The short-lived relief evaporated. "No, Detective, I'm afraid not."

"No one?"

"No, sir."

"I see." Cancini's voice took on a different tone. "I'll be in touch, Mr. Vandenberg. Good-bye."

Fingers trembling, George replaced the receiver. He leaned against the counter and breathed in and out. He straightened when he sensed Mary Helen standing behind him.

"Well? What did he say? What did he want?" He flinched at the accusation in her eyes. "Why did he want to know where you were? What do the police know?"

The tension faded, replaced by a growing irritation with his demanding wife. "What do you mean what do they know? There's nothing to know. How many times do I have to keep telling you that?"

"Oh?" Her tiny hands flew to her narrow hips. "Then why did you have to tell them where you were that night?"

He brushed past her and poured a fresh cup of coffee. He stirred in cream and sugar, speaking over his shoulder. "The detective said they're asking everyone who had an appointment with Dr. Michael on Thursday where they were." With more confidence than he felt, he said, "I think it's routine or something."

"Oh . . . well, that's good then."

"Don't sound so happy, Mary Helen. I swear it's almost like you want me to have done something wrong."

"Don't be ridiculous." She reached for the phone. "I'm going to call Larry."

"What for?"

"To let him know you talked to the police."

He dumped the coffee down the sink. "Do what you have to. I'm going to the office."

"It's Saturday," she said to his retreating back. Phone call forgotten, she followed him from the kitchen to the foyer. Her low-heeled shoes clicked across the marble floor and echoed off the arched ceiling and circular staircase. The mid-morning sun streamed through six-foot windows, brightening the antique furnishings and bathing his wife in light. "George . . ." Her voice was more tentative, less bossy. "What if they call again? What if they want to know why you were seeing Dr. Michael?"

"I don't think they can ask that."

"Oh." She tucked her hair behind her ears. "How much did you tell him, George? Did he know everything . . . about that night?"

The question caught him off guard. Before, whenever he'd tried to bring up the subject and include her in his therapy, she'd scorned the idea. She harped on the importance of family and privacy. She hated that he'd confided in a stranger, told someone outside the family their secrets. Now that Dr. Michael was gone, she'd developed a sudden curiosity. "Yes. He knew everything."

She reached out and pressed her fingers into his forearm. "What do you mean by everything?"

How could he explain? He'd told the therapist about the accident, every detail, from start to horrendous finish. He'd told the man his entire life story, for whatever that was worth. She couldn't understand, preferring to guard secrets and keep unpleasant memories tucked neatly into the past. Seeing a therapist had been his idea, criticized by his wife, and hidden from his children. He pulled Mary Helen's hand from his arm. "Nothing. I don't mean anything."

He left her standing in the doorway, mouth gaping. In the car, he forgot the office and turned eastward toward the family river house. After a little more than an hour, the car rolled down the gravel drive. The new version of the place, renovated by Mary Helen, reminded him of their house in town. But even his wife's commanding hand could not keep nature at bay. Wildflowers crept outside their borders, infringing on the miniature bushes she'd ordered the gardeners to plant. The woods that edged one side of the property were dark and thick, filled with brush and bramble. Getting out of the car, he glanced at the large house and the smaller cottage before strolling down to the dock where the new boathouse stood.

Down by the water, he pulled off his shirt and shoes. He rolled up his pants and let his feet dangle in the river. The cool water lapped at his toes. This was the part of the property he loved, the water itself, the wildlife, the natural beauty. For years, he'd denied himself time at the river, afraid of the memories. It wasn't until he'd begun seeing Dr. Michael that he realized how much he'd given up. When the dreams started, he'd known it was time. He came often and alone, when he was sure the place would be empty.

George looked down at his hand, at the gold ring encircling the third finger of his left hand. It had grown tight over the years with the weight he'd gained, and it was difficult to remove. He touched the smooth metal and tugged at the ring. It wouldn't budge. Leaning over, he dipped his hand into the water, waving it back and forth in the light current. Wet, the ring slipped down to his knuckle. He worked it back and forth until it dropped into the palm of his hand. The ring glittered in the afternoon sun. He held it up and read the inscription, his wedding date followed by his initials.

His fingers closed over the ring and the memories of that day flooded his mind. He'd started drinking early. Bloody Marys with the frat brothers by ten, beer at lunch, and gin in the late afternoon. The ceremony itself was a blur, but he remembered Mary Helen's face as she came toward him. The church had been crowded with their families' wealthy friends, all decked out in black tie and tasteful jewels. His wife-to-be had sauntered down the aisle, nodding at people she recognized and elongating the moment. At the altar, she'd taken his hand, leaned in close, and whispered in his ear. "It's going to be all right, darling. This is how it was meant to be." Stepping back, she'd smiled, so sure, so triumphant.

He didn't remember much else except going through the motions, repeating the vows, doing whatever was expected of him. It wasn't a great start to any marriage, but he had no one to blame but himself. He didn't love Mary Helen then any more than he did now. He was grateful to her, sure, but that wasn't love. They were bound together now only by the life they had built around the children. Love was a distant memory from his past with a different woman. Those days were long gone and the life he'd chosen was the one he'd allowed Mary Helen to choose for him. Opening his fingers again, he stared at the ring, the symbol of commitment in a marriage. Tears pricked his eyes until the gold circle in his palm blurred. George blinked, closed his hand around the ring, and tossed it in the river. He listened for the plink and watched it disappear under the water, gone forever.

Chapter Fourteen

Father Joe sipped the coffee. "Ahh. Dunkin' Donuts. My favorite, Michael."

Cancini grinned, leaning back in the guest chair. "I know." Both men sat quietly a few moments, drinking their coffee. The morning light streamed in through the tall windows of the priest's living quarters. Outside, the streets were quiet; the only sound the chirping birds.

Father Joe balanced his cup in his lap. "Any sins to confess this morning, my friend?" Their relationship, long and filled with mutual respect, was rooted in tradition.

"Same ones as always, Father. Sorry to say, I'm still a sinner."

"Well, aren't we all?" The elderly man chuckled. His face crinkled when he laughed and his nose tipped up toward the heavens. "Keep trying, Michael. Say three Hail Marys and that should do it then."

"Yes, Father," Cancini said.

"Will I see you at Mass tomorrow?"

Cancini grinned again, these questions and answers the same

every visit. "No, Father." He glanced around the room, taking in the new stack of books piled around the priest's armchair. Dark brows furrowed, he squinted to read the wide variety of titles. He saw mysteries, biographies, and history. The old man read books the way some people did puzzles, or went to the movies, or drank coffee. It was his favorite pastime, his only pastime other than prayer. Cancini didn't like to read. It took too long and he preferred reality, but he understood the desire to escape. They sat for several minutes, drinking their coffee, the silence both comforting and familiar.

When the priest did speak again, his words were as much a pronouncement as a question. "It's been a few days since I've heard from you, Michael. I presume there's a new case then?"

"Yes, Father."

"Let me guess? The psychiatrist? The one I read about in the papers?"

"That's the one."

Father Joe clucked his tongue. "Sad. I will never understand what would drive a soul to take another man's life."

Cancini said nothing. It wasn't a new conversation. As a homicide detective, he'd known many violent men, even evil men. In his world, men were judged for their crimes. The appropriate punishment was supposed to be meted out through the justice system, although it didn't always work that way. Still, it was a world that condemned a man for his sins. In contrast, Father Joe accepted all men as sinners, believing fully in repentance followed by forgiveness, no matter the sin. In spite of his all-encompassing compassion, the priest was fascinated by Cancini's cases and the complexities of police work.

"Do you want to talk about it?"

"There's not much to say other than what you've heard on the news. We have no witnesses, no tangible DNA evidence, and as of yet, no motive."

"You're frustrated."

"Yes."

"The method of killing was not a gun. It was a knife. That's unusual, isn't it?"

"Yes." Cancini walked to the large window. The neighborhood had changed since the priest had first come to the parish. He could see the houses across the street with their sagging porches, peeling paint, and dandelion yards. A few homes had been renovated by young couples, but most were run-down with old wiring and older plumbing. New houses and new neighborhoods had sprung up in rings around the city, drawing anyone who could afford bigger and better. The parishioners, like the homes they lived in, were mostly old, or poor, or both. Yet, Father Joe stayed.

"A stabbing then. Like your mother," the priest said.

Cancini's head jerked back. "No, it's not the same." He paused and rubbed his hands on his thighs. "The victim was knifed in the back. I don't even think he saw it coming. And there was no robbery. I think the murderer knew the victim."

"I see."

"My best guess right now is that it was premeditated—at least partly."

"So, you believe it could be someone close to the psychiatrist?"

"Maybe. I don't know. I have no real idea at this point. It's just a feeling." An image of the man lying on the floor, facedown in his own blood, melded with that of his young mother, crumpled and bleeding to death on the hard floor of a convenience store. He remembered the rusty stains on the coat and shoes the police had sent home to his father. Her purse and the rest of her belongings had come home in a cardboard box. He shivered.

"You should trust your instincts," the priest said, interrupting his memories. "Stay with those who had a connection to him." Cancini nodded but said nothing. The priest picked up his coffee and took a long sip. "Well, how's your father then?"

Cancini stared down into his cup. "About the same, I guess. Good days and bad."

"What's the prognosis?"

"Don't know. The chemo's been making him so sick. It's hard to believe that stuff is supposed to make him better." The detective swallowed. "He's seventy years old. How much can he take?"

"Your father is a strong man, Michael. You know that."

"Stubborn, Father, not strong."

"Be that as it may, Michael, your father did survive the murder of his wife and raised you by himself. It was not an easy life for him." Cancini frowned. "We must all learn to accept what we cannot change and make the best of what we've been given. It is God's will."

The detective finished his coffee and stood. "Well, Father, I wonder how my murder victim would feel about God's will right now, or how his wife feels, or his secretary for that matter."

Father Joe gazed at his friend, his kind eyes never leaving the younger man's face. "I will pray for them, Michael."

Cancini looked down at the floor, his face grim. "Yeah, I'm sure they'd appreciate that."

He was almost out the door when the old priest spoke again, his voice soft. "And I'll pray for you, Michael. I'll pray for you, too."

Chapter Fifteen

"So, you think it's a coincidence or what?" The captain sat back in his chair, fingers pressed together into an empty house.

"Can't say yet." Cancini said. He didn't believe in coincidences and he didn't like speculating on another officer's case—the hit-and-run of Nora Michael's brother—especially one for which there were so few facts. "I talked to the guy who caught the case last year but he came up with bubkes. No motive, no suspect, and no real proof that the hit-and-run was premeditated at all. All the witnesses on record stated the car was already speeding and took off after the victim was hit. I'm not surprised it was ruled an accidental homicide." Cancini hated having to go into this, but after one call from Nora Michael, the captain was nosing around both investigations and prodding the detective for answers. "The statement the lady working the magazine stand gave the police is pretty much like all the other witnesses. She said she remembers talking to Nora Michael but not saying anything about the car hitting her brother on purpose. The ladies disagree about what was said." Cancini slumped down in the chair. "To tell you the truth, there isn't a whole lot to go on."

"Doesn't sound like it," Captain Martin said. A toothpick dangled from his lips, bobbing up and down when his mouth moved. Cancini recognized it as an obnoxious habit the man had picked up trying to emulate his favorite TV character, a big-time detective with all the answers. A fresh supply of toothpicks sat on the desk in a small glass jar. "Do you think there's any connection?"

"Honestly? Not based on what we know so far."

"But it is sort of odd, don't you think?"

"Odd? I guess, but I'm a lot more worried about my case, my victim." Cancini shifted in his chair. Neither man was comfortable in the other's presence, the detective's ex-wife always between them. He didn't blame the captain. The marriage was over and it was a free country. Still, dating and marrying another detective's wife was like breaking a code. He cleared his throat. "Mrs. Michael gave me the same spiel she probably gave you, and our guys have gone over that note she brought in, but there was nothing to find. It was clean for prints and there's no way to trace its origin." Gesturing, palms upturned, he said, "I don't think I can help the lady when it comes to the death of her brother, at least not right now. And frankly, other than that note, which tells us nothing, we don't have any reason to believe the deaths are connected except both victims shared the same profession. Now, if we were able to go into patients' histories . . ." He let the implication lie there, but the captain sat stone-faced, silent. Tipping his head to one side, Cancini concluded, "Besides, I would think she'd be a lot more worried about finding the person who killed her husband right now. That's what I call odd."

Martin nodded once. "Maybe, but it is an interesting conspiracy theory. What if it did turn out to be the same killer?"

Cancini swallowed a groan, tired of the subject and tired of

Nora Michael. The detective didn't like to be second-guessed or micromanaged. More than two decades on the force, experience under seven different captains, and nothing had changed. There was always pressure.

"Have we got anything, any leads at all?" the captain asked after a moment passed.

"It's too early to say. We're looking into a couple of things."

"Such as?"

The detective folded his arms across his chest. "Not much to tell yet."

"Try me."

Cancini opened his mouth and closed it again. Usually Martin gave him time and space to put together a case—especially lately—in light of their awkward relationship. He disliked laying out a case when there was no real evidence, only conjecture and guesswork, but Nora Michael and her theories had pushed forward the timetable. "Working on some details about the knife, checking out some of the alibis for the patients he saw that day, and . . ." The detective paused. "There are some discrepancies in the description of the relationship between the husband and wife." The toothpick in the captain's mouth stopped moving. "They may have been having some problems."

Martin tossed the toothpick into the trash and plucked a new one from the jar. "I thought Mrs. Michael had an alibi?"

"She does, but we're trying to get a better picture of what was going on at home. Right now, we're working on phone records and bank records, that sort of thing, check out whether she made any questionable calls or withdrawals recently."

"Well, whatever you do, do it fast," the captain said. He stood, ending the meeting. "I have a feeling Nora Michael's gonna be a royal pain in my ass." Cancini said nothing, hand on the door. Martin cleared his throat. "I heard your father's been sick. How's he doing?"

He stiffened. "He's getting by."

"I wouldn't ask, but Lola is worried about him."

Cancini's chin dropped to his chest. Inexplicably, his father and his ex had liked each other. They talked about television shows they followed or music they enjoyed or the Sudoku puzzles they worked on. When the marriage had ended, his father hadn't said a word, but Cancini had seen the look that said he'd let her get away. He'd wanted to wipe away that look, tell his father about her infidelities and the rest, but he couldn't do it. *What the hell*, he'd thought, *it's just one more thing I haven't done right.*

"She'd like to visit him, if that's okay with you."

Cancini nodded. The company would probably do the old man some good. "Fine."

"Good." The captain spit out another toothpick. "Keep me in the loop on the Michael case, Cancini. I mean it."

"Fine," he said again, grumbling under his breath. He pushed thoughts of Martin, Lola, and his dad from his mind to focus on the case at hand. He didn't have time to waste in the captain's office. Sitting at his desk with a fresh cup of coffee, he sifted through his notes. The medical examiner's report had whittled the time of death down to between nine P.M. and midnight. Most of Dr. Michael's patients had alibis for that time period. Three did not. He circled their names in his notes.

Above those names, he wrote Nora Michael. Alibi or not, he had questions about the widow. Perhaps it wasn't right to judge her based solely on her emotionless reaction to her husband's murder, but he did anyway. Her distant manner rubbed him the wrong way. Scratching at the salt-and-pepper stubble on his chin, Cancini thought he knew her type. He'd been married to it. Although Lola lacked Nora Michael's sophistication, both could turn a man's head. Still, that didn't make them the same. It was the eyes, the deflated expression, the look that told him they didn't care one whit whether the sun came up tomorrow or the next day or the next. There was something similar in the women, some element of emotion or intimacy that seemed to be missing. Was he right about the new widow? Was she like Lola?

Cancini, a man first and foremost, had been excited by his former wife's attention, so flattered he'd failed to wonder why a platinum beauty would notice him, a birdlike nobody whose only distinction was his success in the department. He should have known. After the initial enchantment wore off, he found she lacked feeling, content to share space, giving nothing in return but the benefit of her presence. When she strayed—more than once—he'd left. Marriage over. She was Martin's problem now.

Shuffling through the files on his desk, he pulled out the thick manila folder on the hit-and-run death of Mrs. Michael's brother. There were no interviews with patients, but the file did include a list of those scheduled for appointments that week. He recognized a few, guessing those were the patients who'd transferred to Dr. Michael after the accident. Each of the names had a valid alibi save one, George Vandenberg. He put a star next to that name, already circled in his notes.

Farther down the page, he printed the only clues he had to the description of the murderer. Five-ten to six feet tall and right-handed. That could be man or woman, especially if the woman wore heels. It wasn't much to go on. In truth, it was barely anything at all.

"Hey, Cancini!" Smitty strode into the squad room, eyes twinkling. "I think we might have caught a break."

"Oh? What makes today so special?" the detective asked.

Smitty stopped. "You okay?"

Cancini waved a hand. "Sorry. Just got out of Martin's office. Wants to know where we are."

"Well, maybe this will help. I was able to get the phone records for Mrs. Michael's room up in Chicago. There were four calls the night the doc was murdered." Smitty sat down, his voice excited. "At five—Chicago time—she called a cell phone number we haven't been able to trace yet. Then at eight, which is nine o'clock D.C. time, she got a call from Dr. Michael's office. She was on the line for approximately fifteen minutes. That coincides with the call that was made from the phone in Dr. Michael's private office."

"That fits in with the time of death Kate gave us," Cancini said. "He would still have been alive then."

"Right. She made a third call, right after the call from her husband, to the same cell phone she'd dialed earlier."

"And the fourth?"

"Also to the same cell phone number. Midnight our time."

"Odd she used the hotel phone and not her cell phone."

Smitty shrugged. "Maybe it was dead or she can expense calls made from the hotel. Either way, we got lucky."

Cancini rubbed his forehead. "How likely is it that the cell phone number belongs to the husband?"

"Not likely at all. I checked with his secretary, figuring she'd have the guy's numbers for emergencies and such. She didn't recognize the number at all. Plus, the timing's too weird. Why call her husband on his cell right after she'd just talked to him on his office line?"

"True," the detective said. "Is it a local number?"

"Yep. Trying to match a name to the number, but you know how that can be."

"Yeah, I do." He looked at Smitty. "Anything else?"

"My guy up in Chicago talked to some of the people who had dinner with Mrs. Michael that night. There was some deal in the hotel from six until about eight or so but she left a little early." Cancini paced while his partner talked. "A couple of the people at Mrs. Michael's table said she seemed disturbed. One lady said she thought Mrs. Michael seemed upset about something, kind of sad. That would have been not long after the first call."

"I think I see where you're headed. You're thinking the reason Nora Michael acted strangely at dinner was because she knew her husband was going to be murdered that night. You're thinking she knew because she'd arranged it herself." Cancini stopped pacing.

"You don't sound like you believe it."

He half smiled, voice weary. "Oh, I could be persuaded, believe me. I just think it's a big jump in assumptions. Maybe we should sit on that theory until we know more about the cell number."

"But wouldn't it make perfect sense she would call the killer beforehand to give him a heads-up that Dr. Michael was still in the office? Then she calls again at midnight to confirm the job is done. She's out of town. She knows he works late on those nights. It makes sense."

"It could, but we don't want to get ahead of ourselves."

"Why don't we just ask her about it?"

Cancini shoved his hands in his pockets. "Because it would be better to have the information on the cell phone number first. We don't know the substance of those calls. Besides, there are other explanations. It could've been a coworker or a friend."

"Or a boyfriend."

"Or a boyfriend. Either way, if we wait, we can do a check on the person before she gets a chance to warn them we're on to her." He paused. "If we're on to anything."

The young man brushed the blond hair from his forehead. He nodded, his face glum. "Okay. I get your point."

"Smitty, this is good work," Cancini said. "If the calls turn out to be suspicious, it's more ammunition to subpoena bank records and the rest of her personal information. Let's do it right, make any evidence we get stick."

"Sure. It feels like something though."

"I know." Cancini recalled the smooth, tear-free face of the widow the morning she learned of her husband's death. Shock or something else? "Don't worry. Nora Michael is at the top of the list and if there's something to find, we'll find it."

Chapter Sixteen

Inside the guesthouse, George stood in front of the mirror and peered at his reflection. The years had been kinder to him than he deserved. He'd put on a few pounds like most men his age. His face had grown redder and fleshier, blurring the chiseled bone structure into a softer version of his boyhood visage. He still had a full head of hair, and most of his wife's friends found him attractive—when he was sober. None of it mattered though. He still felt old, used, and incompetent on the inside.

He slipped on a shirt and left the small house, impulse guiding him to the old boathouse. Sagging and weather-worn, it stood in contrast to the solid new boathouse and dock Mary Helen had ordered built. He reached out and touched the splintered wood. His wife was right. It was an eyesore now.

The door creaked open on stiff and rusty hinges. A damp, musty odor hit him in the face, and he covered his nose with his hand. He breathed through his mouth until he got used to the smell. Cobwebs filled the corners, hanging down at eye level, and he brushed them away. Except for a broken canoe and some old paddles pushed up against the far wall, the boathouse sat empty. The opening for his father's boat had been boarded up years ago, plunging the space into near darkness. He left the door open for light and fresh air.

George inhaled the stale air, closed his eyes, and remembered. He'd been cleaning the boat, rinsing saltwater and wiping the interior, when Sarah had surprised him. He'd leaped out and wrapped his arms around her thickening waist. To his great joy, she didn't resist. He pulled her in tighter until her body melted into his, her head falling onto his shoulder. He kissed her hair, the top of her forehead, and her cheeks, afraid to let go. They stood close, arms intertwined. After several minutes, she pushed him away, pressing against his chest with her hands.

"Give me a minute, George." She averted her face, but not before he saw the tears. Her eyes told him what he needed to know.

"Why?" he managed to ask.

Shaking her dark head, she didn't answer at first. When she did speak, the words were barely a whisper. "Because it's for the best, George. God, this is so hard." She took a breath. "I know you're serious about us being together, but I know it would never work. I've spent a lot of time thinking about it, and no matter what you want, you can't change how other people would be. Your parents, your family, your friends. They wouldn't forgive you or me—especially me."

He grabbed her hands. "It wouldn't be that bad, Sarah. I mean, I know my dad would be mad for a while, but he would get over it."

She tried to smile, eyes wet again. "You should hear yourself, George. You can't convince me of something you don't believe yourself. He'd cut you off and you know it." He opened his mouth and closed it again. "If, and this is a big if, they were to accept the marriage, I would always be the outsider. I don't fit in with your kind, with your friends, your life."

"But you're talking about things I don't care about anymore. I want to be with you. We can make it work." He reached out to pull her back into his arms.

"You say that now," she said, voice shaking, "but it would change. I promise you. It would be easier for me. I've always done without, and I can't miss what I've never experienced, but you—it would matter someday. Maybe not in a year, maybe not in five, but eventually . . ." Tears streamed down her face, mixing with the salty sweat beading up on her forehead and nose. Inside the boathouse, the heat was oppressive, the air still and stagnant.

"I'll get a job," he said. "Graduation is right around the corner." She lifted her head, watching him. "I don't understand you, Sarah. You know how much I hate my father. The pressure he puts on me, the expectations. Why are you so worried about what he thinks or what my family thinks? I'm not."

Her words were flat, definite. "He loves you."

"For whatever that's worth."

"He wants what's best for you."

"Is that what this is all about? What's best for me?" George's voice rose and the veins in his neck grew thick. She remained silent. "You're siding with my father now about what's best for me? What about the baby? What's best for our baby? What gives you the right to decide?"

Her face flushed. "Don't get nasty, George." She moved to leave and he grabbed her arm, his fingers pinching the supple skin. "Let me go."

He loosened his grip but held on. "Please, Sarah. You're not even giving us a chance."

She shook her arm free. "There's no point, George. I'm a wait-ress in a bar, no family you'd want to know, no education. We have no chance."

"You can change that, Sarah. You can be whatever you want. I'll help you."

"No! It's too late for us."

He kept talking, offered to get two jobs and support her while she went to school. "It'll be hard for a while but we can do it and—"

"No!" Spit flew from her mouth. "That's not how it's going to be. You are going to go back to your world and everything will go back to normal. It will be like we never even met."

His mouth hung open. "That's crazy, Sarah. I can't change how I feel. I'm not going to forget you because you tell me to. It doesn't work that way. I love you."

She pursed her lips, all trace of tears gone. "No, George, you only think you do. You love the idea of me, the girl who is differ-ent, who represents everything you're not supposed to be doing. You want to be with me for all the reasons your father wouldn't want you to."

His mouth clamped shut. Was she right? Was she nothing more than a symbol of rebellion against his father? He pushed the thought from his mind. "No."

Again, she tried to leave, but he jumped in her path. She raised her hand to slap him, but he caught it, squeezed, and pulled her into him. She jerked her body, but couldn't escape his grasp. "Stop, you're hurting me,"

"You can't leave, Sarah. I need you to listen to me." Sweat poured down his back. He put both arms around her to keep her close. She kicked and punched and he let her. "I listened to you, Sarah. It's your turn to listen to me."

Her body grew limp. "I won't. I can't."

Their bodies slipped to the floor, his arms still holding her tight. He rubbed her back, his hand making circles. "I don't believe you can do this, Sarah. I don't." She bowed her head, and her long dark hair hid her face. He leaned close, voice soft and urgent. "I know I've been a jerk, and maybe everything you've said is true. Maybe my parents would hate you. Maybe they would cut me off. Maybe we'd be completely on our own. I don't care. I know you think I would someday, but you're wrong. Just because I grew up with more than you doesn't mean that's the only life I can live. Even with all I've had, I've never been as happy as I am with you." He stroked her silky hair, his fingers combing its length. "It sounds corny, even crazy, but I need you. I need us to be together." Pausing, he waited, but still she said nothing. "You are the best thing that's ever happened to me. I can't lose you, Sarah. I won't. That's the truth."

She lifted her head and pushed her hair behind her ears. Rocking back on her heels, she staggered to her feet, looking down at him. Shoulders squared, her dark eyes were flat, expressionless. "No, George. The truth is you already have."

Chapter Seventeen

THE SCOTCH DULLED his senses, though not enough Cancini forgot he was sitting alone at the bar with an aching head. He should be getting home, but since the divorce, he felt less and less like being in the apartment. The empty rooms reminded him of the failure in his personal life, of the failure in his judgment. It was one thing to be a loner; it was another to always be alone. Once upon a time, he'd wanted a family and a home life, something that would make his father proud. But he'd picked the wrong woman. He only wished they'd had a kid, wished he could've given his dad a grandson or a granddaughter. Instead, he'd disappointed the old man again. Cancini sipped the scotch and counted the bottles lined up along the mirrored wall. Smitty would have a smart comment, tell him he was delaying the inevitable. Smitty would be right.

A shout in the back corner of the bar made him look over his shoulder. A small group clustered around a dartboard. He lost interest and swallowed another slug of scotch. Picking at a stale bowl of pretzels, he watched an Orioles game playing on TV. It might not be home, but it beat an empty apartment any night. Besides, Monty kept the conversation to a minimum and the drinks ready and available. It was a good relationship, the detective thought, better than most.

A fresh glass with three cubes appeared in front of him. Monty tipped the bottle of scotch, filling it to the rim.

"I didn't order that," Cancini said, looking up.

"I know." The bartender hooked his thumb toward the end of the bar. "The lady did. It's on her."

A sideways glance and he knew the woman who'd paid for his drink. Nora Michael. She sat perched on the end of a stool, long legs crossed. She raised her glass and smiled. He nodded once. She picked up her wine to join him.

"This seat taken, Detective?"

He shook his head. "It's all yours."

"Great. How are the burgers here? I just ordered one."

"Greasy, the way I like 'em." Finishing his drink, he pulled the fresh scotch closer. "Thanks for the drink."

She shifted on her stool, her lithe body facing him. "You looked like you needed one."

"Maybe."

Silent only a moment, her fingers trailed the rim of her glass. "You don't seem surprised to see me, Detective. Why not?"

His gaze flickered over her face. The makeup had been artfully applied, almost hiding the dark shadows under her bloodshot eyes. "What makes you think I'm not?"

She sipped her white wine. "You're not. I can tell."

"Well, maybe I am and maybe I'm not, but something tells me you do a lot of things that surprise people."

She smiled. "I'm not sure if that's a compliment, but I'm going to take it as one anyway." Cancini shrugged but said nothing. "Well, I'll tell you why I'm here. To find you."

Ice clinked in his glass when he drank. "So, you found me. I don't know what you expect to learn."

"It's not what I can learn from you. It's what you can learn from me."

Monty returned with the lady's plate, silverware, and condiments. Wordless, he took Cancini's first glass and swiped at the counter with a damp towel. The detective took another long swig of scotch. Mrs. Michael picked up the large burger, her long fingers pressing into the soft bun. Ketchup, grease, and gooey cheese oozed over the sides and she asked for extra napkins. Cancini remained quiet until she finished.

She pushed the plate away. "That was good." She wiped her lips and polished off the wine. "I haven't had a burger in so long, I forgot how much I liked them."

"Really? Are you one of those vegetarians, or vegans, or whatever they're called?"

She laughed out loud, a throaty, sensual laugh. The lovely red lips parted wide, revealing even, white teeth. "No, nothing like that. Edmund and I had been on this health kick, you know, eating chicken, fish, and vegetables. No beef allowed. No alcohol other than the occasional glass of wine. No fruit. No bread. I guess it sounds pretty boring."

"Very." He changed the subject. "Mrs. Michael, what is it that I could learn from you?"

She hesitated only a second. "It's about one of my husband's patients and I think one of my brother's. Edmund didn't normally talk to me about his cases—never actually—but there was one that kept eating at him. He brought it up a few weeks ago and I thought it might be important . . ." Her voice trailed off.

Watching the lady's reflection in the glass, Cancini considered her words. "Conversations between a husband and wife can sometimes be ruled privileged. Does your lawyer know you're talking to me?"

"I don't need a lawyer, Detective." A tinge of exasperation crept into her voice. "Do you want to hear what I have to say or not?"

He raised his shoulders. "I don't want to get burned if you scream privilege later."

She frowned. "I'm not going to scream anything and I'm not going to say anything I don't want you to know. I'm trying to give you a picture of his state of mind the last couple of weeks and maybe some suggestion as to where to look for answers." Her face softened. "Would that be okay?"

He took a swallow of scotch. He didn't trust her, but he wanted to hear what she had to say. "Sure."

"Good. There's this patient and I don't know a name or even whether it's a man or woman, but whoever it was had been on my husband's mind more and more. He started talking about this person facing a life-changing decision and how this decision could hurt a lot of people."

Cancini's heavy eyebrows furrowed. "Hurt?"

"Yes, that's what he said. It was something like . . ." She looked past him, remembering. "Something about a terrible thing in this person's past they needed to admit. From what I could gather, Edmund was encouraging a confession." She paused and smoothed her hair. "I'm not sure if I've got this right, but this terrible thing might have been a crime. Supposedly, no one knew about it, but once they did, it might wreck people's lives."

"Your husband told you this?" The woman nodded. "Why?"

She looked down at her lap and wiped some imagined crumbs from her slacks. "I think . . ." She hesitated. "I think Edmund wondered if he was doing the right thing, pushing this patient, telling this person to confess. I think he believed it was the only way the patient could get better, but he was worried about the consequences. I got the feeling he wanted my opinion, but I also think . . ." Mrs. Michael bit her lip. "I think he was afraid."

Cancini let out a breath. "Afraid? Do you mean physically afraid?"

"I think so."

"Afraid of this patient, the one you've been telling me about?"

"I'm pretty sure," she said. Her voice dropped to a whisper. "Something happened in his appointment that day . . ." Her lower lip quivered. "He told me about it on the phone that night. He called me in my hotel room. That was the last time we spoke."

Smitty had already given the detective the details of the calls between husband and wife the night of the murder. "What did he say?"

"Not much," she said. "Only that one of his sessions had gone badly and this patient had gotten upset. Something got broken, a lamp or something. He said the patient told him to back off and stop pushing so hard."

Cancini ran his fingertips through his short, spiky hair. *Stop pushing.* Coincidence? Out loud, he asked, "So, this patient may have been violent?"

"Oh, definitely. I think whatever happened in the past, the thing that might have been a crime, I think it was something violent." She sighed. "I wish I'd told him to stop the sessions and tell the patient to find another doctor when it first started bothering him. Edmund had been acting so strangely recently. He wasn't sleeping. He was distracted. It was like he was obsessed." She gave a nervous laugh, "I guess if I was the jealous type I might've been angry, but I knew how much his practice meant to him."

Even though Cancini knew no response was necessary, he said, "Your husband was dedicated to his patients."

She sucked in her breath. "Yes, he was." She dabbed at her eye with a handkerchief. "I admired him very much and now he's gone."

Sipping their drinks, the two sat at the bar for several more minutes, the anonymous patient weighing on both their minds. Could the patient have lost his temper with his therapist? Could he or she have decided they'd had enough? Could a patient have snuck back into the office and coldly murdered the one person who was trying to help him? An unstable patient made for a convincing suspect. *Stop pushing.* The words were eerily similar to the note she'd dropped in his lap.

Cancini set his glass on the bar. "I do have one question for you. I've been wondering why your husband didn't have a picture of you on his desk or somewhere in the office."

She blinked, but not before he caught the look of surprise. "My husband liked to keep his sessions with his patients focused on them. He kept his personal life separate. Why? Does it matter?"

"No, I guess not." Cancini hesitated, then said, "We haven't been able to find your husband's reading glasses. Do you know where they might be?"

Mrs. Michael's shoulders drooped and she polished off her wine. "They could be anywhere," she said. Her eyes fell away from his. "My husband was always losing things. He must have ordered three pairs of glasses in the last year alone. Later, I would find them in the strangest places." Her hand shook as she placed her glass on the bar.

He waited a moment, then slid from the barstool and threw some cash on the wooden bar. There was nothing more he could learn. "Thank you, Mrs. Michael. This has been helpful, but I need to be getting home."

"You're welcome, Detective." She straightened and waved a hand. "I don't know if any of it means anything. After all, this patient may be completely innocent. It's just . . . I thought you should know."

At the door, he glanced over his shoulder. She remained at the bar, a solitary presence. In her suit and heels, she didn't belong in a dingy bar like this one. Did she notice the burnt rings on the bar or the black velvet paintings hung near the bathroom? Did her nose wrinkle at the odors of old beer and stale cigarettes rising from the patchy rug? Monty's was hardly the five-star restaurant he pictured her in. How had she tracked him down and why? He left with a shrug, letting the door swing shut behind him. Was she telling the truth or simply diverting attention from herself? She hadn't asked once about the note or her brother. The urgency in the station had been eclipsed by this new information. It could be something, but even if it was, it would be difficult to prove. No patient in their right mind would voluntarily give up their right to privacy, and without more credible evidence, he was in no position to pursue a subpoena. Her story amounted to nothing more than hearsay in a court of law. Whistling under his breath, Detective Mike Cancini walked home in the dark. Baffled, he was sure of only one thing. The lady was a mystery.

Chapter Eighteen

GEORGE SANK TO the ground, the memory of Sarah bringing him to his knees. Oddly, it felt as close as yesterday. The flowers, grass, and dust smelled the same. The river still rushed past the property, just as it always had. The heat and humidity still spiked in the warm weather months, bringing families, boaters, and fishermen. Life here hadn't changed.

In Richmond, the years had ground to a slow crawl, dragging unmercifully to the dead end he lived every day. He hated his life. He hated his job. He hated his wife. He loved the children, but they were teenagers now and no longer needed him. Did they love him? He couldn't say for sure. In a moment of pure insight, he realized he'd made the classic mistake. He'd done everything he could not to be the domineering, controlling father he'd known. Instead, he'd been mostly absent, barely even registering on the radar, except as an annoyance, pestering them for tidbits about their lives. He didn't know what they felt, who their friends were, what they wanted out of life. He was a man who happened to live in their house—some of the time.

Escaping to Washington, usually on the pretext of business, had grown into a weekly event. Mary Helen had stopped complaining a long time ago. Instead, she used his absences to live her life the way she wanted, free of him. They didn't have a marriage. They had an arrangement. He watched the rushing river and the rapids tipped with tiny whitecaps. He breathed in the warm air and knew he wanted to start over. The fading light cast shadows across the green grass down to the water. He raised his left hand. An indentation marked the third finger, a reminder his wedding ring sat at the bottom of the river. That was different. He was different.

He pulled in his knees and bowed his head. Dr. Michael's words replayed over and over in his mind. *It's time to come forward.* He'd resisted, afraid to lose his children, afraid of his wife. It wasn't just fear. George recognized his reluctance didn't all start with his wife. He'd been unwilling to put his family through a potentially public airing of a nasty accident, one he'd covered up for more than twenty years. Now, crouched in the grass, he wondered why he'd been so unsure.

"George," Dr. Michael had said in one of their last sessions, "surely you must see the depression you suffer, the apathy, is all brought on by your own inability to reconcile your actions in the past with the present."

He didn't answer. He'd barely listened to the therapeutic jargon, so focused on the fear that coursed through him when he considered confessing his sins. "Can you refill my prescription?" he'd asked, deliberately avoiding the subject.

He remembered Dr. Michael had written something in his notebook, the one he always kept in his lap during each of George's appointments. "Do you feel strong enough to have the dosage lowered? You've been on this antidepressant for a long time. Maybe we could cut back a little and see how you do."

"I don't know. I guess, if you think it's okay," he said, adding, "but I'm sure I still need it."

"Perhaps." Stroking his thin mustache, the doctor returned to the topic of a full confession. "You may find, George, that it's not as terrible as you think. I know you're afraid, but you must have faith."

He'd stared at the therapist, eyes wide in disbelief. "You don't know what you're talking about, Dr. Michael. It would be a nightmare. What if the police didn't believe it was an accident? I could even go to jail."

"Is that it? You're afraid you might go to jail?"

"No, no," he'd said, waving his hands. "It's not just about me. There's my family, my wife's family, even . . . uh . . . Sarah's family, wherever they are." George waved his hands in protest. "No, I want to. I do. I'd give almost anything to stop carrying around this burden, but it's not going to happen. I can't do it. It would be selfish of me."

"Who told you that, George?"

He'd left the question unanswered, but they both knew. Now, breathing in the heady scent of honeysuckle and wild roses, George wondered at his misguided loyalty. Maybe he'd been wrong. George had allowed himself to be led down this path, a pretty and windy road that never ended, careening toward a consuming guilt that threatened to eclipse the man who bore it. Drowning in his own shame, sometimes too embarrassed to look at his own reflection, he was more than eager to numb his conscious mind. It was no kind of life. Dr. Michael had tried to help him change, but in the end, he'd shoved the doctor away—in effect killing his own chance at finding happiness. What did that leave him? A wife who belittled him? Children who couldn't count on him? Friends who didn't really know him? His life was a sham, a gorgeous charade of how to have everything and how to have nothing.

Without knowing why, he recalled the summer after the accident. He'd graduated from college. That was followed by his engagement to Mary Helen. It was mostly a blur. He couldn't even remember how he'd become engaged, only that she stayed by his side every day, flashing a ring with a large diamond encircled by sapphires. Years later, he discovered she and his father had picked out the ring and paid for it with the trust fund he'd inherited on his twenty-first birthday. He'd spent most of that summer at home, sitting by the pool and avoiding the river, drinking beer with his frat brothers until they passed out. No one around him seemed to notice; they were too busy planning his wedding, planning his career, planning his future. Mary Helen came over every day, conferring with his mother, their two heads bent over list after list of guests, food, and gifts. When he'd shown up at the ceremony and reception, even he'd been impressed, stunned by the attention to detail. Mary Helen had a talent for creating the illusion of perfection.

The honeymoon had been no more memorable than the months that preceded it. The holiday only gave him an excuse to begin drinking before noon, lie in the sun, and stumble into bed each night. Then he'd made a critical mistake. In an alcoholic haze during a heated session of lovemaking, he'd called her Sarah. His wife had jumped away as though his skin was that of a leper. "Never again, George. Under no circumstances can you ever mention that person's name to me again. Do you understand?" Wrapping the sheet around her naked body, she'd run to the shower. "If you do, I swear I'll take you for everything you have. That part of your life is over. This is your life now." And she'd been right. It was over.

He stood and brushed the grass from his clothes. A soft breeze caressed his cheeks. The sun slipped over the horizon and dusk settled over the property. A calm settled over him and he knew this was where he wanted to be for the rest of his life. It wouldn't be easy to change course after all these years, to veer off the road paved by his wife and family, to drive down the rocky road he'd avoided for so long. They might never forgive him, but none of that mattered now. He needed to do what was right, not what was expected. He climbed into his car, sober, an unexpected surge of confidence in his heart. Leaving the rural roads of the river, he bypassed Richmond. Both hands firmly on the wheel, he kept his focus straight ahead. It was time to start over.

Chapter Nineteen

"DAMMIT! THIS DOESN'T make sense!" Smitty smacked his desk.

"What doesn't make sense?" Cancini came up behind the younger man. In spite of the early hour, the office buzzed. Anyone not already assigned to a case had jumped into the Michael investigation. Cancini sipped coffee and leaned over Smitty's shoulder. "What's the matter?"

Smitty pointed at the computer screen. "This phone number. I don't get it."

"Don't get what?" Cancini put the file folder he'd been perusing under his arm.

"Mrs. Michael. Remember how I told you she made three calls from her hotel room the night her husband died? And they were all to a local cell number we've been trying to trace?"

"I remember," he said. "Did you find out whose cell it was?"

Deep lines appeared above Smitty's long, thin nose. "Yeah, and that's what's weird. That number is hers."

"Hers?" Cancini repeated, and angled his head to see the screen. "Whose?"

"Mrs. Michael's. It doesn't make sense. Why would she call herself? And why three times? Was she leaving herself messages or what?"

"Wait." Cancini's brow creased. "She gave us a number, didn't she, so we could reach her?"

"Different number. She has two phones in her name. The one she gave us isn't the one she called that night."

"Maybe it's Dr. Michael's phone."

"No. He had a different number, different service even, and we found that phone in his car. This number wasn't his."

Cancini straightened. "Have you tried calling the number?"

"Yep, three times. No answer and there's no name on the voice mail. It's automated."

"How long were each of those calls?"

"Hold on," Smitty said. He shuffled through his notes. "The first call was less than ten minutes and the second about the same." He looked up at Cancini. "Now, here's where it gets interesting. The third call was close to thirty minutes long and that was at midnight."

"Midnight D.C. time?"

"Right."

"How long had she had that phone number?"

"Looks like at least a year."

The dark-haired detective nodded and sipped from his coffee. When he spoke, the words gained momentum, an idea taking shape in his mind. "It's possible she was leaving messages for herself, but thirty minutes at that time of night seems excessive. For now, I'm going to rule that out. Just because the phone number belongs to her and she pays the bills doesn't mean she actually uses that phone." He walked the floor behind Smitty's chair. "Let's say she's paying for someone to carry that phone so she can get in touch with them whenever she wants."

"Someone for hire or maybe someone she didn't want her husband to know about?"

"The boyfriend idea."

Smitty spun around to face Cancini. "It's a pretty clever scheme actually. The lady gives the phone to someone else so no one will know who she's talking to. Makes sense if you're trying to hide a lover, especially a lover who'd be happy to help a lady get rid of her husband."

"Maybe," Cancini said, "but remember, we're guessing. She could have given the phone to her housekeeper or a close friend. There could be another explanation."

"Doubt it. From what I've learned, she doesn't have any close friends and the housekeeper idea doesn't seem right. Why spend half an hour on the phone with your housekeeper at midnight? Making sure the laundry gets done?" Smitty snorted. "It's fishy to me. No question about it."

"So, boyfriend is your best guess?"

"Probably," Smitty said with a shrug of his narrow shoulders. "There aren't any kids and the marriage seems weird." His long fingers tapped a tune on the desk. "She's pretty hard to read."

"You're not kidding," Cancini said. He glanced over at the captain's office, then pulled up a chair close to his young partner. For the next several minutes, he detailed Nora Michael's surprise visit to Monty's. Cancini concluded by repeating the story of her husband's preoccupation with the patient who may have been violent. "I honestly don't know what to make of it. She seemed a little more broken up about her husband than she did the other day, but that doesn't mean shit. The whole note thing bothers me and now this, tracking me down at Monty's on the flimsy pretext that she thought I should know." He banged his fist on the desk. "What the hell is she after?"

"She must have followed you. It's not like that dump is easy to find. No offense."

"None taken."

"Either way, she went to a lot of trouble to find you and talk to you alone." Cancini couldn't disagree. "So, that means one of two things. Either she doesn't want us looking too closely at her, which means she has something to hide, or she's telling the truth."

Cancini rubbed his hand across his chin. "Or both. She could be telling me the truth because she has something to hide. A true story that pans out makes her more credible and less suspicious."

"I hadn't thought of that," Smitty said. "So what's our next move?"

The detective's head pounded and he didn't answer right away. The next move was always the question. It kept him awake at night, lying alone between the sheets and staring at the ceiling in the darkness. A mistake, a miscalculation, could change the course of the entire investigation. He'd seen it happen. A detective, convinced he had his murderer, could be wrong, inadvertently wasting time pursuing the wrong suspect while the real killer escaped judgment. Sometimes those situations could be corrected, but other times . . . Cancini had been lucky so far. Still, the knowledge that he might be wrong, that he could fail to avenge a victim because he'd made a mistake, fed the insomnia he lived with day in and day out.

Cancini stood again and returned to his desk. "We need to go with both angles. Let's keep after the wife, see what we can find and look into the patients as much as we're allowed. Any more on Nora Michael's background check?"

"Still working on it."

"Good. Let's get a record of all the outgoing calls from the Michael house and the doc's office for the past month. I want to know if there are any other calls to that cell phone number."

"Okay." Smitty took notes as they talked.

"Have we learned any more about why she wouldn't move from Boston to be with the husband she admired so much?"

"No one seems to know. Everyone assumed it was job-related."

"What about bank records? Have we got anyone working on that?"

"Wilder is pulling Michael's records, personal and private, to see if there's any funny business, large withdrawals, or deposits that can't be explained. There were joint accounts and separate accounts, stocks, bonds, insurance. He'll find it if anything's there."

"Let me know what he comes up with." The second angle, pursuing a patient, could prove stickier. Domestic situations happened all the time, but questioning patients could stretch the boundaries of privilege. He would have to be careful. "I want to find out if what Mrs. Michael said holds any water, too. She claims it's one of the patients he saw on the day he died. We'll bring the patients in, go over their alibis again, and ask a few questions about how their appointments went. There were a couple I wanted to talk to again anyway." He saw the questioning look on Smitty's face. "Don't worry, I'll clear it with the D.A.'s office first."

"And then?"

"Let's see where it takes us. We'll ask each of them if anything unusual happened. What was the doctor's manner? Did he seem himself? Supposedly a lamp was broken. Maybe someone in the waiting room heard something. We'll keep 'em here as long as we can, get as much out of 'em as possible."

Smitty's light eyes narrowed. "Some of them might not talk without their lawyer."

"That's okay. Let 'em have a lawyer. I'm not going to ask why they were seeing the doctor," Cancini paused and grinned. "Unless they happen to want to tell me."

"Yeah, right."

Cancini rose, empty cup in his hand. "There is one more thing. I'd like to bring Sandy Watson in again."

"I thought she was done giving her statement."

"She was, but now I have some new questions to ask her. She didn't mention anything about an incident in the office that day. Either she didn't know about it, it didn't happen, or she deliberately left it out. I want to know which it is. Also, it's been a couple of days now. Maybe she's remembered something else."

"I'll call her," Smitty said without delay.

"And let's make sure that the patients see her here, answering questions, fully cooperating." A smile spread across Cancini's face. "Let's see if we can make any of them a little uncomfortable, shake the tree a little. Maybe then we'll see who's who."

Chapter Twenty

Mary Helen had hung up on him. Not that he cared. George had phoned her on his way to the city, his trip hampered by the ubiquitous Washington traffic. When he'd told her he wasn't coming home for a few days, she'd screamed, hurling nasty words across the phone lines. His head still throbbed, but he didn't mind. For the first time in months—maybe years—he was completely sober. Mind clear, he sat up most of the night, writing letters to his children, their framed pictures in front of him on the wooden table. For much of the time, he stared into space, smoking and dreaming of the years he'd pissed away, the most important years of his kids' lives. He didn't know if they could ever forgive him, but if nothing else, they would know he loved them.

The letters were brief, barely more than notes, but they were written from his heart. He made no promises or sweeping pronouncements. He simply told them he was sorry. Careful not to predict the future, George wrote he might do and say things they wouldn't understand, but none of it was a reflection on them. The choices he'd made throughout his lifetime were his alone and he took sole responsibility. He did not mention their mother at all. As he put pen to paper, he sensed the tide turning, for better or for worse.

Sliding into bed, George's body trembled. Sharp pangs clawed at his gut and he fought the urge to go out for vodka or gin or anything to stop the shakes. Sleep, when it came, proved restless and dreamless. Awaking early, he shivered under the heavy comforter. Overhead, the ceiling fan whirred and he blinked in the morning light. Had he made a mistake? It was one thing to tell yourself you were going to change your life, it was another to follow through on that vow. Still, it felt better than all the days before when—most of the time—he felt nothing. In the past year, hope had only come in sessions with Dr. Michael, dissolving as soon as he was out the door, but this was new. This was hope born of his own planned actions and resolutions. The realization got him out of bed.

George felt like crap. In the early stages of withdrawal, his hands shook and his skin crawled. When the police called and suggested he come down to the station, his stomach twisted and he could barely choke down a piece of toast. He considered calling Larry but pushed the thought from his mind. He hadn't done anything wrong. That was the old George, the fearful George, the man who excelled at the art of hiding. The new George wouldn't do that. Those days were done.

At the police station, he followed a tall blond detective with such long legs he didn't walk so much as lope across the room. Left alone in a dreary room, George hid his shaking hands in his lap. Five minutes stretched into ten. He looked around the room. Three windowless walls were distinguished only by spots of peeling paint. The fourth wall contained a large panel of glass. Squinting, he guessed the glass was of the one-way variety, used to watch interrogations. He crossed his legs and jumped at the squeak of the chair in the soundless room. Goose bumps erupted on his arms. He locked his hands together and bowed his head. His heart pitter-pattered at a breakneck speed and he took several deep breaths.

Detective Smithson poked his head in. "Sorry about the wait. Would you like a soda?"

George licked his lips. "Yes, thank you."

The man waved a hand. "Follow me. I'll take you to the machine." Out of the room, voices rose and fell and phones clattered. People rushed by. George hesitated, frozen by the activity. The detective apologized again. "It's not always like this. The Michael investigation has everyone pretty busy." George remained silent, not trusting himself to speak. Smithson held up a couple of bills. "On us today."

"Thanks." He bought a soda and a pack of crackers. "Will it be much longer?" he asked as they made their way back.

"Probably not," Detective Smithson said. "Some of the questioning has taken longer than we thought. I hope you don't mind waiting."

Looking around, George stopped again. He recognized the detective who'd escorted Sandy Watson from the office building on the morning after Dr. Michael's death. Seated at a desk on the far side of the room, he spoke to a young woman with long, dark hair. A petulant glare distorted her pretty face. The girl seemed familiar, yet he didn't know her.

"Like I told you on the phone," Detective Smithson said, "we're talking to everyone who saw Dr. Michael the day he died. Anything you know might be important."

"Oh. Well, I don't think I know anything, but I'll try." George's eyes returned to the girl at the desk. He watched her jump up from the chair, sling her purse over her shoulder, and stomp away. His lips parted. He did remember her.

"Mr. Vandenberg? Are you all right?" The detective followed his gaze.

"Yeah, sorry," George said. He tore his attention from the retreating back of the young woman. "I'm fine." He hesitated, then asked, "That girl, the one that just left, was she one of Dr. Michael's patients, too?"

The detective shrugged. "I think so. Several of his patients are here today." He walked on and pushed open the door to the interrogation room. "His secretary is here, too."

"Oh." He wobbled on his feet, disoriented as though he'd just stepped off a roller coaster and couldn't quite regain his balance. He put his right hand out and grabbed the table, catching himself before he stumbled. "Mrs. Watson?"

The man looked at him. "Yes. You know her, right?"

He fell into the chair and exhaled. "This must be terrible for her. How is she doing?"

"As well as can be expected, I guess. She's been a big help to us, too."

The door clicked shut and George was alone again. A chill crawled up and down his spine. Nausea clawed at his belly and he chugged the soda, the bubbles temporarily vanquishing the urge to throw up. He could leave. He didn't have anything new to tell the police anyway. In spite of his wife's sly insinuation, he knew he wasn't involved. He couldn't be. He loved Dr. Michael. Even in death, the therapist loomed large in George's mind. The one person he wished for in that moment was the same reason he sat in a police station. He smiled at the irony.

"You certainly look pleased with yourself, Mr. Vandenberg." The dark-haired detective stood in the doorway, a thick file folder in his hand.

The smile vanished. "No, not really." He stood and extended his right hand, wiping it on his trousers first. "Call me George."

Chapter Twenty-One

Lauren Temple was a pain in the ass. Her know-it-all attitude combined with her reluctance to answer any questions made her a difficult interview. Detective Cancini sincerely hoped he would never have to question the young woman again.

"I told you where I was that night," she said through clenched teeth. The long and shapeless dress she wore hid whatever figure she possessed. Her hair, dyed almost black, hung across her face and spilled over her narrow shoulders. A dozen or more bangles clattered on her thin wrists. "Did you check it out or not? That's your job, isn't it?"

"We talked to your boyfriend. It looks like you were telling the truth."

Her mouth dropped open. "It looks like I was telling the truth? I was telling the truth." She folded her arms across her chest. "Why do I have to answer all these questions again? Why am I here at all?"

In spite of her manner, he managed to keep his tone neutral. "We're talking to everyone who saw Dr. Michael that day."

"You already did that. Why am I doing it again?"

"Because he was your therapist and because you and some others had appointments with him just hours before he was stabbed to death. That makes you one of the last to see him alive. That's why."

Her mouth opened and closed again. She uncrossed her arms and put them in her lap. "What do you want to know?"

"Did anything unusual happen that day when you saw Dr. Michael?"

"Unusual? Like what?"

Cancini swallowed a groan. "Was everything normal when you saw him last?"

Lauren Temple frowned. "I guess. As normal as it usually was."

"Meaning?"

"It was a bore." She waved a thin arm and the stack of bracelets jangled. "I was close to quitting anyway. It's not like it was doing me any good or anything."

He made a note to speak with Mrs. Watson about the young woman. "Was that because you were disappointed in Dr. Michael? Was he an incompetent therapist?"

Her top lip curled. "That's good, Detective. You're trying to make me say I didn't like him or something. The truth is I didn't care about him one way or the other. I already told you going to him was kind of a lark. I thought it would be cool." She snickered. "It wasn't."

"Okay, I get it. How long had you been seeing Dr. Michael?"

"Off and on for about a year, I guess. I wasn't a regular or anything. I went once in a while, when I felt like it."

"So, did you think Dr. Michael seemed like himself at your last appointment?"

She tossed her head and the fabric fell away from her bony frame. Her collarbone protruded awkwardly and spoiled the smooth line of her shoulder. She noticed his raised eyebrows and yanked the dress back up. "He was fine."

"What did you talk about?"

Her dark eyes flashed. "You're not allowed to ask me that. I know about patients' rights, you know."

"No one said you have to answer." Her face reddened. "Since you were only seeing Dr. Michael because you thought it was cool, I didn't think you'd mind telling me what you were talking about. Unless there's something you don't want me to know."

Lauren jumped to her feet. Her oversized purse grazed his head when she yanked it from the floor to her shoulder.

"Was seeing Dr. Michael more important than you would have me believe, Miss Temple?"

She stood over him, both hands on her hips. "Not the way you're implying, Detective."

"If you say so."

"Oh, for God's sake," Her hands fell and she exhaled. "All I ever talked to him about was my parents, okay? I'm just another kid who has issues with her parents. You wouldn't understand . . . what it was like." Her lip quivered as she spoke.

It was the first real emotion he'd seen from the girl. What wouldn't he understand?

She regained her composure, voice brittle. "Satisfied?"

He wasn't, but he had no room to press the point. "That wasn't so difficult was it?"

Her face hardened. "Are we done?"

"One more question. Would we have your permission to review Dr. Michael's files as they pertain to you?"

She glared at him, her mouth contorted in an angry gash. "Jerk," she said, and stomped away.

He grinned, but it faded quickly when he realized she'd shown a quick temper. In his experience, people with hot tempers could be prone to violence. This young lady had a chip on her shoulder that matched her unpleasant demeanor. He thought of the odd broken bone. An accident or something worse? Whatever the nature of her problems, she had a solid alibi and this murder appeared to have been at least partially premeditated, not solely the result of an angry outburst. He flipped through his notes. Lauren Temple hadn't been one of the doctor's most frequent patients, having seen him only a dozen or so times in the past year. She'd been telling the truth about that. She might have had issues, possibly deep and disturbing issues, but she also had no apparent motive.

Watching her weave her way through the desks, he wondered how a young woman working as a restaurant hostess could afford a high-priced shrink like Dr. Michael. She shared a dingy apartment with two other girls and drove an older car. Where did the money come from? Were dear old mom and dad footing the bill and if so, would they find the irony amusing? He made another note to check on it.

Smitty appeared with a fresh cup of coffee. "George Vandenberg is in the interrogation room. Seems kinda nervous."

"Yeah? How so?"

"I don't know. A little jumpy maybe," Smitty said. "Seems like a nice guy, though."

"Don't they all?" Cancini sifted through the folders on his desk until he found the one he wanted. "Mrs. Watson?"

"I put her in the empty office down the hall and took her some coffee. I let it slip to Vandenberg she was here."

Cancini looked up. "Good. How'd he seem?"

"Shaken at first, but he made a nice recovery. Asked how she was doing. Oh, and he recognized the Temple girl from Dr. Michael's office."

"Did she see him?"

"I don't think so."

"Doesn't matter," Cancini said. "Check on Mrs. Watson again, feel her out a little, and then take a look at Vandenberg for me. I want your opinion about how he checks out. He's one of the only patients from that day that doesn't have an alibi. Plus, he's a transfer patient from Mrs. Michael's brother."

"On it," Smitty said, and headed down the hall.

Cancini swallowed the steaming coffee, drinking it as fast as his mouth could stand. He imagined the caffeine flowing down his throat and traveling directly into his bloodstream. It had already been a long morning and promised to be a longer afternoon. He didn't mind as long as they came up with something, some lead they could work with. So far, they hadn't gotten much. Still, they hadn't had a chance to talk to Mrs. Watson again and he felt sure she might know more than she realized. They just had to ask the right questions.

Questioning Vandenberg, Cancini suspected Smitty was right about the man and his level of anxiety. A light sheen of sweat covered his upper lip and he had difficulty maintaining eye contact. Early in the interview, news he was one of the last three people to see the therapist alive had left him at a momentary loss for words. The detective tried to take advantage.

"You were his last appointment for the day."

Vandenberg raked his hand through his hair. "I didn't know that."

"How was your session with Dr. Michael? How did it go?"

"Fine. Why wouldn't it?" He wiped his brow with a white handkerchief. "Is it hot in here?"

Silent, Cancini made notes. From under his lashes, he studied the man across the table. His skin was the color of putty and Cancini was sure the man's hands were shaking. "You did say you did some heavy drinking later that night. Maybe you'd had a bad day?"

The broad shoulders sank lower. "I drink too much every day, Detective. Well, at least I did. Just ask my wife." He attempted a smile, a sheepish grin. "I'm trying to quit. The truth is, I'm not feeling so well."

Cancini ignored the small joke and glimpsed the man's bare ring finger. "Does your wife live in Richmond or here in D.C.?"

"Richmond."

Writing again, he asked, "How many days a week do you spend in the city?"

"About four, I guess."

The pen kept moving. "Does your wife ever join you? Spend any of those days—four days a week you said—here, or is she always home in Richmond?"

"Is that important?"

"It's not," Cancini said, although he thought it was. How had the man's relationship with his wife factored into his sessions with Dr. Michael? A strained marriage was not out of the ordinary, but he knew of cases where people had killed over less. He wrote in his notebook: *Mrs. Vandenberg?* "How did Dr. Michael seem to you during your last appointment?"

"How did he seem?" Vandenberg stumbled over his words. "I don't know. He seemed like Dr. Michael always seems." A sad expression flitted across the handsome face. "He was a good man."

"Yes, I've heard that." Cancini sat forward, bringing his body and face closer. "What I mean is, did he seem upset at all or rattled or scared?"

Blinking, Vandenberg didn't answer right away. "No, he was fine."

"Well, that's it then." Cancini closed his notebook and offered his hand. "Thanks for coming in." He led Vandenberg to the door and smiled. "By the way, we've been asking some of the patients if they might allow us to view their records, their case files. It could give us a feel for Dr. Michael's mental state and all that. What kind of pressure he was under, his workload, that sort of thing, you know."

"My records?"

"Yes. I was wondering if you'd be willing to grant us permission to review your records?"

"I . . . I don't know," the man stammered.

Cancini clapped him on the back, steering him toward the exit. "Well, it would be a help to us and I'm sure you have nothing to hide. Think about it and let me know."

"Sure. I'll think about it," he said, the words thick and uncertain.

Vandenberg gone, Cancini hurried to the viewing room where Smitty sat waiting. "You saw the interview?"

"Oh yeah," Smitty said. A wide grin split his face. "Guess what I found out from Mrs. Watson."

"Tell me."

"Mrs. Watson saw Vandenberg and she remembered something. That last session between Dr. Michael and Vandenberg? She doesn't know how it happened, but a lamp got broken."

"Did Vandenberg break the lamp?"

"She didn't know. She passed Vandenberg in the hall when he left but said he ran past her like he was in a hurry. Then she went in the office and found Dr. Michael cleaning up the lamp. He didn't say Vandenberg broke it, but she said he was distracted. Then he told her to make sure she locked the door when she left that night."

Cancini dropped into a chair. George Vandenberg was a complicated man. "Well, there you have it. Vandenberg lied."

Chapter Twenty-Two

GEORGE LAID HIS head against the steering wheel and took long, deep breaths. The lie had been stupid. Mrs. Watson had to know about the broken lamp and might even have been the one to clean it up. He'd been so upset when he left that day, he'd run out without speaking to her. His mind spinning, he tried to gauge how much it mattered. No harm had been done and the doctor had assured him everything was fine. Although he hadn't told the truth, he hadn't entirely misrepresented the situation, either. His head dropped. Who was he kidding? If the police found out about the lamp, about his outburst, they'd know he lied. If only he could take back his words and his anger. The sound of Mary Helen's voice rattled in his head. *What have you done?*

Back at the apartment, George picked at a peanut butter sandwich and pored over newspaper reports on Dr. Michael's murder. According to the articles, his therapist had been stabbed to death. Could he do that? Was he capable of sticking a knife in someone? Sober, he didn't think so, but drunk? George closed his eyes, straining to put together all the pieces of that night. He pushed the sandwich away. It was useless. He had nothing left but to have faith in his innocence.

He rose and tossed the plate in the sink. His fingers shook and he clutched at his stomach. Not for the first time, he was grateful he'd thrown out the liquor. He didn't need the temptation. He staggered to the couch, determined to focus his energy on his resolution to be strong and do the right thing. Had he already failed by lying to the police? Why had he been overcome with fear? He pulled a pillow over his head to block the afternoon glare. George felt awful. He lay with his arms folded across his chest and prayed for sleep. Dozing fitfully, he dreamed of another time and place and the one night he could never forget.

Mary Helen had touched him on the shoulder, her fingers pressing lightly into his skin. He'd jumped backward, nearly knocking her over.

She regained her balance and came closer, taking small steps. "God, George," she said, choking out the words. "Did you do what I think you did?"

The young man couldn't answer. His face buried in his hands, sobs wracked his body.

Reaching out, she caressed his hair and whispered soft words in his ear. "It's okay, George. I know you didn't mean to. It's okay. We'll fix everything."

At first, he didn't hear her, the grief and loss so sudden and terrifying. When her words did penetrate his conscious mind, he shook his head. "How will it be okay? Nothing will ever be okay again."

She never stopped touching him, rubbing his back and stroking his arm. When she brushed at his tears, he flinched as though her hands burned his skin. Momentarily startled, she pulled away.

"I know it doesn't seem like it, George, but it will be okay. We'll get through it together."

Anger bubbling, he shouted, "We? You didn't kill the woman you love, the woman you wanted to marry. You," he said, spitting out the words, "don't have anything to do with this."

She took a step backward. Seeing the fear flit across her face, he sank to his knees, sobbing louder and harder than before. Rocking back and forth, he cried for an hour, the tears flowing until he couldn't cry anymore, his eyes red and stinging. When he looked up, she was still there, sitting cross-legged on the grass.

"What are you doing here?" His throat raw, he struggled with the words.

"I came to find you," she said, no apology in her voice. "I missed you and thought I might find you here." She looked past him to the boathouse and the dark figure lying on the ground. Her blue eyes looked older. "I got here a few minutes before . . ." Her voice trailed off. "I heard you fighting."

"Oh," he said, unable to return her gaze.

"I thought it was over."

A single tear slid down his face. "It was, I guess. I just didn't want it to be."

"So I gathered." Her tone was short, the words clipped. Sitting apart, the evening dusk grew denser as night approached. "What should we do now?" she asked.

George pushed himself up. His arms and legs hurt. "I don't know. Call the police, I suppose."

She stood, too. "I don't think that's a good idea, George."

He couldn't move. What did it matter? He'd lost her forever. The sudden empty space in his heart made him stumble. How could this be real? Aloud, he said nothing, but Mary Helen talked and talked. Her words filled the darkness. She promised to take care of him, offering the slimmest glimmer of light. She told him to go home, she would handle everything. Dazed and heartbroken, he followed her to his car, stopping at the shadow of Sarah's old clunker. He sobbed again. Mary Helen waited, then pushed him into his car and handed him the keys. "Go home, George. Get some sleep. You look like hell." He drove the roads in a fog, stopping once for cigarettes. Home, he fell into bed, crying, alive but dead inside.

George woke with a start, the dream still fresh and terrifying. A light perspiration covered his face and chest. His stomach swirled and gurgled and he rushed to the bathroom, vomiting the bit of sandwich he'd eaten. He washed and raised his head, barely recognizing the ashen skin and sunken eyes of the man staring back at him. He wasn't well. It was the lie, the one he'd told that detective. Maybe it was small compared to the lie he'd lived with for more than twenty years, but both were wrong. For him, lies came with a price. No one understood the tumorlike guilt that coursed like wildfire through his veins. He bowed his head, no longer able to look at himself. The crossroads had come and what had he done? He'd vowed to change. He'd written letters to his children based on that vow. Then he'd gone to that police station and done what he'd always done. He'd lied. It had to stop. He lifted his head again, repeating the words out loud. *It had to stop.* He said the words over and over until his face lost the slack, loose look it had acquired over the years. His jaw hardened even as he clutched at the pain in his gut.

Finding the card with the detective's phone number, George dialed quickly before he lost his nerve.

"Cancini here."

"Detective, it's George Vandenberg." George could hear the tremor in his voice. "I was calling about something I said this morning. It wasn't exactly true."

"What wasn't true, Mr. Vandenberg?"

"My last appointment with Dr. Michael. It was terrible, not normal at all."

"I see," the detective said. "What happened?"

George angled his face up to the window, drinking in the warm sunlight. His stomach rolled again, but he ignored it. He had to finish what he'd started. The words came without thought. "I yelled at Dr. Michael. I was mad at him and I yelled at him. Then I jumped up and knocked over a lamp. It smashed to bits. I calmed down then. Dr. Michael knew I didn't do it on purpose, but he was upset. The truth is, I think he was disappointed in me. He told me not to worry about the lamp though and I left right after that."

"And that's when you went to your club?"

"Yes."

"I'm glad you've decided to be honest with us, Mr. Vandenberg. Maybe you should come in so we could talk about this some more."

"Oh." George's shoulders sagged and he fell back on the sofa. "I don't feel well. I think I'm sick."

"I'm sorry to hear that," the detective said. "Are you sure you don't have more you need to tell us? I can send a car for you."

Doubling over, George breathed in and out, waiting for the stabbing pain to pass. When it did, he spoke again. "No, but there is something else. It's about my records."

"Your records? What about them?"

He closed his eyes, sat up straight, and tipped his chin toward the sky. There was no telling what could happen, where the truth might lead. Over the last year, he'd told Dr. Michael everything, leaving out nothing. Mary Helen might never forgive him. His children might shun him. His friends might pretend he didn't exist. He didn't care anymore. He couldn't erase the past or eradicate the guilt that had shaped his life, not completely anyway, but he could—finally—take responsibility for his actions. For the first time in a long time, he made a tough decision and carried it through.

"Mr. Vandenberg," Cancini asked again, "what about your records?"

"What you said before." There was a brief pause. "You can have them."

Chapter Twenty-Three

"Goddamn!" Cancini held the phone in his hand, staring at the handset. Had Vandenberg really just offered up his records? Shaking his head, he placed calls to the department lawyer, the district attorney, and the captain. When the appropriate paperwork arrived, he sent Smitty to Vandenberg's apartment with instructions to get it signed before the man changed his mind. He sat at his desk waiting and sifting through his notes. Vandenberg had lied. The nature of the lie, the omission of an angry outburst that ended with a smashed lamp, had already made the detective suspicious. Then the man called and confessed the lie. Hell. Was Vandenberg trying to impress the detective with what a good guy he was? In a murder investigation, especially a murder so premeditated and brutal, that was a near impossibility. Even the widow had to be a suspect.

Vandenberg's brief explanation of events during his last session had not satisfied the detective, but the man's voluntary release of his patient records had. Vandenberg intrigued the detective. Cancini had known the man was lying, his intense discomfort evident in the interrogation room. Smitty's observation that he appeared anxious seemed like a mild understatement after the fact. Still, the man had a vulnerability that Cancini recognized. He tapped a pencil against the desk. In spite of Vandenberg's size and charismatic masculinity, he seemed broken somehow. His eyes lacked light. Cancini recognized a man who'd experienced loss and pain. He knew and understood loss, too. Was that Vandenberg's problem? Was it something with his wife? He pushed the questions from his mind. It was useless trying to guess what was in the man's head. Vandenberg could just be a terrific actor.

Cancini pulled together his notes, rereading the brief background they'd collected on Vandenberg. The man had led a privileged life. Expensive prep schools, fancy lessons, prestigious university, multiple homes. He'd married, settled into a career, and had a couple of kids. He'd raked in the rewards with a big house and a big social life. None of it sounded too bad to Cancini, a D.C. boy born and bred, but then again, one never knew. The man had been seeing a psychiatrist. Maybe his life wasn't as perfect as it appeared.

Vandenberg had started out seeing the victim's brother-in-law, but after only a few weeks, his doctor was dead in a hit-and-run car accident. Within a few weeks of transferring to his new therapist, Dr. Michael, Vandenberg increased his sessions to twice a week. Was that a vote of confidence in the doctor or an indication of the depths of the man's problems? Either way, whatever it was that made Vandenberg believe he needed to see a shrink would be in those case files. And if the detective got lucky, there might be a whole lot more.

Smitty met Cancini outside Dr. Michael's office building, a manila envelope clutched in his hand. "I got it," he said.

"Any problems?" Cancini asked.

"None, but I gotta say he didn't look too good. Reminded me of a few guys I've picked up off the street—withdrawal, the DTs."

Cancini nodded. He recalled Vandenberg's trembling hands and nervous twitches. The man had also hinted he'd recently given up drinking. "Wouldn't surprise me. C'mon, let's go up."

Together, they pulled aside the yellow crime scene tape and entered the reception area. Both stopped short of the large blood-stain in the middle of the room. The blood appeared almost black against the creamy-white carpet. Cancini averted his eyes, stepped around the blood, and moved farther into the office.

"What do you want me to do?" Smitty asked.

"According to this, we can't take anything out of the office." Cancini waved the document signed by Vandenberg. "But we can review anything the patient has given us permission to see. I want to put everything that has to do with George Vandenberg in this box. Any forms with vital information, payment records, notes on sessions, all of it."

The blond man frowned. "Wouldn't this be easier if we had Sandy Watson pull everything for us? I mean, she'd know where stuff is."

"It would be," Cancini said. "Except then she'd know we're looking at Vandenberg. She's a sweet lady and everything, but . . ."

Smitty nodded. "I get it. There's a reason why maybe the doc didn't tell her anything about his cases."

"She means well and I could be wrong, but I don't want to take any chances." His face screwed up in a grimace. "Besides, the captain was pretty specific. No leaks to the press about anything or anyone."

"Right."

Cancini moved into the doctor's private office. "I'm gonna start in here." He set the box on the floor. A large cherrywood desk sat to the right, its surface clear of pictures, staplers, and piles of papers. He stepped closer. There was nothing but a notebook and pen, a tape recorder, a phone, and a lamp. A bookcase against the wall behind the desk was neat and orderly, decorated with vases and medical books; no clutter spilled from the shelves. To his left, he saw a sofa flanked by a pair of end tables. On one of those tables was a lamp. The other was bare.

He found the wastebasket by the desk. It was empty as he expected. The cleaning service would have emptied the basket, any obvious remnants of the broken lamp long gone. He crouched and peered into the bottom of the basket. He ran his finger along the curved base, feeling tiny scraps of ceramic. Holding up his finger, he stood and walked to the lamp on the end table. The slivers on his finger matched the lamp.

He returned to the desk and sat down. Had the doctor been working at his desk that night? Cancini opened and closed the drawers, stopping on the last one. Inside, under an unopened package of cassette tapes, was a framed photograph of Nora Michael. He pulled out the picture, turning it over in his hand. The glass was intact and he stood the heavy frame up. The photo looked recent, no more than a couple of years old. Why had the doctor buried it in the bottom drawer? Was it just to discourage distractions during sessions or was there a deeper meaning? He returned it to the drawer.

Cancini picked up the single notebook and flipped through it page by page, but saw only random notes. Setting it aside, he pulled the tape recorder to him and popped open the cover. He reached out and fingered the tape inside. The label read, "G.V. Session 51." He inhaled and removed the tape, turning it over in his hand. The crime scene catalog had listed the tape recorder, but not the tape. Was this what he thought it was? Did Michael tape every session? He pushed away from the desk and yanked open the desk drawers again. Nothing. He spun around. Behind him, built into the bottom of the bookcase, were large drawers. Opening the first one, he hit pay dirt. He sat back, holding a large box in his lap. It was filled with cassette tapes, each labeled with the initials G.V. and a session number. Cancini's heart pounded.

He uncurled his fingers and looked from the tape in his hand to the ones neatly aligned in the box. There were almost one hundred tapes in the box, all arranged in numerical order. In the outer office, Smitty rummaged through files, slamming drawers shut. Cancini considered the cassette in his hand. Why was tape number 51 in the machine? It couldn't be Vandenberg's last session because it was out of order and pulled from near the middle of the box. Had Michael been listening to it in the minutes before he was murdered? Or had the killer intentionally put the tape into the machine for the police to find? Was it a message?

Cancini put the tape in the cassette player and pushed the rewind button. He needed to hear the tapes and this was as good a place to start as any.

"Tell me again about the accident." A man's voice, quiet and insistent, filled the room. Cancini leaned closer. "Tell me exactly how it happened and everything you remember."

The next voice belonged to Vandenberg. "What's the point? I wish I never had to think about it or be reminded of it—ever again!"

The doctor spoke again. "Please, George, indulge me. It might be more important than you think."

Reclining again, the detective listened, riveted by the recollections of a middle-aged man, the memories sometimes clear and other times rambling, all ultimately leading up to a startling and despicable act. The voice of George Vandenberg carried across the office. Smitty stood in the doorway, his face stunned.

Near the end of the tape, the patient's tone was subdued, sadder. "I wanted to confess then, but I didn't. Then later, when I had the chance, I still didn't come forward. And then, of course, it was too late." Cancini clicked off the cassette.

"Jesus! Have we got two murders here? Right there on the tape, he admits what he did to that girl!"

Cancini said nothing for a moment. He removed the tape from the machine and placed it back in the box between numbers 50 and 52.

Smitty stepped into the room. "What do you think? Is he guilty?"

Bony fingers trailed the edges of the tapes. It would take days to listen to all of them. The man's life could be in that box. How many people could say that? How many people would want to? A low pulsing at the back of his neck promised a throbbing headache and he sighed. "Yeah, he's guilty. I don't know of what yet, but he's guilty of something."

Chapter Twenty-Four

CANCINI RUBBED HIS eyes and checked his watch. Four o'clock in the morning. He stood and stretched his arms, trying to shake off the feeling that the office walls were closing in on him. For the first time in hours, there was silence instead of the voices of George Vandenberg and Dr. Michael. He looked down at his notepad filled with scribbled observations and questions, and wondered how long it would take to get the sounds of the two men out of his head.

After Smitty returned to the station, Cancini had stayed. He'd planned to listen to only a handful of tapes, but as the evening wore on and the gnawing hunger in his belly faded, Cancini was hooked. As a cop, he saw most people and their actions in black and white. The law made it easy, but the story on the tapes didn't fit into a category. Yes, Vandenberg was guilty, but it wasn't clear of what. Was the girl's death an accident or homicide? There was so much gray.

He'd started with the first tape, then skipped ahead several sessions after he realized it had taken the patient weeks to trust his therapist. When Vandenberg did finally reveal the accident, Dr. Michael had remained aloof, not voicing any shock or surprise. Although impressed by the doctor's impartiality and ability to remove himself from the ugliness of what had occurred years earlier, Cancini was also horrified.

"Why didn't you call the police right away?" asked the doctor on one of the tapes. Silence. "That's not an answer, George. You must know why you ran away."

Vandenberg's tone was sullen. "I didn't run, exactly. I just let her handle everything because it was easier."

"Easier? That night, you mean, or later?"

"Both, I guess."

"I see." This was a phrase the doctor used frequently. "I seem to recall you told me once you wanted to come forward later. What happened that time?"

Vandenberg whined. "She didn't want me to. Mary Helen told me to let sleeping dogs lie. She likes expressions like that. Let sleeping dogs lie."

It hadn't taken long for the detective to recall that Mary Helen was Vandenberg's wife, the woman he'd spoken with briefly when he phoned George in Richmond.

"Did you always tell Mary Helen when you were considering telling the truth about what happened to Sarah?"

"Of course. She's my wife and, you know, she already knew everything."

"Yes, George, I do know." Dr. Michael zeroed in on his patient. "But here's what I'm trying to get at, have you think about a little." The therapist paused briefly. "Why let your wife know you're planning to come forward unless you want her to talk you out of it?

Surely, you must've known she would try since she had all the other times."

"Oh my God, do you think?" There was the sound of a low moan. "You do, don't you? That's what you think of me, that I never really wanted to tell the truth."

"It's not what I think that matters," said the doctor. "It's what you think." There was a long period of silence before Dr. Michael spoke again. "Let's approach this from a different angle."

Vandenberg's tone changed. "What do you mean?"

"Well, let's examine the present and your actions now. You come to see me regularly, which your wife does not like, and—"

"Hates," interrupted Vandenberg, "not doesn't like. Hates."

"All right, hates," said the therapist, "and yet you still do it. George, you've told me many things you've never told anyone else. You must look at this as a positive action. You must view this as an important first step."

"Maybe, but she doesn't know I've told you about her or that night," the patient said. "Not everything anyway. She'd probably kill me if she did."

"Nevertheless, you continue to come here. Doesn't that show you that maybe your wife doesn't have the ability to dictate every-thing you do? Maybe you don't want her to anymore."

"Maybe." The voice was doubtful.

"Perhaps you're close to making your own decisions about this. After all, it was a long time ago, George."

The detective realized he'd been right about Vandenberg. He was a broken man, scarred by far more than a shaky marriage. He'd lived a life built on a lie. That knowledge, crushing to a man as sensitive as Vandenberg, left him weak and paralyzed. Finding it increasingly difficult to live with his guilty conscience, but unable to break completely free from the bonds of his wife, his depression intensified. Whatever love he'd once had for the woman he'd married had been overshadowed by his resentment of her role in what he termed the worst night of his life. Was that why he'd given the police access to his medical records? Was he trying to assuage his guilt for Sarah's death or punish his wife? Or was it a confession to a more recent crime, the murder of the man who was trying to help him?

"It happened again, Doc," Vandenberg said on a recent session tape. "She was in my dream, like she was still here, alive."

"Sarah, you mean?"

"I could see her so clearly. I thought I forgot all the little things, but I didn't. She had this great laugh and could tell a dirty joke with the best of 'em. Sometime we'd go swimming naked at the river and she'd stand there on the shore, dripping, just amazingly beautiful. I even remember how soft her hair was and the way it smelled after she worked at the tavern serving drinks all night, kinda smoky and greasy, and still sexy." His voice broke off, the reminiscence over. "Jesus," he said, "what a sad sack of shit I am, still lusting after a woman who's been dead for more than twenty years. You must think I'm pathetic."

"Of course not. I am interested, though, in what happened in your dream. Was it like the other one?"

"The one where we fought about the baby?"

"Yes, that one."

"No. In this dream, we talked and laughed." Vandenberg seemed to lose his focus for a second before continuing the description of the dream. "We actually did that a lot, you know. It wasn't just about the sex. She was smart and funny and . . . I guess none of that matters now."

Dr. Michael indulged his patient. "I disagree. All of it matters. Everything you remember about her is important."

Cancini had clicked off the tape there. Over several sessions, Vandenberg described Sarah's personality, her beauty, her relevance in his young life. Dr. Michael encouraged him, advising his patient that his memory would help him strengthen his resolve to do the right thing. The detective wasn't sure he agreed, wondering if perhaps the doctor wasn't pushing George toward a deeper depression. His worries seemed to be confirmed in one of the final sessions.

"I don't think I can do it. I don't know if I want to," Vandenberg said.

A hint of irritation crept into the therapist's tone. "George, don't back out on me now. This is important. You must keep the faith that it's the right thing to do."

"Right for who?" questioned the patient, unenthused. "Even if I confess now, it won't bring Sarah back, will it?"

"No, George, but it might bring you back."

"Ha! And who the hell would care about that?"

Although he'd skipped around, Cancini had saved the most recent session for last, holding out the final tape until he'd learned more about Vandenberg. The man had lived an entire life responsible for the death of another human being, yet accepting no consequences for that act. While the patient was obviously troubled by these facts, he'd made a mess of that life and the second chance he'd taken. Vandenberg considered himself a failure as a husband and, at best, an ineffective father. Adrift in his guilt, he seemed incapable of living in the present.

Cancini sat down again, stretching his legs under the desk. Despite his disgust for what Vandenberg had done, the detective could not bring himself to hate Vandenberg. After hours of listening, he'd learned enough about the man to understand what a leap it was for him to relinquish his medical records as well as attempt to give up drinking. Clearly, Vandenberg had reached some sort of impasse, but that didn't excuse his behavior. Cancini had a job to do and a list of questions. What prompted Vandenberg to give up drinking and reveal his past? Was it a consequence of tragedy or something more sinister? Having taken a life once before, even accidentally, would it have been easier for him now? Had he graduated to cold-blooded murder?

Cancini stifled a yawn and withdrew the final cassette from the box. He placed it in the recorder, already knowing he would hear some kind of argument resulting in the broken lamp. Now, he wondered if there was more. What had really happened that day? If Mrs. Michael was telling the truth, her husband was afraid of this patient following Vandenberg's furious tirade. Had the doctor pushed too hard, angering the man? Had it been enough to push George over the edge? Pushing the play button, Cancini closed his eyes, waited, and listened.

Chapter Twenty-Five

GEORGE TOOK BREATH after breath, barely hearing Mary Helen. Pot after pot of coffee, salty snacks, and half a pack of cigarettes couldn't stop the cravings or the sudden bouts of nausea. When he could look at her, the disgust and loathing on her face was almost enough to make him vomit again.

"So, let me get this straight . . ." Her teeth clenched, there was no trace of the former debutante in her icy tone. "You went to the river Saturday when you said you were going to work. Then claiming you needed time to think, you drive up to Washington for the weekend. I suppose I should at least be grateful you had the decency to call me and tell me you weren't coming home. Now you tell me you want to move to the river, as if we could just pick up our lives at a moment's notice." She didn't wait for him to respond. "And to top it all off, yesterday you go to the police station and meet with a detective without a lawyer?" Her tiny hands opened and closed with her words. "Without a lawyer! For God's sake, George, what is your problem? Are you insane or just plain stupid?"

He wrapped his hands around the heavy coffee mug. Her words bothered him less than he expected. He remained quiet, letting her rant. Even so, he was grateful his son and daughter were at school, oblivious to the fight brewing at home.

"What if the detective thinks you're a suspect? What about us? What about your family? Do you know what this could do? The police might start asking questions, talking to our friends. This is unbelievable! Again, you act without thinking of anyone but yourself. What did I ever do to deserve this?" Mary Helen paced the length of the gourmet kitchen, moving around the granite island in circles until he felt dizzy watching her. "My God, do I have to do everything?" She stopped and glared at him. Wagging her finger, she said, "There will be no more statements. You have to cooperate, of course, but I'll call Larry right away and have him talk to that detective. That way, they'll know they can't question you again without him there. And you are to stay here where I can keep an eye on you."

"It's too late for that," he said with as much confidence as could muster.

Mary Helen started to object, but something in his quiet manner stopped her. "What do you mean?"

He swallowed but held her gaze. "I signed a document allowing them access to my records with Dr. Michael."

She frowned, head cocked to one side. "What did you say?"

"I signed away my patient confidentiality." All the color drained from her face. "They probably know everything by now." He dropped the bombshell. "He taped all of our sessions, you know."

His wife fell into a chair, her lipsticked mouth opening and closing, issuing only squeaks of outrage.

He tried to explain. "I was tired of hiding the truth, of living a lie every day of my life. You and I both know I'm responsible for Sarah's death, whether I like it or not." His wife flinched at his former lover's name. "I couldn't take the secrets anymore." He paused and sipped the steaming coffee. Under the table, his legs trembled. "It's what Dr. Michael wanted me to do for a long, long time. I wanted it, too, but I was afraid. The truth is I didn't have the courage then, the courage to tell the truth, or . . . or the courage to stand up to you, Mary Helen."

"And now you do." She cut into his confession, her words dripping in sarcasm.

Blood rushed to his head and his breath caught in his throat. "Yes, I do."

"Are you drunk?"

George counted silently until he could speak. "No. For once, I can honestly say I'm completely sober."

She stared at him, then said, "Well, goody for you."

They sat in silence, the air charged. The dynamic of their relationship had shifted. He put his hands in his lap and waited, comforted only by the knowledge he'd followed through on his vow and hadn't backed down. It was something he hadn't done in a long time. Still, Mary Helen was not ready to concede him this small victory.

"I'll ask you again, George, what about us? If you don't care about me, how could you do this to your children? How dare you risk ruining their lives?"

He winced. Even more than his fear of his wife, it had been his reluctance to involve his children that had kept him from coming forward these last few weeks. "I wrote them letters."

"Excuse me?" The red lips curled in scorn. "You wrote them letters? Are you kidding?" She stood up, shoving the chair out of her way. "What did you say to them, George? I'm sorry I'm a murderer, kids, please forgive me?"

"It was an accident," he said.

Mary Helen stepped toward him, hand outstretched, and slapped him across the face. "I hate you," she said, and stormed out of the kitchen.

His shoulders slumped. Mary Helen stomped up the stairs and slammed the door to their bedroom, the loud bang echoing throughout the quiet house. He rubbed his cheek, feeling the sting of her hand and the hurt of her words. Had he made a mistake? Had he done the wrong thing again? Shaking his head, he couldn't accept that. Revealing the truth was right, and knowing it gave him strength. By now, Detective Cancini might have listened to enough tapes to know about Sarah, to realize that George bore the guilt of a horrible accident and the subsequent cover-up. Mary Helen had a point about the kids though. They would be humiliated by him, embarrassed, and maybe even disgusted. Maybe someday they could forgive him and even be proud. After all, how could the truth be worse than the drunken, useless man he'd turned out to be? If they learned nothing from him, he prayed they would recognize they must be true and honest or their lives would be as false as his had been.

George trudged up the stairs. He stood outside the bedroom door, listening to the muffled sound of sobbing. After a moment, he tried the handle. It was locked. "Mary Helen? Mary Helen? Open the door." Whatever they once had was lost, yet George didn't want to hurt his wife any more than he already had. Over the years, he had shifted a great deal of the blame for his mistakes to her, but in moments of clarity and sobriety, he knew she was as much a victim as he. "Please open the door. I want to talk to you."

"Go away," came the choked response.

He jiggled the doorknob again. "Please, I don't want to leave it like this. We need to talk and figure this out. I'm sorry that you have to be involved. I really am. I wish . . ." He hesitated, shaking off the thought. "Well, it doesn't matter what I wish, I'm sorry I ever got you into this." The sobbing had stopped. He felt like a fool, standing in the hallway, calling to his wife through the door. "Can't we talk about this? Please."

Silence. Then the soft pad of footsteps across the thick carpeting. He heard the click of the lock before she pulled open the door. He looked down into her tearstained face, smudged with black mascara and eyeliner. The red lips were blurred in her pale face. Mary Helen turned away and flopped on the bed, a wad of tissues in her hand. "There's nothing to talk about," she said through sniffles.

In two strides, he crossed the room and sat beside her. Reaching over, he held her hand. It lay in his palm, lifeless and cold. She did not look at him. "I never meant for things to happen this way. You know that." Mary Helen pulled her hand away, sliding farther from him on the bed. "I know you're angry and I understand. It's scary, but we have to be realistic. The damage is done. In truth, it was done a long time ago. We should have told the truth then, but we didn't and now we're both going to pay for that. It's my fault. I don't blame you." George took a breath, deciding to be honest again. "I did for a while, but I was wrong. It was my decision and I was weak and stupid. I have to say all this because it's on the tapes. Everything about that night is on those tapes. And a lot more than that night." Without looking, he could feel the heat of her eyes as they shot into his soul. Mary Helen could not have despised him more at that moment. "The police will probably want to talk to you. I'll tell them you were only trying to help, that you were scared for me, that you were young . . ." His heart tightened. Even if she had been hard on him, it wasn't always that way. Long ago, before the accident and before Sarah, they had cared for each other. After, she'd stuck by him when she didn't have to. Why? She huddled against the headboard, her face buried in the pillows. The mother of his children, she looked small and fragile. "We both made mistakes, Mary Helen. You deserved better than me." He touched her shoulder gently. "I'm sorry."

"Me too," came the lilting voice after several long minutes, the soft sound so low he almost didn't hear her. "I'm sorry, too." Uncurling her body, she squared her shoulders. With her painted fingernails, she pushed the mussed hair off her face. "I want a divorce."

Chapter Twenty-Six

"You look like hell," Father Joe observed, his eyes glowing in the morning sun.

Both men smiled at the lifelong Catholic's language. "That's what I love about you, Father. You call it like you see it."

"Aye. The truth shall set you free and all that, you know."

The smile faded from the detective's face. He heard George's voice in his head. After hours of listening to bits and pieces of Vandenberg's life, the truth seemed less clear and more ambiguous than ever.

"It's true, Michael." The priest cocked his head to the side, voice soft. "You do look terrible."

Cancini swallowed the piping hot coffee. After a moment, he said, "I didn't get much sleep."

"It's the case then? The psychiatrist?"

The detective nodded. He set the coffee aside and talked, outlining what he'd heard on the tapes, including Vandenberg's confession to a death decades earlier and his most recent outbursts of temper.

"Do you think he might have killed his doctor?"

"I don't know yet."

"It sounds like he's a troubled man." There was no judgment in the old man's face. "You will find the truth."

Cancini said nothing. His eyes wandered to the cross hanging over the doorway. He'd once asked the old man why he'd hung it there.

"My mother, a good Irishwoman if there ever was one, believed a cross over the door kept the bad spirits away. The truth is, it's probably just an old wives' tale, but it's a good one, don't you think?" The priest had chuckled telling the story.

Looking at the cross now, Cancini wished he could believe. "It's not as easy for me as it is for you, Father. I don't think I have that forgiveness gene or whatever it is that makes you see the good in people."

"That's not true, Michael."

"Sure it is. I live in the real world. I can't forgive things like you do and push things out of my mind like they never happened. I think there should be justice, punishment for those that break the law." He thought of Vandenberg's dead girl, her death unnecessary and unpunished. "There should be a price to pay."

Father Joe took a sip from his cup, his eyes never leaving the face of the younger man. He spoke slowly. "Maybe there is, Michael. Just because it's not your kind of price doesn't mean it hasn't been paid."

Cancini's face darkened. "That's hogwash, Father, and you know it. Murderers, thieves, crooks. They walk the streets every day and live their lives any way they want. We do our best to catch them and punish them but plenty get away with it, too." He hesitated, then added, "Vandenberg killed that girl."

"I thought you said it was an accident—"

"Maybe it was and maybe it wasn't. Either way, he ran away. It's not right."

The priest bent his head. "No, it's not right. Still, I'm sure there has been, as you put it, a price."

"Maybe," Cancini admitted.

"Could he be a suspect then?"

Cancini shrugged. "I guess. Possibly."

"Is the widow still under consideration?"

"Yes. She's a cool customer. Too cool for my taste." He frowned. "And something doesn't seem right about the marriage. They spent a lot of time apart, multiple cell phones, maybe separate bank accounts . . ."

The two men sat quietly then. After a few minutes, Father Joe stood and set his cup on the side table. He faced the empty street, his starched white shirt reflecting the bright sun. He inhaled deeply, his broad shoulders rising and falling with each breath. When he spoke, his voice was quiet, contemplative. "The distance between what's good and what's bad is less than you might think." Cancini opened his mouth to say something but thought better of it. He'd heard Vandenberg crying, grieving over the death he'd caused and been unable to forget. He could allow that Vandenberg had suffered, but it didn't compare to what the girl's family and the girl herself had gone through. Father Joe spoke again. "Within each of us lies the ability to go either way. We can do good and strive to be good or we can be led down another path. One path, of course, leads to another." The priest paused, shoving his hands deep into his pockets. "I believe a man's worth cannot be defined solely by his goodness, but also by his desire to battle that in him which is not good. No man can fully understand another's struggles. We can judge them and we can condemn them, but we cannot truly understand." He turned back to face his young friend. "That is why I believe in forgiveness."

The detective stood, shaking his head. He reached out and patted the old priest on the shoulder. "You're a good man, Father, but I'm not you."

"Of course not, Michael. You are you and you're a better man than you think. And you're a damn good homicide detective to boot." He grinned. "You have a job to do and I know you will find Dr. Michael's killer."

"And he or she will go to prison, as they should."

"Their price to pay?"

"Yes."

"Well, that is the law," Father Joe said, then dipped his head, looking Cancini in the eye. "But remember, you are your mother's son, and a more forgiving woman I never knew."

He left the priest's quarters deflated. All the talk of forgiveness and goodness did not sit well with the detective, and the reference to his mother seemed unnecessary. Why had Father Joe said it? It had nothing to do with this case. It had nothing to do with the brutal slaying of Dr. Michael or with the violent death of the young waitress twenty years earlier. And it certainly had nothing to do with George Vandenberg.

He slammed the steering wheel with his hand. "Damn."

Chapter Twenty-Seven

Being summoned to the captain's office did not improve Cancini's morning. He slouched low in the chair, bone-weary, heavy bags encircling his eyes.

Martin hit him with questions. "Did you talk to the D.A.? Can you get the search warrant or what? How soon do you think?"

Cancini swallowed a slug of coffee, his head aching already. "I talked to her and she's going to see Judge Cramer as soon as he gets in, around ten or so. Jackie's gonna call me or Smitty when she has it. Until then, I'm going back to the doc's office to see what else I can learn."

The toothpick in the captain's mouth splintered and he spit it into the wastebasket. He plopped another between his lips and nodded his approval. "You'll meet at Vandenberg's apartment?"

"That's the plan."

"Good. Listen, I got a call from Mrs. Michael's attorney this morning at seven. Do you think she knows what's up?"

Cancini scratched his head. "Well, she was the one that gave me the tip that one of the patients had scared her husband, but I don't see how she could know how far we've gotten. Even I can't believe Vandenberg gave up his privacy rights so easy."

The captain agreed. "So, tell me, how solid is what we've got on this guy?"

Cancini bristled. George Vandenberg had been moved to the top of the suspect list. He was prone to wild mood swings that might make him capable of capital murder. Adding in that he'd already killed a girl and covered it up did not help. Still, without more evidence than the tapes and the broken lamp, it was circumstantial at best. "It's a beginning—not conclusive, though."

"But the widow's out as a suspect? Is that right?"

Cancini finished his coffee. Most of the reasons he'd liked the wife as a suspect had not gone away. Her reluctance to move from Boston to be with her husband, the repeated trips back to Boston for long periods of time with no explanation, the calls to the unknown cell phone the night her husband was brutally murdered—these questions had not been answered to his satisfaction. In spite of her helpful revelation about the violent patient, he resented the wasted time spent on the note and the brother's hit-and-run accident. The missing glasses bothered him, too. They'd verified the widow's story that Dr. Michael had a habit of losing them, but his secretary was sure he'd had them the day he was murdered. "Sorry," Cancini said. "I can't rule her out yet. Why?"

The captain flicked another toothpick into the trash can. "The talking head says the widow wants to know when she can go back to Boston. I didn't even think the husband had been buried yet."

"He hasn't. His body's still at the coroner's." He sat up straighter. "What did you tell him?"

"What could I say?" Martin said with a shrug. "She's not under arrest."

Cancini leaned forward, the headache pounding. Until the searches of Vandenberg's apartment and his car were done, he'd prefer to have Mrs. Michael close by where they could watch her.

"Then he got snotty with me, implying we were bungling the case." Fingering the toothpicks in the jar, the captain selected one. "Naturally, I told him if she left town, it might be construed as a hostile action to the investigation. After all, what's the rush?"

Cancini sat back, breathing a sigh of relief. He and Martin would never be friends, could never be friends, but he could usually count on the captain to do the right thing on the job. Never a great detective, Martin excelled in management, possessing that special talent that let him deal with the brass and kiss up whenever it was required. It was a job Cancini could never do. The two men were polar opposites. For Cancini, it boggled the mind they had both chosen the same woman. Not surprisingly, his ex-wife preferred a captain to a lowly detective.

The captain stood. "I want you to keep me posted on all developments. This ain't no one-man show here. No bullshitting around, Cancini."

Cancini stood and frowned. Yes, sometimes he preferred to work alone. He didn't like mistakes. It wasn't about the glory or anything else. Martin should know that by now. Cancini didn't need the additional hassle of keeping the captain updated on each and every tidbit, constantly reminding him who was boss. On the other hand, Martin had handled the lawyer and he'd kept the widow local. It was something. He bit back on his resentment and nodded once. "No problem, Captain. Promise."

Smitty and Wilder, faces grim, waited for him at his desk. Smitty spoke as soon as the older detective came within earshot. "Someone doesn't want us to find out much about the widow."

"What do you mean?" Cancini asked, sinking into his chair.

"We've got the basic stuff—you know—graduation date, marriage date, job history, all verified by the city of Boston and Northeastern University, but that's it. There's no credit card history we can find, no real paper trail. Most everything was in her husband's name. House, cars, everything. There was nothing out of the ordinary we could find there. She does have her own bank account and a 401(k) through work but without a subpoena, I don't know if there's been any unusual activity."

"See if you can get one."

"Sure."

"Anything from neighbors, coworkers?"

Wilder chimed in. "No one will say much. The neighbors liked the doc a lot, but I can't find anyone who can tell me much about the wife. Everyone kinda clams up."

"Maybe she doesn't make friends easily," Cancini said. With her icy manner, it didn't shock him she might put people off. "What about anyone in Boston?"

"So far, the same," Smitty said. "It's tough not being able to canvass the neighborhood, and I've run into the same thing as Wilder. It's almost like she barely lived there."

Cancini ran his hands through his hair. Why was she so eager to return to her hometown of Boston? "Do we have anyone who can do some legwork up there?"

"I can ask my buddy," Smitty said. "If he's not on a case, he might be able to lend us some help."

"Good."

"I don't get why no one will talk about her." Smitty folded his arms across his chest. "You'd think she'd have at least one good friend who could tell us something. It feels like we're getting blocked at every turn."

Cancini couldn't disagree, but it wasn't enough. "Not much to find is not the same thing as someone not wanting you to learn anything." He eyed Smitty and Wilder. "Just find out what you can. Wilder, try her local grocery, dry cleaner's, anyplace she would have frequented. Smitty, maybe you can have your friend go a little further back, before she was married. She must have dated, had high school or college friends, something, anything . . ." He stared at the file folder lying on his desk. "George Vandenberg" was written across the front. Thoughts of Nora Michael disappeared as the man's voice, his confessions and his crying, seeped back into the detective's brain.

Smitty reached across his shoulder and tapped the file. "The background on Vandenberg. It pretty much jibes with what we heard on the tapes. But there is something else—an arrest."

Cancini opened the folder and looked up at his partner. "The assault charge?"

The blond man's eyes bugged. "How did you know?"

Weary, the detective decided he could never bear the burden borne by therapists and psychiatrists. Knowing every facet of a person's life, particularly the spots where they were weak and ashamed, was more responsibility than he ever wanted. "Vandenberg told Michael in one of their sessions." Shortly before his marriage, young George had gotten in a fistfight in a bar and been charged with assault. "It was dismissed, wasn't it?"

"Yes, but I think it goes to show a pattern of violence. I wouldn't be surprised if we find some other incidents that weren't reported."

Cancini agreed but said nothing. George had a temper, particularly when he drank, which it seemed to the detective he'd done regularly for most of his life. It hadn't been lost on him that the fight in the bar occurred shortly after the girl's death but prior to his wedding. Still, if the evidence supported charging him with the murder of Dr. Michael, the earlier arrest would not look good in court. The broken lamp showed that even more than twenty years later, Vandenberg still wrestled with his demons.

After Wilder returned to his desk, Smitty spoke again, voice low. "Did you get the name?"

Cancini had told everyone on the case a girl had died and only Dr. Michael knew George's most horrible secret. Around the squad room, the woman had only one name, Sarah. He'd had to listen to dozens of tapes before he ever heard the last name, and even then, it was only once.

"She was the prettiest thing I'd ever seen," George had said, his tone gushing as he described their first meeting. "She brought a pitcher of beer and walked away. I wanted to talk to her, but she had a bunch of other tables so I had to wait to get her attention again." Vandenberg had chuckled a little. "I was with one of my frat brothers and he caught me mooning after her and started ribbing me right away. I didn't care. We finished the pitcher and she came back. I don't know why, but I couldn't talk for a second. So, my friend did it for me. He pushed me to my feet and told her my name, laughing because I was so nervous. God knows I was." The patient had paused.

"And then what happened?" asked the therapist.

"She told me her name. She said, 'I'm Sarah Winter. It's nice to meet you.' Just like that. Not embarrassed at all."

"Ah." Dr. Michael let out a long breath as he spoke, elongating the word as though he'd just been told an extraordinary thing.

"Yeah. She was something," George said, the voice fading away, "but that was a long time ago."

Cancini picked up the slip of paper with the name, folded it, and handed it to Smitty. "I want you to look into this quietly, okay? No leaks."

Smitty shrugged, his face blank. "Whatever you want."

Cancini tucked the file under his arm and grabbed his keys. He had tapes waiting, and while there was no doubt the therapist had been brutally murdered, the cause of death for Sarah Winter remained undetermined. He hoped the results of an autopsy or a police report would turn up, though he knew old records were often hard to locate. Cancini needed facts, not hearsay and emotions. As fascinating as he found the tapes, they were not the complete story. Was Sarah's death an accident or homicide?

Chapter Twenty-Eight

"I did something terrible this weekend, Dr. Michael." Cancini settled back in the chair, Vandenberg's voice familiar to him now.

"Terrible? How do you mean?"

"I scared my son. Really scared him. I didn't mean to. I didn't even know he was there. He can barely look at me. God, I'm an idiot, a damn idiot! I know what you're thinking. He's pathetic and—" Vandenberg stopped when the therapist interrupted him.

"Take your time, George, you're not making sense."

"Right. I got drunk," he said, his tone bitter. "Big surprise, huh?"

Cancini thought he caught the sound of a sigh. "I thought we'd agreed you wouldn't drink, George. It doesn't seem to help."

"I know, and I was only going to have a couple of pops, but then Mary Helen started in on me about something or other. I swear I can't even remember what it was now and Wills wasn't supposed to be home yet," the patient said, voice breaking. "Jesus, it must have been awful for him."

"You can't blame Mary Helen for your drinking, George."

"Why not? She drives me to it. You don't know what she's like."

Dr. Michael disagreed. "She is not the reason you drink."

"Well, she sure as hell's part of it," the patient said, the words louder now. "She drives me crazy! Always pick, pick, picking at me."

"Calm down, George. That's not what we need to talk about today. Remember?"

Vandenberg did not respond for several minutes. The detective waited, listening to dead air. On a notepad, he wrote Mary Helen's name, thinking it might be time to pay the lady a visit.

"Better?"

"Yeah, I'm sorry. I guess I got off track," George said.

"It's okay. But the drinking . . . it's not good. Let me remind you about that treatment facility, the one I told you about." Cancini listened as the therapist described a rehab hospital.

"I know you mean well, Dr. Michael, but I'm not sure I can do that right now. I'm not ready."

"Even after scaring your son?" There was a gasp. "I apologize for the way that sounded," came the voice of the therapist, "but I don't think I'm wrong in guessing you had another one of your episodes."

The detective sat up straighter in the chair. What was an episode? Had there been other episodes discussed on the tapes he'd skipped?

"No," George said, reluctance in his voice, "you're not wrong."

"Do you want to tell me about it now?"

Cancini leaned forward, turning his ear toward the tape recorder.

"Yeah. Okay." He heard the indrawn breath, no louder than a whisper. "I'd had a few, like I said before, and Mary Helen was screaming at me. I'm such a disappointment. I'm a miserable husband. Her father tolerates me at work. Why can't I do more? So, I had a few more, and, you know, she screamed a whole lot more. It must have been about eight or so and Wills wasn't supposed to be home from the movies until nine. I grabbed the scotch bottle and started chugging. I know it was stupid . . ." The man sounded sorrowful. "I did it to piss her off."

"Did it work?"

"Oh sure. Then again, everything I do pisses her off." There was a brief pause.

"What happened next, George?"

"Do you want her version or mine?"

"I think it might be best if we start with hers." Cancini noted the doctor's response. Why would he choose to hear what the wife said happened?

"Yeah, okay." He cleared his throat. "I started in with my own insults, something I don't usually have the courage to do when I'm sober."

"And she got angrier?"

"Yeah. She'd had enough and tried to leave the room. I grabbed her hard and yanked her by the arm." George's voice got quiet. "She showed me the bruises the next day."

"I see. Is there more?"

"Unfortunately." Vandenberg's voice cracked and a few seconds passed. He spoke again. "When she was struggling to get away from me, I stumbled and we both fell. Mary Helen thinks she sprained her wrist. Then she jumped up and ran out. I was so incensed, still so drunk, that I threw an ashtray at her head. Luckily, I missed, but it hit the wall and shattered into a million pieces. I don't think I meant to hurt her. I would never do that on purpose." There was silence for a full minute. "Mary Helen told me Wills was standing in the doorway and saw the whole thing." A choked sound came over the tape, the sound of a muffled sob, then quiet again. "You should have seen his face the next morning. I think he hates me. I can't say I blame him. I'd hate me, too."

Cancini's shoulders tightened and he clutched the pen until it dug into his hand. The man had physically hurt his wife. He'd bruised her skin and become violent when she tried to leave. The detective dropped the pen and stopped the tape. He understood the hatred between the couple, familiar to him after his own disastrous marriage. He even understood the fleeting desire to inflict harm, but it was a line no man should ever cross. Vandenberg had crossed that line, yet Cancini sensed the man's remorse was genuine. He shook his head. The man had assaulted his wife. There could be no excuse. No matter how vulnerable the man seemed, this recording told the story of a different man, a violent man. He pushed play again.

"So, you had a fight," Dr. Michael said. "You were drunk and things got a little rough. Sadly, your son had to witness this."

"Yes."

"George, I have to ask. Did you and your wife argue about the accident?"

"I don't know. I can't remember."

"Do you remember your son's face or what happened right after he witnessed the argument?"

"No. I don't even remember throwing the ashtray or Wills being in the room."

"Then you did have another episode," the therapist said. "Everything you've told me today is strictly what your wife told you happened. Is that correct?"

"Yes."

Cancini's eyes locked on the turning wheels of the tape. Did the doctor doubt the veracity of Mary Helen's story?

"You don't remember the fight? You don't remember hurting your wife? You don't remember your son being there?"

"No," Vandenberg said. Cancini thought he sounded sad, defeated. "No, I don't."

Dr. Michael's tone weary, he asked, "George, do you remember anything at all?"

"Not after I chugged the scotch. No." His answer was no more than a whisper.

"What happened next?"

"Nothing. She said I passed out after that. I woke up on the sofa, still in my clothes."

Seconds ticked by and the meaning of the episode seemed to weigh on both men. Cancini could not turn away from the recorder. The therapist cleared his throat. "Look, our time is up for today, but this is important. It means something."

"Means something? Like what?"

"Well, I think we can both agree you've been carrying around some deep emotions for a number of years, repressing them most of that time."

"Wow. It sounds a little better the way you put it."

"Either way, in tandem with your increasing inability to repress these emotions, your drinking has escalated, too. With that comes behavior you can't control, don't even remember. Don't you see that?" There was no audible response, but the doctor went on anyway. "Good. You and I are working hard on the emotional areas, but the drinking is something else. It's getting out of control. You can't continue to use alcohol as a drug." Dr. Michael's words became more insistent. "George, this is your second episode of alcohol-induced amnesia in two months. Do you realize how dangerous this is? We need to get you into a program."

Cancini listened and wrote, *Alcohol-induced amnesia?*

"I'm afraid. I don't know if I can do it, Dr. Michael."

"I understand, but surely you realize all of this, our sessions and the blackouts and the accident, they're all related."

"I guess."

A touch of exasperation crept into the therapist's voice. "You can't afford to guess anymore, George. These blackouts are not benign. It's not as though you are passing out here. To everyone else, you're functioning, aware of what you're doing. Mary Helen is not going to be understanding forever. Plus, the next time, you could hurt someone, maybe seriously. Is that what you want, George? Is it?"

The detective shut off the machine. According to the doctor, Vandenberg experienced blackouts where he remained functional. During those blackouts, he often became violent but remembered nothing. Was it possible? On the night of Dr. Michael's murder, Vandenberg drank heavily, a fact corroborated by the bartender and several witnesses. Had he become violent that night as he had other nights when he was drunk? He'd fought with the doctor earlier in the day. Did he return to the doctor's office and brutally stab him to death? And if George had committed the murder, slaying his own therapist, did he even remember?

Chapter Twenty-Nine

"A divorce," George said. "I don't know what to say." He slumped on the bed, stunned. Anger he'd anticipated. Hatred, too, but not this. He touched his bare ring finger. Wasn't that what he'd been wishing for when he'd tossed his wedding ring into the river? Even so, he'd never believed it was a possibility, no matter how much she hated him. Divorce was too sordid, too low class for Mary Helen.

"Not right away, of course," she said, her drawl heavy. "We'll have to get through this. I'll stand by you because that's what's best, but after that, I want a divorce." She sat down at her dressing table and wiped away the smeared makeup. She brushed the tangles from her hair, rearranging the blond locks into a smooth bob. "I don't think we need to say anything to the kids just yet, do you?" Mary Helen allowed a trace of sarcasm to creep back into her tone. "After all, they'll have your letters to prepare them for the police and all."

He watched Mary Helen's reflection in the mirror. She applied fresh lipstick and pursed her lips three times. "I have a meeting at the upper school," she said, referring to the private school their children attended. She went into the closet, emerging several minutes later in a different outfit. "You can move your things into the guestroom on the third floor. You can stay there when you're not in D.C."

"I'm giving up the apartment. I put my notice in this morning." He paused. "I thought I might stay at the river." Her face froze and he knew he wasn't mistaken this time. She did hate him. "Unless you don't think I should."

She blinked, then pasted a smile on her red lips. "Suit yourself."

George wandered from room to room after she left. He stood in his son's room amid the piles of books, clothes, and athletic wear, and the reality of divorce—the loss of his family—hit him and his stomach twisted. William, or Wills as he was known, was nearly grown. Soon he would be away at college, a man in his own right, able to make his own decisions. George swallowed and leaned against the wall. Would Wills understand? Could he forgive his father?

He packed a bag and left the house. As the miles rolled by, his despondence gave way to hope. He rolled down the windows and let the warm air blow through his hair. He smelled the blooming azaleas and marveled at the dazzling display of colorful tulips on the oak-lined streets of Richmond. The hard part was over. The police knew the truth and would do with it what they wished. If they wanted him to, he would cooperate. If not, at least his conscience was a little clearer. No matter what the police did and no matter how his children reacted, he could never erase the lifelong guilt or forgive himself, but he'd made a start. His confidence swelled with the realization that he'd acted like a man, standing up and doing all the things he should have done so long ago.

George stepped from the car, his back drenched in sweat. In the guesthouse, he poured a Coke and finished it in three swallows. The tremors had lessened, but at times, his head still pounded and his stomach churned. He threw his bag into one of the bedrooms and unloaded the groceries he'd picked up along the way. He forced down a handful of crackers. Things were happening fast. Within a week, his therapist had been murdered, he'd allowed the police to learn his most terrible secret, and his wife had asked him for a divorce. His body ached and he went outside, gulping the fresh air.

He crawled into the hammock by the river and welcomed the memories. They no longer scared him, although their innocence made him sad and a little confused. Why did everything seem so much clearer to him now that he was older, no longer distracted by the selfish tendencies of youth? He pictured her as she had been long ago, teasing and coquettish on a hot spring day.

"What makes you think I'm so perfect?" Sarah had asked, lying naked in the rope hammock, a coy smile on her face.

Standing over her, George pretended to consider. "Well, maybe I've been too quick to judge." He stepped closer, allowing his hands to travel over the length of her body. "Yes, the hair is good. The breasts. Hmm. Let me see." He reached out and circled each nipple with his index finger. "Very nice." His fingers trailed down to her belly button. His eyes widened and he pulled his hand away. "Nope. I'm sorry. I was wrong. You're not perfect after all."

Struggling to sit up, she looked down at herself, then back at him. "What's the matter?"

A stricken look crossed his face. "You have an outy," he said, shaking his head in disappointment.

"What?"

"It's such a shame. Almost perfect, but . . ." He laughed then. She reached out and he caught her hands in his. He looked at her sideways, from under his lashes, and kissed her belly button. "See, an outy!"

Pushing him away, she laughed, too. "You jerk." She jumped from the hammock. "Catch me if you can." She raced to the dock, diving from the edge, her perfect form slicing the water. He'd found himself running, too, desperate to keep up with her, to hold her, to keep her perfection close as long as possible.

Then reality had set in and she'd discovered he had a girl-friend. The sweetness he'd taken for granted had been replaced by accusations and mistrust. They tried. She'd put on a gallant face, pretending none of it bothered her, but he'd known it wasn't true. Sarah hadn't been that good at playing it casual. That had been his special talent.

The sun blazed in the sky and George walked back to the house. He ate a grilled cheese, sipped a second Coke, and daydreamed of days gone by. The call jolted him from the past and forced him back to the present.

"I'm sorry to bother you, Mr. Vandenberg. It's Danny Fielding. I tried your cell phone earlier today and you didn't answer." The man spoke in a rush.

"It's okay, Danny, I didn't have it on. It's not your fault."

His apartment building superintendent seemed surprised. "Oh. Well, you did tell me to call you if I needed to reach you, didn't you?"

George agreed that he had. "Is everything okay? Did I not give you enough notice or forget to sign something?"

"No, no. Nothing like that." The man stumbled over his words. "The police are here with a warrant. They want to search your apartment."

George's fingers tightened on the phone. "A warrant?"

"Yes, I think they're going in now. I didn't want to let them in, but they had the warrant."

A cold fear coursed through his body and he shivered. "Did they say anything else, like why they wanted to look in my apartment?"

"I did hear something—one of the detectives I think." Danny hesitated, then said, "They said it was a murder investigation and to search everything real good. They said it was that murder that's been in the papers, you know, that psychiatrist that got stabbed." George's hands shook and he struggled to hold on to the phone. "I'm sorry, Mr. Vandenberg. I just thought you should know."

George choked out a thank-you and hung up. His throat tightened and his skin crawled. Why? Was it because of the lamp? Maybe Mary Helen's fears had been more justified than he'd been willing to admit. Maybe he should have had Larry's counsel when he'd spoken to the police. He had no alibi after he left the club. He'd been alone. He'd fought with Dr. Michael that day. Worse, he'd given the detective motive, spoon-fed it to him with the tapes. Wouldn't Mary Helen find that rich? It wasn't Sarah's accidental death he'd needed to worry about. It was Dr. Michael's murder. Sweat trailed down his face and pain exploded in his head. He jumped to his feet, staggered to the sink, and threw up.

Chapter Thirty

Cancini stood in the living room of Vandenberg's apartment. Dark plaids, stripes, and soft leather covered the solid wooden furniture. A large window overlooked a small park. Neat and clean, but not showy, it was the kind of place Cancini wouldn't mind having if it were in his budget. On a detective's salary, it wasn't. The assistant D.A. and a handful of forensics officers bustled around the apartment. Vandenberg had returned to Richmond, and according to the superintendent, given a lengthy notice on the apartment.

The forensics team ripped open drawers and dumped the contents on the floor. They searched under and behind furniture, pulling the cushions from the chairs and sofa. Picture frames were removed from the walls and books were pulled from the shelves. Cancini rifled through Vandenberg's desk and papers, but found nothing. Wandering back to the bedroom, he watched as the sheets were stripped from the bed. He thumbed through the suits, shirts, and khaki pants that filled the walk-in closet. Belts and ties hung from two arms on the wall. There were no female clothes or accessories to be found. Clearly, Mrs. Vandenberg did not stay over.

"Detective?" A wiry young man approached. "So far we haven't found anything significant. Do you want us to collect hair samples from the brush or sheets?"

"No." Cancini shook his head. The killer had left only the dead therapist lying on the floor. There were no strands of hair, unexplained fingerprints, or samples of blood other than the victim's. Standing in the middle of the room, he turned his head in a semicircle. "Have you checked the shower and sink for trace bloodstains?"

"Yes, sir. Nothing."

"All the clothes and shoes? Maybe there's spatter we've missed."

"I'm sorry, sir, but there isn't anything. Everything is clean here."

"Clean?"

"As in there are no dirty clothes at all. Everything's been laundered."

Cancini sighed. Sometimes it worked like that. You did a search and whatever might have been there was gone. It wasn't a stretch to assume that if Vandenberg did murder his therapist, he was smart enough to get rid of the clothing he wore that night. A flash of gold caught his attention then, and he moved toward the items piled on the floor. He picked through books and papers but found only a shiny pen. He looked back at the man from forensics. "Anyone come up with a pair of reading glasses? Gold, wire-rimmed?"

"No. Sorry," the man said.

"Cancini, got something." Smitty's voice came across the apartment. "In here."

He followed the voice to a tiny kitchen, an L-shaped room with just enough space for a table and two chairs. "What is it?"

Smitty gestured to a butcher's block next to the stove. "A knife is missing."

Cancini's heart skipped a beat. He stepped closer. Six steak knives were tucked into slots on the bottom row of the block. A sharpener and four larger knives occupied the slots above those. One slot, however, was empty. Cancini pulled out the knives and laid them side by side on the counter. He looked up at Smitty.

"The butcher knife is gone," his partner said. "I'm betting our murder weapon belongs to this set."

"It's the right brand?"

"Yep."

"Not in the dishwasher? Or a drawer?"

"Nope."

He considered the hole in the knife block. There would be no way to prove the knife that killed Dr. Michael came from this kitchen unless it had markings like initials, but it was still damaging from Cancini's point of view. If they got lucky, someone in the lab could make a match. Either way the empty slot in the block would put the image of George holding the large knife into the minds of a jury. "Good work," he said to Smitty, and turned to one of the forensics officers. "Bag these knives and the block."

The detectives walked out of the apartment together. "I think it's time we pay a visit to Mrs. Michael, don't you think?" Smitty shot him a questioning look. "Call it a courtesy visit."

"Sure," his partner said. "After that?"

"Heading to Richmond to meet Mrs. Vandenberg, maybe see if she can shed some light on her husband's activities."

"Why would she do that?"

"Don't know, but I've got a feeling there's no love lost between them."

Smitty nodded and turned the car toward the Potomac. "You get that from the tapes?"

"Yeah, and something else." As they rode, he told his young partner about Vandenberg's blackouts. "He admitted he drank heavily the night Dr. Michael was murdered. Maybe he doesn't remember what happened?"

Smitty snorted. "Sounds like psychological mumbo-jumbo to me."

"Maybe." Cancini rolled down the window, breathing the sweet scents of spring. "Probably."

"My buddy in Boston got back to me."

"Did he find anything?"

"I gave him her maiden name, Nora Burns. From that, he found out she shared an apartment with her brother through college and right up until she got married. Now, here's the weird thing." Cancini watched Smitty's face. "The rent, tuition, books, all of it was paid for in cash. No credit card. Never even a check. Always cash."

Cancini sat back against the seat. His shirt stuck to the cracked leather and he rolled up the window again. It was weird, but that alone didn't make it suspicious.

Smitty pulled up in front of a large redbrick estate with dark shutters and double doors. "Nice place," he said.

Cherry trees, evergreens, and brilliant flowers dotted the landscaping. A sweeping drive curved around the side of the house, keeping the garage hidden from view. Tall windows faced the street and glittered in the bright sun like jewels. "Big for two people." Cancini scanned the street. An old Toyota, rusted in spots with hubcaps missing, sat parked on the street in front of the house. It seemed out of place in the quiet, well-manicured neighborhood and he made a quick note of the license plate.

"Hey." Smitty elbowed him. "Look."

A woman stood on the front steps, her back to them. Golden hoops hung from her ears and her dark hair was piled into a high ponytail. A flowered skirt billowed around her long legs. Mrs. Michael, standing inside the house, leaned toward her, arms outstretched. The woman pulled away, whirled on her tiptoes, and skipped away. She shaded her eyes from the blistering sun, jumped in the old car, and revved the engine before driving away.

"Isn't that—" Smitty started.

"Lauren Temple," Cancini said, cutting him off. "One of the patients I interviewed the other day." He got out of the car and headed up the drive, Smitty by his side.

The door opened after one knock. "Oh, it's you." Mrs. Michael looked over their shoulders, red-rimmed eyes searching the street. "I'm sorry," she said. "I wasn't expecting you." She sniffed and held up the wadded-up tissues in her hand. "I'm kind of a wreck today. It's just, well, you know . . ."

Cancini glanced back at the now-empty street. "Is that because of Lauren Temple?"

She winced, then raised her shoulders in a shrug. "I guess you saw her leaving."

"Why was she here?"

Her lips parted and she blinked. With a shake of her head, she waved them in and led them to the living room. "Make yourselves comfortable," she said. "Let me wash my face, and I'll be right back."

She carried a tray of coffee when she returned. Cancini noted the freshly applied lipstick and dry eyes. Her rich brown hair had been swept up into a French twist. The crushed tissues were gone. Her voice, broken just minutes earlier, was crisp, businesslike now. "How can I help you today, Detectives?"

"You were going to tell us why Lauren Temple was just leaving?"

Mrs. Michael sat down across from them. "Oh, that. She came to pay her respects. I'm afraid she caught me in a low moment." She crossed her smooth legs. "Actually, I'm glad you're here. Do you have any news for me?"

Cancini ignored the change in subject. "How do you know Miss Temple?"

"I don't," the widow said. "She came because she said she was a patient of my husband's. I thought that was nice of her, don't you?"

"Yes," Cancini kept his tone noncommittal, unable to reconcile this considerate act with the hostile young woman he'd interviewed. "Very nice."

Mrs. Michael sipped her coffee. "Has what I told you the other night helped you?"

"We're pursuing some leads." Cancini avoided naming Vandenberg. "I can't tell you anything specific though."

"But you have something?"

He wasn't ready to reveal how far her tip had taken them. "Maybe. It's too soon to tell."

"I see," Mrs. Michael said. "Can you tell me anything?"

"No."

She uncrossed her legs and stood. "Detectives, why did you come here?"

Lips twitching, Cancini realized he might be enjoying the woman's irritation more than he should. Underneath the icy exterior, he suspected there was a fiery and passionate woman.

Surely the tears they'd seen earlier were a sign she wasn't as cold as she appeared. "I have a couple of questions." he said, no longer smiling. "About the calls on the night Dr. Michael was murdered."

Pinched lines appeared above her full lips. "What about it? I told you my husband called me that night and how worried I was about him. That was around eight. I'd just gotten back to my room after dinner. Do I need my lawyer for these questions?"

"That depends. Do you have anything to hide?"

"Don't be ridiculous," she said, hands on her hips. "What do you want to know?"

"I'd like to hear again why you were worried about him."

"Why? I told you he was anxious. A patient had gotten angry during a session. He was a little nervous about it. Any wife would be worried, too. We've been over this already."

"Yes, but I've been thinking. You knew he was feeling a little scared. Did you call him back and check on him? See if he was all right?"

Head bowed, she sat down again. "No, I didn't."

"So, you didn't call to check on him," Cancini said. "But you did call someone."

Her head snapped up, her face pale. "Wh-what?"

Cancini nodded at Smitty, who took over the questioning. "Mrs. Michael, there were four phone calls that night. One was from your husband, exactly as you said, and the other three were made from your room to a Washington-area cell phone number."

She came to her feet. When she spoke, her voice shook with anger. "You checked my phone calls? You had no right to do that."

"This is a murder investigation. We have every right."

"I won't have it."

Cancini asked again, "Mrs. Michael, who did you talk to three times on the night your husband was murdered?"

"Leave!" Two white spots stood out on the smooth skin of her cheeks. She pointed one slender finger at the front door. "Now!"

They walked out, the heat of her gaze on their backs. She slammed the door after them.

"I'd say you pressed her buttons," Smitty said.

Cancini agreed but said nothing. Like it or not, the calls meant something. Any pretense of an innocent explanation was long gone. A lover? An accomplice? He didn't know, but he was more determined than ever to find out.

Chapter Thirty-One

George sat at the table, slack-jawed, and stared into space. Stunned, he rocked back and forth in his chair, going over everything in his mind. His apartment had been searched. He'd expected to be questioned in light of his relationship with Dr. Michael—but investigated? He couldn't get his mind around the idea he was a suspect in the murder. He laughed out loud, the sound harsh and short, trailing off into a quiet moan.

He held his head in his hands. It was his own fault. He'd broken that vase and lied about it. He'd gotten so drunk he couldn't remember driving home. He gave them the tapes. It made a sick kind of sense. Still, the idea he could have murdered Dr. Michael was ludicrous to him. He'd needed the therapist, relied on him. His hands trembled and he shivered with cold. Dr. Michael believed in him.

"George," his therapist had asked, "has it occurred to you that you were in shock?"

"Shock?" he'd repeated. "Yes. Oh my God, I was completely shocked. I didn't mean for any of it to happen. I didn't."

"That's not what I meant," Dr. Michael said. "Yes, you were shocked, but I'm wondering if you were in medical shock. Specifically, it's called acute stress reaction, although you may have heard of it as psychological shock. Your behavior, as you've described it to me, fits the symptoms." George sat dumbly, his mind dredging up the horrible night. "You did as Mary Helen told you, barely thinking for yourself. Isn't that true?"

Even if it was, it didn't make the old George feel any better. "That's not her fault. She was trying to help."

"That's not what I'm saying. Just listen for a moment." The doctor pulled off his reading glasses. "After the fight and accident, you said you just sat there for what could have been hours, as though you were in a daze. You said your heart was racing and you were sweating. These are all symptoms of acute stress reaction. When Mary Helen arrived, having witnessed what happened, you never even heard her. And when you did become aware of her presence, you yielded all control to her, allowing her to make the decisions."

"But I couldn't—" George interrupted.

"Studies show the brain can shut down when it's traumatized." Dr. Michael plowed on. "The body protects itself by maintaining function, the heart pumping, blood flowing, but the brain itself is off, so to speak, too shocked to comprehend and incapable of working properly."

George said nothing, remembering the utter helplessness he felt at the sight of the woman he loved lying crumpled on the ground, her blood soaking her shining hair.

"It's my medical opinion you were in a state of shock at the accident. That's why you didn't call the police or go for help. You told me you stayed in your apartment for two days, eating nothing, lying on the bed. That's because something inside your brain simply shut down, turned off. So when Mary Helen took over, you let her because your mind wasn't able to process the events as they were happening. You even allowed her to steer you away from phoning the police, your first instinct, because you had no power to make decisions. You were helpless."

George sprang from the couch and paced the small office. Could Dr. Michael be right?

Dr. Michael stroked his mustache. "What do you think might have happened that night if Mary Helen had not shown up?"

He stopped pacing and ran his hand through his hair. He faced the doctor, mouth screwed up. "I . . . I don't know."

"Neither do I, George." He paused. "But the shock had to wear off eventually. Symptoms can last a couple of days or up to a few weeks. Either way, if you had been alone when that happened, your actions that night might have been different. Maybe they wouldn't have, but we'll never know."

George flopped back on the sofa, his eyes flat. "I don't get it, Dr. Michael. It's like you're saying I was in shock so that's my excuse but then the next minute, you act like I might have run away anyway, with or without the shock."

"Would you have? Run away?"

"No!" George pounded his fist on the armrest.

"Very good. That's what I thought. But still, you've spent your entire life blaming yourself, wearing your guilt like a curse. It's possible the circumstances of that night may have been more than you were equipped to handle at the time. Because Mary Helen showed up, we'll never know for sure whether you would have done the right thing, but I'd place my bet you would have."

George's head came up. Gratitude shone in his face. He'd never before considered those events from the perspective offered by Dr. Michael. For just a moment, he imagined he wasn't the monster he'd always believed. Then reality set in and other memories, just as terrifying, came flooding back.

"But I never did come forward. I could have the next day, or the day after that, or any time. But still, I did nothing." He could no longer look his therapist in the eye. "I failed to do the right thing even when I wasn't, you know, in shock."

"Don't you see, George? That night set things in motion. After that, you had to protect Mary Helen. You couldn't come forward later because she was afraid she would be seen as complicit in the events. Isn't that the way it happened?"

George nodded. "But she wouldn't have been there if it weren't for me. Crazy as it seems now, she just wanted to be with me. I had to protect her, even though I don't know what I was protecting her from." Putting his head in his hands, he mumbled an apology. "I'm so sorry for everything, so sorry."

"Guilt is an insidious bedfellow, George. It can . . . it can change a person if it's left to fester, to grow. That night led to a series of mistakes that compounded into your life as it is today."

Seated on the couch, he felt tears prick his eyes. Yes, it was all true. He'd made a mess of his life. If only that night had ended differently. If only he'd let Sarah walk away. If only he hadn't been so afraid to lose her, she might still be alive. Would he still have chosen Mary Helen as his wife? Would he have followed the path laid out for him by his wife and his family? Did it even matter anymore? It was done now and he couldn't change it.

Sniffling, George blinked back tears. When the therapist spoke again, his tone was firm. "George, I think you know that there is only one way to undo everything that's been done. You must go all the way back, to where your guilt originated."

His heart sank. The pronouncement was not new, nor was it outrageous, but to George, it was potentially fatal. The tiny bit of a life he had left, the tenuous threads of his marriage and the relationship with his children, could all be severed beyond repair. That was a risk he wasn't sure he could take.

"You don't have to answer now, George. We can discuss it some more next week."

Relief had flooded through his body. "Okay."

George lifted his eyes to the ceiling. Dr. Michael deserved better from him in death. He wasn't sure how, but he knew he would no longer watch his life from the sidelines. Dr. Michael's murder was not an event from the past. He couldn't hide from it or pretend it would go away. No, George reminded himself, he was a different man than he was two days ago. This was the present and unless he took action to prove his innocence, it could very well be his future.

His head ached and the pounding pressed against his skull. How had it come to this? He'd done the very thing his doctor had wanted. He'd allowed the truth to be exposed and risked the wrath of his wife, but it had come at a price neither he nor Dr. Michael could have anticipated. The truth had elevated him to the role of murder suspect. What next? A search of his Richmond home? His office? His car? It was insane. The irony made him sick to his stomach. He swallowed back the bile and looked down at his hands, willing them to be still. He breathed in and out until his heart rate slowed. Dr. Michael had been wrong. The truth had not set him free. It had made him look like a murderer.

Chapter Thirty-Two

Cancini rarely escaped the capital city. His travels in recent years had been limited to the city's vast suburbs and occasionally a tiny beach in Delaware. Richmond, with its vibrant history and deep Southern overtones, felt like a foreign country to the homicide detective. Mary Helen Vandenberg, with her soft drawl and honeyed tones, reminded him of parasols, waltzes, and large plantations. Small and slender, she wore a lemon silk suit and pearls that matched her shiny blond hair. She possessed a waiflike beauty, although her delicate looks were not the type to which he was usually drawn. With gracious manners, the sort he'd heard of yet rarely encountered in the gritty life he led, she ushered him inside the small mansion as though he were an old and dear friend. She waved a delicately boned hand at an elegant sitting room and excused herself to prepare tea and coffee. Cancini eyed the room with its antiques and dainty chairs. Ill at ease, he took the largest armchair in the room, although it still appeared fragile enough to shatter under his modest weight.

Returning with a silver tray and china cups, Mrs. Vandenberg set the service on an intricately carved cherry table. He sat stiffly, afraid to move. His former wife had aspired to this type of house, this type of decor, but he preferred a recliner and sturdier stuff. Mrs. Vandenberg handed him a cup and perched on the edge of an ornate sofa. Several picture frames sat on top of a gleaming black piano. It wasn't hard to spot the photos of the Vandenberg children, both blond with coloring similar to their mother's.

"Your kids, I take it?" he asked.

"Yes," she said with a broad smile. "Both are in high school now. Wills is a senior, going to college soon, and Elizabeth Grace is a freshman. Do you have any children of your own, Detective?"

His attention was drawn back to a formal portrait of Mary Helen's daughter. The girl bore a strong resemblance to her father in spite of the light hair and eyes. Her attractive face, smooth and noble, was familiar to him, leaving him with the vague feeling he'd met her before. The boy, however, seemed to favor his mother in every way.

"Detective?" She broke into his thoughts, her voice honey-sweet. "Do you have any children of your own?"

"No," Cancini said. "I'm divorced."

She lowered her lashes. "I'm sorry." She waited another moment before asking, "How can I help you, Detective?"

"Well, ma'am, it's about a couple of things." He jiggled the dainty cup and saucer and placed it safely on the table to his left. "You are aware that Mr. Vandenberg's therapist was murdered a few days ago?" Mary Helen nodded, face somber. "I assume your husband told you he was in the station yesterday," the detective said, "and that he gave us access to his medical records with Dr. Michael?"

If he'd hoped to take her by surprise, he knew in an instant he had not succeeded. "Of course, Detective." She smiled again. "When you've been married as long as George and I have, you don't keep secrets from one another."

"Yes, ma'am," Cancini said with a tiny smile of his own. "You only keep secrets from other people."

Her lips twitched. "Pardon me?"

The detective stood, arched his back, and stretched his knees, which had already grown achy on the uncomfortable chair. He was no longer smiling. "Dr. Michael had a habit of taping his sessions with his patients. I don't know whether you knew that." Her placid expression remained unchanged. "I've listened to a lot of your husband's tapes."

The lady didn't flinch. "And?"

"And I think you know something about keeping secrets, Mrs. Vandenberg."

Setting her cup aside, she folded her hands in her lap. "I don't usually discuss personal issues with strangers, Detective, and I find this conversation going into a very private area." George's wife smiled again, the lilt in her voice softening the words. "I understand you're only doing your job. Still, I think it would be best if these matters were handled with an attorney present."

The detective studied the woman in front of him. Mary Helen Vandenberg was a woman used to getting her way, and she did so with a Southern hospitality and manners so sweet a person would hardly notice. If she wanted it to, the interview would end as quickly as it started. He did not intend for that to happen. "That's up to you, of course, Mrs. Vandenberg. I'm more concerned at the present, however, with your husband's blackouts. Like the one he had in front of your son."

This time, Cancini hit his mark. Her face paled. When she regained her composure, her voice was firm. "George is my husband, Detective, and whatever happens in this house stays between us."

"Did he have a lot of blackouts, Mrs. Vandenberg? I'm curious because Dr. Michael seemed to be concerned about them. Were you concerned, too?"

"Still private, Detective, although I do admire your persistence." The smile accompanying her words turned chilly. Standing, she smoothed the lines of her skirt. "Well, thank you for coming, Detective. If you need to speak with me again, please phone in advance and I will arrange a meeting." She put out her small hand. "It was a pleasure to meet you."

Cancini studied the woman in front of him. "What happened before, with the girl Sarah, was a long time ago." He paused and caught the hint of long-standing disgust coming from Mary Helen. "Your involvement in that is one thing, but Dr. Michael's murder, that is another."

She dropped her outstretched hand. "Meaning what, Detective?"

His eyes lit on the tiny vein throbbing in her neck. "Meaning this: I don't know for sure what happened twenty years ago, although I mean to find out. But I do know a man was stabbed to death in my city by someone who wanted him quiet. And I'm going to find that someone and put them away for the rest of his, or her, life."

"Well," she said, the Southern drawl now sounding forced, "I hope you do find that someone, Detective. Murder is a terrible thing."

"Yes, ma'am, it is."

"Is that all then?"

Poker-faced, she was much better at hiding her feelings than her husband. Dr. Michael's tapes played through the detective's mind. Mary Helen was more than complicit in covering up Sarah's death and her actions made her an accomplice. George wasn't the only one who might suffer if the past were revealed. How much did she know about what led up to Sarah's demise? How much did she see? Certainly, she had benefited from her rival's untimely death, marrying George only a few months later. What would Wills and Elizabeth Grace have to say about that?

"Just curious, Mrs. Vandenberg, did you ever meet Dr. Michael?"

The lines around her mouth deepened. "I told you, Detective, that I would rather have an attorney present if you had any more questions."

"Yes," he said, "you did say that, but this isn't really a personal question. And as I said, I'm just curious."

She clucked her tongue. "Really, Detective? I'm quite sure your reasons for wanting to know something aren't as innocent as idle curiosity."

"If you say so. But I am interested."

She tipped her head to her shoulder. "Why? What does it matter?"

He pretended to consider the question. "It's something I picked up on from one of those tapes. Dr. Michael had proposed a joint session with you and your husband."

"I'm sure I don't know why he would do that," she said.

He pushed aside his jacket, putting his hands in his pockets. "Something about working out how you might come forward about that Sarah business. I gathered from the tapes that Dr. Michael thought you might be the primary reason George was unable to confess."

"I am not even going to dignify that with a response," she said, all trace of Southern manners gone.

"You still didn't answer the question. Did you or did you not ever meet Dr. Michael?"

She remained silent, her face averted.

He took a step toward her. "Well?"

She looked up at him, blue eyes hard as glaciers. "You said you listened to my husband's tapes, didn't you? Did you ever hear my voice on those tapes? Did you?"

"No, but I didn't listen to all of them."

"That's your problem," she said, voice cold. "The next time you want to talk to me, call my lawyer. We're finished here." She raised her heart-shaped face and showed him the door.

On the drive back to D.C., it occurred to the detective he'd been dismissed by two women that day, both angry and both bothered by too many questions. Mrs. Michael, with her secret cell phone calls, was hiding something or someone. Where was that phone now? He understood that even with a subpoena, he might never learn who was in possession of that phone on the night of the murder. Then there was Mary Helen Vandenberg. Her secrets were of a very different nature and she'd spent more than twenty years protecting a secret far more criminal than an affair. Just how far would she go to keep protecting it?

Chapter Thirty-Three

Georgestared up at the ceiling and blinked, eyes adjusting to the darkness of the night. A faint breeze blew in through the open window, stirring the flowered curtains. An owl hooted in the distance, its plaintive sound sending a shiver up his spine. He breathed in and out, his mind going over every event of the past week. Everything he knew to be true was wrong.

He'd made several calls during the evening, embarking on his own personal line of questioning. Attempting to retrace his steps on the night Dr. Michael was killed, he'd started with his arrival at the club. The manager had filled in some of the blanks.

"Yes, Mr. Vandenberg, I did try to get you a cab, but you refused."

"I'm sorry, Mr. Lewis." George paused, unsure what he was hoping to learn. "I shouldn't have driven home. You were only doing your job."

"Yes, sir."

"Mr. Lewis, other than having a bit too much scotch, did I behave badly?"

The man hesitated. "I don't think it's my place, sir, to judge that sort of thing."

George sighed. "I see. Well, if you think of anything, it could be important."

"Well, there is something, Mr. Vandenberg." The man clucked his tongue. "You did seem angry at someone but you never said who. I'm not sure I heard you right, but you kept saying something about how you couldn't take the pressure anymore." George's heartbeat sped up and he clutched the phone. Mr. Lewis's tone was apologetic. "That's all, sir."

George rubbed his temple and swallowed. He didn't remember saying anything about being angry. Had he simply blanked it from his mind? "Thanks, Mr. Lewis, you've been a big help."

"I didn't tell the police, sir."

"Excuse me?" His head began to throb.

"About what you were saying. They were here this morning, asking questions, but I only told them I tried to call you a cab. I didn't say anything about you being under pressure. I hope I did the right thing, sir."

He'd lied and assured the manager everything was fine. Most of the calls had been more of the same. Nothing he'd learned had helped. A gust of wind blew open the curtains. George pulled his legs up to his chest and curled into a ball. He had been under pressure that day, yet it wasn't so much more than any other day. There were times it seemed every important person in his life was always pushing him, Mary Helen, his father-in-law, and lately, Dr. Michael. Was that what he'd been ranting about?

George had to assume he'd driven straight from the club back to his apartment, although he had no memory of the act itself. Worse, he had no way of proving this assumption. His building had security, but it was so private that cameras had been vetoed by the board of directors. While there was always a guard on duty at the front desk, coded passkeys allowed entry into the underground parking lot, thereby eliminating any witness who might have seen him return to the building. A dead end.

His head, neck, and shoulders ached, and he craved a warm scotch or a cool gin martini. Tiny goose bumps dotted the flesh of his arms. It was his blank memory that scared him most of all. Not knowing what he'd done, even though he believed it was as innocent as going to bed, was unnerving. The knowledge that he couldn't explain his actions, didn't even know for sure what they were, was even more disturbing. A claim of memory loss would not hold much water with the police. Of that, he was sure. And not knowing the details did not give him the freedom to hide from the truth. He'd already had a lifetime of that, and he could not allow himself to repeat the errors of his past. He pushed the negative thoughts from his mind and straightened his legs, stretching the length of the bed. The movement released some of the tension from his neck to his toes. The wind whistled again, brushing the hair on the back of his arms. George renewed his vow. The truth must be found.

A swath of light cut across the room from the open window. George sat up and held his breath, staring into the darkness. Had he been mistaken? No, there it was again, another beam of light. It was too close to be from a boat out for a moonlight sail. Coming closer, the light bobbed up and down. Someone was on the property. He tiptoed to the window, stood to the side, and peeked around the curtains. The light, a flashlight, stopped moving, and cut in the direction of the cottage as though searching for something. He jumped back from the window, crouching low. His breath ragged, he tried to remember if he'd heard a car or a boat. No. All had been quiet until he spotted the light. Trembling, he rose and pushed the curtain aside again. The light was gone. He peered into the darkness until he caught the light from the corner of his eye. A dark figure moved down the stone path toward the old boathouse. The light shone on the wall of the building, stopping at the door. George's heart raced and he wiped his damp palms on his shorts. Who could possibly be out there? Why were they sneaking around? The figure moved forward again. George gasped. The stranger slipped inside the boathouse and out of sight, the creaky door slamming behind them.

Chapter Thirty-Four

EXHAUSTED FROM THE drive to Richmond and back, Cancini sipped cold coffee and stared at the pile of manila file folders spread across his desk. Handwritten notes and messages filled a wire box next to the phone. With one hand, he shoved the files to the side and flopped back in his chair. "Damn."

"Something wrong?" Smitty said from behind him.

"No. Yes." Cancini crushed his empty Styrofoam cup. "This goddamn case is a hornet's nest. I go in one direction and then I don't know what I've got." He gestured at the papers and folders strewn across the gray metal desktop. "We don't have enough to get an indictment, not with what we have so far, and frankly, I don't know what we've got." The evidence, circumstantial as it was, pointed at Vandenberg, but it wasn't enough for Cancini. He didn't feel it the way he thought he should. A lot of the other guys called it going with their gut, and that was as accurate as anything else, but with Cancini it was more than that. He didn't have a degree or letters after his name, but he had people smarts, a radar he counted on to clue him in to when he was hearing the truth and when he was being told a lie. It wasn't foolproof, but it was usually good enough. "Damn."

Smitty pulled up a chair, flipped it around, and sat. "Anything specific?"

Cancini's face screwed up, the creases in his forehead deepening. "Yeah. For one thing, it's not just Vandenberg who's been keeping secrets or who might have had a motive for wanting the good doctor dead. He's the most likely suspect, but still . . ."

"Meaning the widow."

"She's one."

"I'm not sure I'll be able to help clear things up then. My buddy got some more background on the lady, so I followed up with a couple of calls."

"And?"

Smitty held up a picture of the Michaels and pointed at the widow. "It seems that Mrs. Michael was once a patient of her husband's."

"What?" Cancini sat forward. Nora Michael had been in therapy with the man who ended up her husband? "Are you sure?"

"Yep." Smitty nodded. "That's what I've been told. Kinda blows the mind, doesn't it?"

Cancini let out a low whistle. "Talk about your doctor-patient relationships." His bony fingers drummed the old government-issue desk. From the corner of his eye, the detective saw the captain come out of his office, glance in their direction, and disappear again. He turned back to his partner. "Was that before or after the wedding?"

"The way I was told, she started seeing him when she was pretty young, before they were a couple." He held up a second picture. Nora Michael wore a white suit and hat. Her husband gazed down at her, smiling broadly. "Wedding picture. The marriage took place later, after she was no longer a patient."

"Who told you?"

"One of Dr. Michael's old buddies back in Boston. They were in med school together, along with Nora Michael's brother. That's how they all met. It was the brother who asked Dr. Michael to start treating his sister. How crazy is that?"

Cancini struggled to picture the beautiful widow lying on a couch in an office, spilling her guts about her problems. He couldn't see it. The woman he'd met, so controlled and private, didn't seem like the type. Then again, still waters ran deep, and in his line of work, he'd learned anything was possible. No one was above suspicion. "I don't suppose we have any idea why she was seeing the late Dr. Michael, do we?"

"Nope," Smitty said. "I don't think his friend knew. I don't think he would have told me as much as he did, though, if he didn't wonder about Mrs. Michael. Both of the men closest to her are gone now. I think he was a little worried." He slid the pictures back into a file. "That's all I got. You know how tight-lipped psychiatrists can be."

"Yeah, unfortunately, I do." Cancini recalled his own limited experience with a therapist, a marriage counselor he'd hired to save his marriage. The detective had discovered early on the therapist would not share the contents of his wife's sessions, thereby leaving him exactly where he was before the counseling—in the dark. Maybe with other couples it worked better, but his ex delighted in letting him know she was talking about him, and he couldn't do anything about it. He fired the therapist after only a couple of appointments. Shaking off the bitter memories, he asked, "Do we know if she's still under a therapist's care?"

"No idea."

Cancini scratched at the evening stubble on his chin. Vanden-berg was still their best suspect. He had motive, opportunity, and a history of violence and blackouts. On top of that, he'd already lied to them once. But still . . . Cancini couldn't let the widow go without knowing more. "Since Mrs. Michael is no longer a patient of her husband's, I don't think it would hurt for us to ask her about it. We'll take the direct approach."

"Sure, and right after that we can ask, 'When did you decide to stop seeing your doctor and start, you know,' " Smitty said with a wink, " 'seeing your doctor?' "

Cancini laughed. "Why not? What have we got to lose?"

"Who's got something to lose?" Martin eyed the men, a tooth-pick stuck in his teeth.

"No one, Captain." Cancini's smile faded. "We're just talking."

"Good." Martin bounced on the balls of his feet. "We've got something brewing, anyway." He held up a bulky envelope. "It's a tape from an all-night convenience mart. Sent anonymously. The date is the same as the night Dr. Michael was stabbed. Eleven-thirty P.M. Anyone wanna take a guess who the star is?"

Cancini and Smitty exchanged glances. Neither said a word.

"George Vandenberg. I just got done watching it. It puts him at the store closer to midnight, not home by ten-thirty like he told us."

"He didn't have an alibi anyway," Cancini said. "He told us he was alone."

"True. But this tape shows him coming into the store, buying cigarettes."

"So?" Smitty asked. "How does this help us put him at the crime scene?"

Martin frowned at the young detective and spit the toothpick into his hand. "For one thing, because he wasn't home. And for another, because he didn't seem falling-down drunk like it said in your report. Also, if you look closely, there's something splattered on his shirtsleeve. I don't know if the lab can enhance the tape enough to see, but it could be blood."

"We didn't find any bloody shirts at his apartment, but he could have disposed of those clothes," Cancini said. He picked up the Vandenberg file off his desk. "Has the tape been authenticated?"

"Not yet," Martin said. "I was getting ready to take it down to the lab, but I thought you guys might want to see it first."

Cancini's hazel eyes strayed to the envelope holding the tape. "We do."

"Good. After seeing this, I think you'll find George Vandenberg is looking better and better for the Michael murder. Let's get this thing wrapped up."

Cancini's lips clamped shut. He preferred to reserve his judgment until after he saw the tape for himself. "You said the tape came in anonymously? No return address?"

"That's right. Before you ask, I had someone phone the store to find out who the clerk was that night. I've got the name, and someone's bringing him downtown, along with the manager."

"I'd like to talk to them," Cancini said. Martin led them back to his office. Cancini nodded at Smitty, eyebrows raised. It was the opposite of the old saying that when one door closes, another one opens. There were so many doors opening, he didn't know which one to go through. Where was the truth? Mrs. Michael was hardly the grieving widow he'd expected. What was she hiding? And why was Mrs. Vandenberg, George's wife, so intent on protecting the secret of Sarah's death? How much did it matter to her? Then there was Vandenberg himself. If the tape did turn out to be legitimate, there could be little doubt that he'd lied to them again. No matter how one looked at the facts, that did not bode well for the Southern gentleman from Richmond.

Chapter Thirty-Five

GEORGE SLIPPED ON a pair of shoes and threw on a T-shirt. He raced down the stairs to the door, then hesitated. The front door was in plain view of the boathouse. Heart pounding, he rushed through the kitchen to the rear door. Outside, the evening sky was dark, the stars and moon hidden behind dense clouds. He crept from the back of the house step by step, hands pressed onto the siding. He blinked, straining to see. Across the lawn, he could just make out the shape of the old boathouse. A flicker of light told him the trespasser was still inside.

Watching, he held his position. Should he call the police? Before he could decide, the old door swung open, the sound of the creaky hinges carrying across the yard. The intruder froze and waved the flashlight across the property. George ducked behind the house. He counted to ten, took a breath, and moved back around the corner. No one was there. He scanned the property until he spotted the dark figure near the trees. George followed, then regretted it almost immediately. A twig snapped under his foot, the crack echoing across the lawn. He dropped to the ground. The light arced over his head. His chest pounded and he held his breath. One minute passed, then two. He lifted his head and peeked at the tree line. The trespasser was gone.

George sprang to his feet and ran. Reaching the trees, he picked his way through the brush. The night sounds—crickets, frogs, and owls—seemed louder and closer in the darkness. He struggled to track the bobbing light of the trespasser, losing it time and time again, unable to judge the distance between them. A moment later, he heard the engine of a car. He broke into a run and burst through the woods to a dirt road. The car and the intruder were gone. He bent over, gasping for breath, his hands on his knees. When he recovered, he made the trek back through the trees to his property.

George carried a lantern down to the old boathouse. He held it out in front of him, mind racing. What had the intruder found so interesting. He pushed open the door and waved the light across the room. Dusty footprints marked the floor, but nothing else seemed out of place. Why? This building hadn't been used in years and there was nothing of value inside. Why would anyone care?

He gave up and returned to the house. On edge, he poured a glass of milk and made a sandwich to pass the time. He couldn't understand it. The boathouse didn't mean anything to anyone but him now. No one had used it since the accident. Mary Helen hated it.

"It needs to come down, George," she'd said. "Who knows what kind of bugs and animals are living in there by now?"

He'd argued until she gave up. He'd needed it to stand. He'd needed it to remember.

Sarah had loved cleaning the boat, squirting saltwater from the hull and spraying him in the process, a twinkle in her dark eyes. She'd belonged on the water. The first time he took her out for a sail, she couldn't stop smiling, her long hair blown back by the rushing wind. He taught her to fish, how to bait a hook, and how to water-ski. She loved the power of the boat in her hands, although he made sure they avoided the northern end of the river where Mary Helen's family had a house. If Sarah suspected, she never said.

"Have you ever gone out in your birthday suit?" she asked him one day, a wicked grin on her face. She'd sidled up next to him, edging her way into the driver's seat.

Laughing, he gave her the wheel and wrapped an arm around her waist. "No, I can't say that I have."

"Want to sometime?"

He ran his hands over the length of her body. "With you?"

"Sure. Think how much fun it would be."

The image of her motoring up and down the river stark naked made him smile. The look on her face told him she wasn't kidding. "Maybe."

She sensed his reluctance, taking a different tack. "I've never been skinny-dipping at night. Have you?"

She leaned back into his chest, pressing against him. Desire flooded his loins. "Not yet I haven't. How about tonight?"

"Tonight it is."

George embraced the beautiful memory, but it didn't last, just as things with Sarah hadn't lasted. The years had rolled by and, for the most part, were entirely forgettable. Still, not everything had been awful. He had two children he loved, and by any measure, a comfortable life. Was everything in jeopardy now?

He poured the milk down the sink and tossed the sandwich in the trash. The telephone on the wall came to life, and he jerked his head around at the sharp ring. Other than Mary Helen, no one knew he was there, and after the way they had left things, he was pretty sure she didn't want to talk to him anytime soon. He took two steps toward the phone, but before he could answer it, the ringing stopped. He rubbed his bare arms and looked around the small kitchen, reminded how isolated he was. If anything were to happen to him, how long would it take before anyone knew? The ringing started again. One ring, two rings, three rings. Again, he moved toward the phone in slow motion, expecting with each step for the caller to hang up. Four rings, five rings, six rings.

Breaking out in a cold sweat, his fingers trembling, he put the phone to his ear. "Hello?"

The voice on the other end was unrecognizable, barely more than a hoarse whisper, but the words were coldly clear before the line went dead. "Murderer. Murderer."

Chapter Thirty-Six

THE TAPE BOTHERED him. Cancini had watched it three times, and still there was something about it that seemed staged, unnatural. But the captain was right. Vandenberg did not seem drunk on the tape. He didn't stumble or sway. Instead, he was stiff, head up and back straight, no wasted movements. If the surveillance video was authenticated, it would not look good for Vandenberg. He'd left his club at ten—alone. A slew of witnesses had corroborated this part of Vandenberg's story. The tape placed him at a convenience mart just before midnight. The question was, where had the man been for nearly two hours? Cancini had no doubt what a prosecutor could do with that time and how it might be spun before a jury. The compounding lies added to the evidence mounting against him. So why did he waive his patient's rights and allow the police to access his sessions with Dr. Michael? Was he that clever or that stupid?

Cancini pounded the desk. He knew what was bothering him. Even with the surveillance video in their possession and the knife missing from Vandenberg's apartment, the detective had questions about the man's guilt. "Damn." Listening to those crazy tapes was making him soft. He'd actually begun feeling sorry for the guy. The detective could even pinpoint the moment when it had happened and the session that had touched him most.

"Do you still hate your father, George?" Dr. Michael had asked.

"Yes," Vandenberg cried. A moment later he retracted his answer. "No, I guess not. I don't know what I feel toward him."

"I see. Well, let's look at why you disliked him in the first place."

"Not disliked," the patient said, correcting his therapist. "Hated. I hated him."

"Okay, hated. But surely you didn't always hate him. It must have started somewhere."

"Do we have to do this, Doctor?"

"Yes." The doctor was firm. "I think we do."

There was nothing for a moment and then, "He didn't know how to leave me alone. He was obsessed with controlling everything I did, where I went to school, the classes I took, what sports I played, who my friends were, even who my girlfriend was. I couldn't do anything on my own." Vandenberg's voice rose an octave. "He had every detail of my life planned out for so long, I can't remember when I didn't hate him."

Dr. Michael's tone was noncommittal, but the question was all encompassing. "So, your whole life then? It was always that miserable?" The therapist waited. Listening, Cancini leaned forward, waiting, too.

"No, I guess not. Not always. When I was little, it was different. I remember going to the park with him and growing things in the garden. We had fun then. He would take me to baseball games and out for ice cream and fishing at the river." Vandenberg's voice grew quieter. "I loved him then. I loved him a lot."

"When did it change, George?"

Cancini heard a tremor in Vandenberg's voice. "I'm not sure. It did change though. He changed." There was a long sigh. "Before high school, around then maybe."

"You were growing up. You were a teenager about to become a man."

"But that's no excuse. He changed. It was as though nothing I did was good enough anymore unless it was exactly the way he'd ordered me to do it. I mean, he'd always been tough on me, don't get me wrong, but we got along. Then, one day, we didn't."

"Are you sure it wasn't normal teenage rebellion and your father trying to protect you?"

"Yeah, I'm sure. I might have been a little rebellious, but it wasn't about that. Every night he would drill me with things he wanted me to learn so I could go into the business. He'd describe my life in detail, what kind of wife I needed, where I should live, what clubs I should join. My opinion was irrelevant. In fact, I don't remember him ever asking me what I wanted. I don't think it mattered."

"What about your mother? What did she think of all this?"

"I don't know. She never said much when he was around. He kind of dominated the house in every way." He paused, then added, "I'm sure she loved me, but she couldn't do anything."

"I see." The therapist cleared his throat. "Then your father was what some people might call a control freak?"

Vandenberg snickered. "No, I wouldn't say that. That would be too easy. Besides, he wasn't that way with everything. There were plenty of things he let go, just none that had to do with me. What I would say is that my life became an obsession with him. Whenever I did anything that wasn't in the plan, he went ballistic."

"Was he ever violent?"

"No!" George cried. "No way. But he would threaten to take everything away, and I knew he would do it, too."

The doctor said nothing for a few minutes, allowing his patient some time to calm down. When he spoke again, he focused on more recent years. "So how were things after you were grown and married?"

The answer was grudging, "Better, I guess. Okay. I had the right wife and a good job."

"Was he still so obsessive?"

"For a long time he was. I was following the plan by then, but he kept after me anyway. I had as little to do with him as I could." Vandenberg's breathing sounded ragged on the tape. "Mom died and then he seemed older. He stopped badgering me. It was like he gave up. I could tell I was still a disappointment, but at least he didn't harp on it anymore."

Stopping the tape for a minute, Cancini swallowed hard. He knew a little about what Vandenberg had felt with his father. His dad, too, had wanted more from his son. But it wasn't always that way. Unlike George, he knew exactly when his relationship with his father had changed, Sunday, August 14, the day he lost his mother. Cancini was twelve years old. She'd been an innocent bystander, a customer who walked in the door on the wrong day at the wrong time. None of that changed the fact that she was gone. Together, he and his dad had gone to the morgue, both their lives irrevocably changed by events neither could understand. Sadness replaced joy. Duty replaced play and spontaneity. At home, laughter became a sound from the past. As a boy, Cancini tried to fill the void, tried to live up to his father's expectations, but as the years passed, he knew nothing he did would ever be enough. Graduation brought new misery to the small family when he'd applied to the police academy, squashing his father's dreams of a career in medicine or law. Even then, the young man had seen things in black and white, eager to right the wrongs in the world. When he'd made detective, his father had said, "It's something, I guess." While the elder Cancini never came out and said so, his son knew, could see it in the old man's eyes. He was a disappointment. Divorced. No children. He didn't know Vandenberg, but he understood the man's problems with his father. He pushed play again.

"And the last year, when he had cancer? How was your relationship then?"

For a long moment, there was dead air.

"George?"

"I don't know what to say."

The doctor used his most reasonable voice. "Tell me what you felt during that year."

"I felt the same thing I always felt. My father was an asshole." Cancini flinched at the words. Even to him, the attitude seemed harsh, unnecessary.

"Did he do something different than before?"

"Yeah." George could not hide his bitterness. "He goes from being obsessed with me, then not giving a shit, to then, when he's sick, saying I'm not allowed to see him. My wife could visit. My children could visit. Hell, my friends could visit. But I was barred from the house I grew up in."

"Oh." Dr. Michael seemed stunned, unprepared for this turn of events. Cancini could understand his surprise.

"Yeah. You know when I was allowed to see him again?" George paused for only a half second, answering the question himself. "Never."

"I see," the therapist said.

"No, you don't!" There was sound of a book or magazine falling to the floor. "I wasn't allowed to see my father the whole last year of his life, the whole time he was dying. He refused to see me! Do you have any idea how that feels? Do you know what it's like to know you were such a colossal disappointment your own father doesn't want to see you even when he's on his deathbed? Do you?" Cancini held his breath, waiting. When Vandenberg spoke again, he was quieter, anger spent. "He didn't want to see me."

"I'm sorry, George."

Vandenberg's voice caught. "Do you know how much I hated him for that?"

Cancini sat at Dr. Michael's desk, body leaning toward the cassette player. His bony hands gripped the arms of the chair, his fingers leaving deep impressions in the leather. Engrossed in George's paternal struggle, he forgot the late hour and even that the man on the tape was a suspect in a murder investigation. Fathers and sons. Sons and fathers. The relationship could be the most formative of a young man's life or the most destructive.

"George, would you like to take a break?"

"Do you know what hurt the most?" Vandenberg ignored the question. "After he was gone, after he died, the lawyers told me he'd left everything to me. I got the house, his share of the company, the place at the river. And he left me a journal, his journal. The damn thing was filled with stories about me, all good stuff. There was a letter stuck in the back. It was to me, written right before he died. In it, he told me he loved me and he didn't deserve me." Vandenberg sniffled. "Can you believe it? Almost my whole life he makes me feel unworthy and then he leaves me a letter like that." Cancini blinked, eyes misty. "You want to know how I really feel about my father? I have no idea." Vandenberg broke down sobbing.

The detective had heard enough, the family dynamics striking a little too close to home. He'd turned off the tape and placed it in the box. He'd left the office, tired of complex people and complex suspects. But the complications would not go away. Between Vandenberg, his wife, and the Michael widow, Cancini felt surrounded by secrets. None of that was supposed to matter. He had a dead man and a case to solve. That was his priority. He needed to keep his own feelings out of it. It was evidence that counted. Black and white.

"That convenience store manager and the clerk on the tape are here," Smitty said, breaking into his thoughts. "Are you ready?"

"Yeah, you take the lead. Anything from the lab guys?" The two men strode side by side to the interview room.

"Not yet."

Cancini recognized the clerk from the tape, an elderly man with a shock of white hair. A second man, big-boned with a large paunch around his middle, wore a sweat-stained sport shirt and sweatpants. Perspiration dotted his forehead and upper lip. He mopped his face with a hand towel.

"Thank you for coming in." Smitty made introductions and recapped what they'd seen on the video. The clerk sat wide-eyed, but his manager appeared bored, tapping his fat fingers against his thighs. "Is there anything either of you can add?"

"No," the burly man said, "an' I don't know why we're here. Far as I can tell, there ain't been no crime committed. So what if a guy came in and bought cigarettes? Who gives a crap?"

"I give a crap, Mr. Turner. Mr. Vandenberg could be instrumental in a case we're working on. We're trying to verify the sequence of events that night. Of course, if you're uncomfortable cooperating with the police . . ." He left the thought unfinished. The clerk shrank farther down in his chair, eyes downcast.

"I ain't sayin' we won't cooperate with the cops, but I got a business to run, you know. We ain't done nothin' wrong. I don't need any trouble."

"That's fine." Smitty turned toward the clerk. "Sir, I was wondering if you could tell me how Mr. Vandenberg seemed that night. Did you notice anything unusual?"

"Like what?" the manager interrupted. Cancini shot him a look. The manager folded his arms across his chest but closed his mouth.

"Anything at all?" Smitty repeated.

"I . . . I don't think so. He was kinda quiet." The clerk picked at his fingernails and swung his leg back and forth. "He smelled like he'd been drinking but other than that, he seemed okay."

"Mr. Vandenberg comes in regularly?"

"Once or twice a week, I guess."

"And nothing was different Thursday night?"

He screwed up his small face, hands clenched. "It's hard to remember, but I don't think so. Except he did look like he might have fallen or something. There was something on his shirt. I asked him if he was okay but he didn't answer. I remember now because usually he's real friendly."

"Are we done?" the manager said, standing. "I think we've talked plenty enough."

Cancini stood, too. "Actually, I have a question for you, Mr. Turner."

"Why?" the man asked. "I wasn't workin' that night."

"It's about the tape and how it came to be in our possession." Cancini caught the flicker in the other man's eyes.

"I don't know what you're talking about."

"Did you send the tape to Captain Martin, Mr. Turner?"

"Absolutely not," he said, and puffed out his chest. "Can I go now?"

"No." Cancini took a step closer to the big man.

The manager's face flushed. "You can't keep us here."

"True. But unless you can enlighten me, I'm going to assume you did send the tape, and if you did, I'm going to start wondering why. Maybe I need to subpoena all of your surveillance tapes so I can take a look for myself what kind of business is going on over there." Mr. Turner's face went white. "Unless you happen to know how I got that tape."

The fat man glanced at the floor and out the door, then shrugged. "I sold it," he said. The clerk gawked, openmouthed. "I looked at it first and I dint see nothin' on it. How was I s'posed to know it was important?"

Smitty looked sideways at Cancini. "You sold it? To who?"

"I don't know." Turner shrugged again. "I dint get a name. Got paid in cash and that was that. Dint see no harm."

"Do you think you might recognize this person if you saw them again?" Cancini asked.

"I don't know. Maybe. She was wearing a wig or somethin'." The man frowned. "But I don't wanna get involved. No way!"

"She? It was a woman who bought the tape?"

"That's what I jus' said, ain't it," the manager said irritably. The two detectives exchanged glances. "Jesus Christ! Are you deaf? It was a lady that bought the tape."

Chapter Thirty-Seven

George slammed down the phone. He raced around the cottage and checked the doors and windows, flipping every lock. Upstairs and down, he turned on all the lights, the yellow glow spilling out through the windows into the darkness. Trembling, he'd never felt so cut off from everything and everyone. Maybe it was time to leave. Maybe it wasn't safe to stay in the house alone. Already there had been a trespasser sneaking around the property, and then that horrifying, creepy phone call. He could hear the words echoing in his head. *Murderer. Murderer.* Who? Why?

He grabbed the phone off the wall. A sleepy voice answered, "Hello?"

"Are you all right?" He clutched the phone, pressing it into his ear. "Are the kids all right?"

"George? What time is it?" Mary Helen's voice sharpened. "Are you drunk?"

"No." He paused, struggling to light a cigarette with fingers that refused to be still. "Is everything okay there? The kids fine?"

"They're fine. Why?"

His body coiled with tension. "Has anyone called for me? Did anything weird happen tonight?"

He heard the switch of the lamp. "No. George, what's wrong? You sound upset."

"I . . . I don't know," he said, inhaling on the cigarette. "It's nothing, I guess."

Mary Helen didn't believe him. "Something happened, didn't it?"

"There was somebody here tonight, an intruder."

"Oh my God," she gasped. "Did you call the police? Was anything stolen?"

"No, no, they didn't take anything. It wasn't like that." George hesitated but decided the truth was best. "Someone came onto the property tonight, after dark, with a flashlight and investigated the old boathouse. I couldn't see who it was. Then they went through the woods, got in a car, and drove away."

"The old boathouse? Why?"

He sat down at the kitchen table, his legs still shaking. "I don't know. There's nothing to see there. It was so weird."

"Maybe it was a vagrant, someone looking for some place to hole up. I think you should call the police, George, even if it was a . . . a homeless person." She was firm, the same old Mary Helen he'd known for so long. "If you don't want to do it, I will. That's private property."

He said nothing. In his heart, he knew the trespasser wasn't a vagrant. The homeless don't have cars and carefully park them where they won't be seen or heard. Vagrants don't sneak onto properties, search old boathouses, and take nothing. The trespasser's actions had a purpose. He just didn't know what it was. "There's something else."

Mary Helen sighed. "What is it, George?"

"Someone called here a few minutes ago. I didn't recognize the voice. They only said two words. 'Murderer. Murderer.' " Saying it out loud made him shiver again. "Then whoever it was hung up."

"Oh, for Pete's sake, George, it was probably a crank caller. Don't kids still do that sort of thing?"

Stubbing out the cigarette, he exhaled. He hadn't thought of that. She could be right. Maybe. "Yeah, I guess. Are you sure everyone is all right there?"

"Yes, everyone is fine." A trace of tenderness tinged her words. "Are you okay, George?"

"Yeah. I'm sorry I woke you, Mary Helen. Go back to sleep. I'll call you in the morning."

He hung up. It could have been a prank caller and the intruder might have been a vagrant. Both were logical explanations, but George was not convinced. Maybe he was growing paranoid in the wake of Dr. Michael's murder, but strange things were happening. These were not random occurrences. There had to be a connection. He prowled the house, checked and rechecked all the locks again. Every light in the cottage blazed. He settled on the sofa, drifting off into a fitful sleep. Images of the boathouse loomed up in his dreams, prickling at his semiconscious state, blurring the lines of what he thought was true and what he knew to be real.

The glare of the sun had made him squint and Sarah had started to cry.

"You hurt me." She rubbed her arms and hips where purple and yellow bruises already marked her olive skin. He hurt, too, his knees and elbows hitting the hard wooden floor when they had fallen together, bodies joined in battle. "George, let go of me." She pushed him away.

His hands fell away and he stood, looking down at her. Tears slipped down his cheeks. How had it gotten this bad, this awful? He loved this woman and she didn't want him anymore. She didn't trust him, and he could hardly blame her. The perfection, the purity of their love had imploded, leaving only ugliness and hurt. Hanging his head, he wiped at his tears.

"Help me up." She held out her hand. Sniffling, he reached down and pulled the young woman to her feet. She stood in front of him, bruised and beautiful. Her slender fingers traced his lips and wet cheeks. Her chocolate eyes glowed, shining and wet. "George, you have to let me go. It's for your own good. Please, trust me that I'm doing the right thing."

He couldn't face her, couldn't face the end. How could the brightest time in his life come to such an abrupt and unnecessary conclusion? Everything before seemed so gray, until this gorgeous and captivating creature appeared before him in a smoky and sour-smelling bar. How could she ask him to forget? How could she expect him to go back to his boring and predictable life? Was that what she thought was best for him?

"I can't."

Sarah's hand dropped. "You don't have any choice, George. I'm ending this relationship. It's over."

"No."

"It's over," she said again, louder, firmer.

In a flash, he saw his future, the dull life his father had laid out for him. Before Sarah, he'd resented it, hated it, but hadn't bothered to find his own way, his own alternative. Young and spoiled, it hadn't seemed urgent. Now, after Sarah, he could say with conviction what he did and didn't want.

"I need you," he begged.

"Jesus," she said. "You're going to make me do it, aren't you?"

George stared, his arms hanging limp at his sides. "I didn't want to do this." She gazed past him up at the house and the drive. "Dammit. This is not going to be easy." Sarah breathed and raised her chin. "I won't ruin your life, George. I won't do it."

"You're not going to ruin my—"

She cut him off, a steely edge to her voice. "There's something I have to tell you. The truth is, I haven't been completely honest with you."

A loud, insistent banging snapped him from the fitful dream. He sat up and blinked. Sunlight streamed through the windows. The banging came again. There was someone pounding at the front door. He rose, joints stiff, and leaned over to look out the front window. Parked in the gravel driveway was a black and white car. The police.

Chapter Thirty-Eight

CANCINI RUBBED HIS bloodshot eyes. The phone calls, interviews, and random bits of information swirled around his brain, giving him a raging headache. He opened his drawer and fumbled for the bottle of ibuprofen. Three empty coffee cups littered his desk. A greasy sandwich wrapper sat crumpled on top of his notebook, the one filled with more questions than answers. A million thoughts raced through his head.

Who bought the surveillance tape? Who was the woman? A vague description—dark wig, oversized sunglasses, and khaki-colored coat—wasn't much to go on. The manager thought she might have been tall, but he wasn't sure and he didn't notice her shoes. Why would the anonymous woman go to so much trouble? What was her connection to Vandenberg? To Michael? Just a good citizen? Highly unlikely.

The two women connected to the investigation and with the most to lose sprang to mind. Closest to Vandenberg, of course, was his wife. It wouldn't be the first time a wife had turned on her husband, but her involvement with the surveillance tape seemed improbable, although not impossible. Still, to buy the tape, she would have to know about its existence in the first place. How could she unless she was in Washington the night of the murder and had followed her husband? Cancini made a note to confirm her alibi.

Nora Michael had also drawn his suspicion, but her involvement seemed less likely. Even if Dr. Michael had revealed the troublesome patient's name, the widow couldn't know Vandenberg had been in a convenience mart just before midnight. She was in Chicago. Again, he wondered if she had a partner but dismissed the thought. There was no evidence of a connection between Mrs. Michael and Vandenberg.

As a person of interest, however, Nora Michael remained a case of smoke and mirrors. A subpoena of her cell phone records turned up little, but did reinforce his suspicion someone other than Mrs. Michael carried the second phone. Discovering who was far more difficult. The more they dug, the cloudier her past seemed. Friends and acquaintances from Boston couldn't enlighten them, admitting she maintained a distance and aloofness that most had given up trying to penetrate. The late Dr. Michael appeared to be the one person who knew her well, and he, of course, could tell them nothing. More than once, the detectives heard how Michael revered his wife, fond of telling everyone how lucky he was to have her. She, by all accounts, kept to herself. A talented tax attorney, she took long leaves of absence and extended vacations for weeks at a time. No one seemed to know why. Furthermore, they could find no additional verification she'd been a patient of her husband's or whether she had sought additional treatment since. He was stymied.

Martin brought in the precinct shrink to listen to Vandenberg's sessions and work up a profile on their suspect. His report sat on Cancini's desk, unread and untouched. He slurped the cold coffee, eyeing the folder. How close would the report be to his own analysis of the man? Would it be an affirmation of Vandenberg as a man who had reached the end of his rope, no longer able to withstand the doctor's pressure, a hatred festering and growing, ending in a cold-blooded murder? Would the shrink paint George as a killer? He picked up the report, fingering the corners of the pages. Tossing the coffee, he skimmed the report, flipped back to the middle and reread the parts that caught his interest.

Vandenberg is prone to fits of temper. Alcoholic tendencies combined with periodic doses of antidepressants do not help the patient exhibit self-control. There is a lack of forethought to many of his actions and little evidence he considers the consequences. The blackouts are a major concern and the patient should seek additional treatment in a substance-abuse facility.

Suffering from mild bouts of depression, the patient wants to change his life but lacks belief it can be done.

The one thing that is consistent about the patient is his fear of the truth being known regarding the incident with the girl and her death. Most of his fear seems to originate with his wife. His loyalty to her wishes and demands does not waver in spite of his deep resentment toward her.

The guilt the patient feels about the dead girl is the source of his depression; however, it is the years since that have fed his sadness. The doctor's insistence that revealing the truth would relieve the depression seems naive and unfounded. How could he know that it would work and not plunge the patient into a deeper depression if his family were to abandon him after the fact?

Vandenberg was not an innocent man. He had done things that were wrong—how criminal was debatable—but clearly wrong. Was he a bad man? The detective couldn't decide. He'd lied. He'd exhibited a volatile temper and a propensity toward violence. Black and white. Right and wrong. So, why did he have questions? "Jesus," he mumbled under his breath and dropped the report back on his desk. "I'm getting too old for this shit."

"You bet you are," Smitty said, smiling broadly. He handed Cancini a fresh cup of coffee. "Why don't you retire and give the rest of us a break?"

Cancini tried to smile, but his head ached and the exhaustion born of nonstop work had seeped into his bones. "Damn, that sounds good about now."

Smitty's smile faded. "I was kidding."

"Yeah," Cancini told the younger man. "Me too."

"Is that the shrink's report?" Smitty pointed at the papers on Cancini's desk. "Anything we can use?"

Cancini nodded. "Have at it." He leaned back and rested his hands on his chest.

Smitty read, turning page after page until he'd finished the report. He cleared his throat. "I don't think our shrink liked Dr. Michael much."

Cancini unfolded his hands. "Why do you say that?"

"Something he wrote that seemed like a slam to me. I don't think he liked the way Michael was treating Vandenberg, didn't agree with him about what the guy should do."

"I saw that, too. How could Michael be sure it was right? What about the family? Blah, blah, blah. It's shrink bullshit."

"I meant the other part, about getting too personal."

Cancini sat up. Maybe he had skimmed too many parts. "What about getting too personal?"

Smitty turned to the back page. "Here it is: 'After listening to many samplings of tapes, it is my opinion that the patient was becoming increasingly dependent on the therapist, placing all hope in the treatment. This was counterproductive, however, considering his reticence to take the doctor's advice to come forward about the girl's death. Most troubling though was not the patient's dependence, but the therapist's.' See what I mean?"

"Wait. Did you say the therapist's?" Cancini asked, twin lines between his dark brows. "As in Dr. Michael was dependent on Vandenberg?"

"Yeah, listen. 'Reviewing the doctor's written notes, it appears the therapist was becoming more personally involved in the patient's decision-making process, even trying to steer him in a particular direction. This is, of course, borderline unprofessional, but of more concern should be the consequences. Too involved with the patient, acting as though he had an almost personal stake in the man's treatment, he may have inadvertently pushed the patient to a violent act by forcing him into a life-changing decision he was not ready to make. It is not clear why Dr. Michael was so adamant it was the only solution for the patient or why he would not accept the patient's reluctance.'"

When Smitty stopped reading, neither man said anything for a moment. The shrink's words further incriminated Vandenberg and gave the police reasonable motive, but they meant something else to the detective. Shrinks weren't supposed to get personal.

Not that he cared one whit whether Dr. Michael behaved unpro-
fessionally, but it mattered if it led his death. Why was Michael
so adamant? For what reason? Cancini jumped up, knocking his
chair backward. "I'm going over to Michael's office." Smitty stood,
too, a quizzical look on his face. Cancini shoved his notebook into
his pocket and moved toward the door. Over his shoulder, he said
with a grin, "You can cancel the retirement party, wise ass."

Chapter Thirty-Nine

THE HAIR ON the back of his neck stood up and goose bumps rose on his arms. He drove slowly, unable to shake the feeling he was being watched. George's eyes darted between the rearview and side mirrors, but he saw nothing. He loosened his grip on the steering wheel. The police visit had left him spooked. Dispatched after a terse call from Mary Helen, the young policeman at his door did not inspire confidence. Possessing more pimples on his cheeks than hairs on his chin, he brought to mind a kid playing cops and robbers. George doubted the boy would be much use stopping a trespasser, especially as he didn't appear to carry a gun.

George wanted a drink so badly his stomach hurt and his hands still got the occasional shakes. He felt like shit and he couldn't avoid the glazed eyes and sallow complexion that greeted him in the mirror. George took several deep breaths and concentrated on the road. He uncurled his fingers and let them rest lightly on the wheel. At least the car was still under his control.

George checked the time on the digital display. Larry had agreed to meet with him on short notice. "I took the liberty of contacting Washington yesterday at Mary Helen's request, and I think you were right to call me. It's fair to say you've been elevated to more than a 'person of interest,' " Larry had said. "I'll need to know everything, George. Otherwise, I'm afraid I can't help you." George knew he did not misread the warning, but it didn't matter. He would cooperate. Larry was his best chance to learn what was going on with the investigation into Dr. Michael's murder.

He pulled off the twisty road and stopped at a dusty convenience store. Since giving up drinking, he'd found himself chain-smoking at an alarming rate, substituting one addiction for another. At least his head was clear, he told himself—sort of, anyway. A small dark sedan pulled in behind him. Inside, he bought cigarettes, Coke, and a candy bar.

The old man behind the counter grinned, dark tobacco stains on his teeth. "Helluva breakfast, buddy."

George shrugged and smiled. The guy was right, but he'd eaten nothing that morning and not much the day before, either. "You know how it is. A little caffeine, a little nicotine, a little chocolate. The three basic food groups."

The old man cackled and shoved the items in a paper bag. "Come on back anytime," he called after George.

Driving away, George lit up, inhaled and exhaled, white wisps of smoke curling from his nose and mouth. He relaxed against the seat. He finished the cigarette and pulled another from the pack. Checking his rearview mirror, he frowned. The dark sedan followed a few yards back. Had he seen the driver go into the store? Had he not been paying attention? He stubbed out the burning cigarette, his fingers trembling again. Could the car be following him? He thought it through and dismissed the idea. Surely it would hang back and try not to be seen.

He sped up, his thoughts returning to the dream of the night before. It usually didn't get that far. Yet now that Dr. Michael was gone, the dreams and recollections had taken on a more foreboding tone. Worse, the dreams were haunting him long after he was awake. He'd never relived the entire fight before, not the worst part anyway, and certainly never the life-altering event itself. He sensed it would happen now. The memory was there, always threatening to break through, floating just on the edge of his conscious state. The nausea returned and he swallowed hard. George glanced up and saw the sedan was closer, almost on his bumper. He considered waving the driver around him, but passing was difficult on these curvy, one-lane roads. He sped up again and gave the car some space.

He dreaded the meeting with Larry. Things were moving fast. He felt trapped on a railroad track, his foot stuck in the tie, the rails vibrating with the power of an oncoming train. Larry needed to hear everything and George knew that was right, but he was afraid. Giving the tapes to the police had been easy. That hadn't required him to do anything. The knowledge he'd been labeled a suspect in Dr. Michael's murder changed everything. He sensed the locomotive barreling toward him at full speed.

The sedan tapped his bumper. George's eyes snapped to the rearview mirror. The car followed closely, no more than a foot or two behind him. What was the hurry? The car hit him again, this time harder, and his head bobbed forward. He looked ahead, to the left and to the right. Dense trees and heavy overgrowth lined both sides of the old road, dirt shoulders practically nonexistent. Although he'd never minded, his wife had always complained about these roads, too narrow for two cars, one going east and the other west.

He checked the rearview mirror again. He would pull over into the oncoming lane as far as he could and let the driver pass. Flipping his blinker on, he slowed and moved his car to the left, careful to keep an eye out for oncoming traffic. He breathed a sigh of relief as the sedan moved to pass. When the other car came parallel, he slowed further. The sedan slowed, too. He strained to see the other driver, but the car's opaque windows made it impossible. The sedan matched his speed, turned toward him, and forced him farther onto the shoulder. Pine branches scraped the side of his car. Something was wrong. He jammed his foot on the gas pedal and jerked his car out in front of the sedan. He turned the wheel to the right, taking him back to his lane. The sedan sped up, too, instantly regaining its position on his rear bumper. George increased his speed, watching the needle creep higher and higher on the speedometer. His eyes shot back and forth between the car behind him and the road ahead. His tires squealed when he took the turns at crazy speeds and he clutched the steering wheel now as though it were a lifeline. Sweat dripped from his temples and wet moons appeared under his armpits. There were no sounds other than the pounding in his chest and his own raspy, labored breathing.

He drove on, his fingers cramped and aching. Coming out of the last turn before the one-lane bridge, George spotted a pickup truck barreling toward him. The driver flashed his headlights and blared his horn. The truck slowed, waving his arm for George to get out of the way. Behind him, the sedan gained speed. Trapped between the two vehicles, George slammed on his brakes. His car spun once, the rear end catching the trees. The pickup, screeching to a stop, crashed into the side of his car, throwing George's body against the steering wheel and the driver-side door. George heard glass smash and the crunch of metal. An airbag punched him in the face. Eyes fluttering, he lost consciousness, vaguely aware the sedan had slowed and inched by the two wrecked vehicles before speeding away and out of sight.

Chapter Forty

Cancini slipped into Father Joe's office late in the day.

"Michael. To what do I owe the pleasure?" The priest waved his arm at an empty chair.

"Thanks, Father," Cancini said. He remained standing. "I only have a minute."

The old man folded his hands in his lap. "Of course. How can I help you?"

Cancini stood, feet spread, his hands deep in his pockets. "I'm thinking that being a priest, one who hears confessions, is not completely different than being a shrink, someone who listens to problems and gives advice."

Father Joe spoke slowly as though considering his words. "Yes, there are similarities, but I wouldn't say they're the same. As a priest, I'm in the business of helping people toward absolution. Of course, we offer counseling, but we don't have medical training and can't handle chemical issues or severe mental disorders."

"But you're still bound by a code of ethics. You can't repeat what's been confessed to you and neither can a shrink. Right?"

Deep lines creased the old man's forehead. "Where are you going with this, Michael?"

"What if you gave someone advice and they didn't want to take it? Maybe they were even afraid to take it. Maybe they even got angry when you kept telling them what to do. Would you keep pushing that advice?"

Father Joe hesitated, then said, "That depends. There are so many circumstances where that would not seem wise or in the best interest of the other party and I'm not even sure it's entirely ethical. Then again . . ."

Cancini's body shifted forward. "Then again, what?"

"If you could be absolutely certain of the outcome and there were no other logical solutions, you might feel compelled to insist on a certain course of action."

"What if you weren't certain? Couldn't be certain?"

The priest raised his palms up to the sky. "Then I would probably limit my advice to gentle suggestions and leave it at that."

"That's about what I thought," Cancini said, unsmiling. "Thanks, Father."

"Any time. By the way, your father phoned this morning. He told me you came to see him last night. Said you stayed until he was asleep."

Cancini avoided the priest's eyes. His father had seemed frailer than usual, tiring after only a few minutes of idle small talk. He'd stayed, watching the old man sleep, counting his labored breaths. "Yeah, well, I had some free time. Thanks again."

"In the middle of a case?"

Cancini hesitated. He understood the priest thought he was being a good son. Cancini decided he didn't have the time to remind him otherwise. He offered a quick thanks and ducked out, leaving the question unanswered.

Later, seated behind Dr. Michael's desk, he turned his ear toward the droning voices of the psychologist and his patient. Dr. Michael urged Vandenberg to confess over and over. Cancini had to agree with the department shrink. The advice seemed reckless and naive. Not only could Vandenberg face legal consequences, he stood to lose his family and friends. Why was Dr. Michael so relentless?

"You know the old saying, Doc, the one about the truth shall set you free?" George had asked on one of the most recent session tapes.

"Yes, George, I know it."

"Is that what you're trying to do with me? If I tell the truth, I'll be set free. My pain will go away. I'll stop feeling guilty. The sadness won't come so often. Is that your theory?"

There was a rustling sound, like the sound of pages being turned or papers being shuffled. "Something like that. I do believe the truth is like a healthy drug. It can make you better."

The patient didn't sound convinced. "Let's suppose I did confess. Who would I talk to? The police?"

"Yes. A lawyer or someone in law enforcement."

"What if they decide to charge me with something?"

"It was an accident, George. Isn't that what you've told me?"

"What if they don't believe me? I kept it a secret so long they might not find me credible. They might want to arrest me."

"I doubt that, George. Besides, if I'm not mistaken, some crimes have a statute of limitations. Maybe it wouldn't even matter."

Vandenberg was quiet. Cancini stood up and paced the small

office to keep his blood flowing. "You think I should do this, don't you?"

Dr. Michael didn't give a direct answer. "George, you've felt guilty all these years because you never took responsibility for your actions. Once you have, then I think some of the guilt will slip away. You'll start to feel better."

"I don't know."

"Look, I'm not suggesting you're not going to feel bad about what happened ever again, but it will be better. It will be a lot better. This is the road to recovery. I promise."

Cancini hurried to the tape player and played the last minute again. *This is the road to recovery. I promise.* He thought back to Father Joe's words. He decided the promise seemed reckless.

"I don't know, Dr. Michael," George said, sliding back from the suggestion again. "I'll have to think about it."

Cancini changed tapes again, listening to the men discuss the events immediately following the death of Sarah.

"When I left, she was still lying on the ground. I could see the blood. It was so hot that night." George's description took on an ethereal quality, as though he'd been merely an observer. "I wanted to stop looking at her but I couldn't. It was Mary Helen who made me get up, move away, stop acting like a zombie."

"She told you to go?"

"Yes. She pulled me to my feet, pushed me toward the car. I remember that because my feet felt like lead and I don't think I've ever moved so slowly in my life. One time I tripped or something and started crying again."

"And Mary Helen?"

"Mary Helen?" George repeated the question. "She waited. She probably wanted to comfort me, but I think she could tell from before, when I wouldn't let her touch me, that I didn't want her to. I remember I could barely stand to look at her. I mean, I knew she was trying to help me, but she was alive and, well, Sarah wasn't."

The doctor cleared his throat. "So, you left and didn't come back that night?"

"That night? Hell, I didn't go back for years."

"That's right, you said that before." There was the sound of pencil to paper and a sneeze. "What did Mary Helen do with Sarah's body?"

Cancini's head came up.

"Excuse me?" George asked.

"Well, Mary Helen is a fairly small woman, what did she do with the body? How did she move it?"

The detective sat forward, his face only inches from the tape player.

"Jesus, I don't know. I never asked her."

"And she never told you?"

"Shit, no. She came to see me the next morning, at my apartment. I think I was still pretty out of it. It's such a blur. I do remember she looked pretty beat. She said something like there was nothing to worry about. She said she took care of everything, stuff like that. Then she said she never wanted to talk about it again. At the time, that was fine by me. All I wanted to do was drink myself into oblivion and forget any of it had ever happened."

"I see."

"You know what's so ironic about that?" George asked, and answered his own question. "Forgetting is exactly what I told Sarah I didn't want to do. She was the one who wanted me to forget about her and I said I couldn't. I wouldn't. And then I wished I could. But it didn't work. I guess you already know that."

Cancini clicked off the tape. He banged his notebook against his leg. He'd learned more than he anticipated. While Vandenberg's actions might not have been premeditated, his behavior after was irresponsible and criminal. Not reporting a dead body, especially when you caused the death, implied something to hide. He'd allowed Mary Helen to act as coconspirator, and then later recast her in the role of scapegoat. It crossed his mind that perhaps Sarah had been more right about her partner than she realized. He pushed play again.

"George, I still don't understand how the accident happened. Could we possibly go over it one more time?"

"I'd rather not." The patient sighed. "I don't like to remember that part."

"I know you don't, but we'll do it differently this time."

"What do you mean, differently?" Suspicion crept into the patient's tone.

"Let's lay it out sequentially. Try to tell me each thing in the exact order that it happened. Don't skip around. If you do remember something later, tell me where in the timeline it occurred." The doctor's voice took on an expectant edge. "I'll write everything down and sketch it out."

"Timeline? What would be the point?" Cancini's hand lingered over the fast forward button. He'd heard about the accident several times already. "I've already told you everything before."

"True, but not in the exact order it happened. Your story jumped around, and other times we only talked about certain parts." The therapist was undeterred by his patient's reluctance. "It could be useful later, if you decide to confess."

"I still don't see the point."

"George, we need to try different things, look at the accident in a new way. Think of it as an analysis exercise, part of your treatment. It might be helpful."

There was a moment of silence, typical for the patient whenever he was expected to make a decision or answer a tough question. "Okay, I guess."

"Great," Dr. Michael's voice pitched higher. "Just let me get a fresh pencil and notebook."

Cancini stopped the tape again. He scratched at his chin, then spun the chair around to the cabinet behind him. In the last drawer, he found a pile of notebooks. He sifted through the books until he located the timeline. He spread it out with his hands, pressing down the pages and smoothing the creases. Four pages in width, it covered Sarah's arrival at the boathouse and the ups and downs of their fight, and ended with George's departure. He read it from left to right, noting the erasures and scratches where events had been added and moved. His gaze drifted to the single lamp next to the sofa, its twin destroyed in a moment of passion. He swallowed and studied the pages again, his fingers stopping at each tick on the timeline. Finished, he folded the timeline over three times and replaced it in the notebook. A question—less than an idea—popped into his head. He dismissed the thought with a shake of his head and pulled the next tape from the box. His outstretched hand paused over the play button and he looked again at the empty space where the lamp had stood. The minutes ticked by in silence until the question grew to a hunch and then to a full-fledged idea that promised to keep him up most of the night.

Chapter Forty-One

George opened one eye. The sun blazed and he turned away, groaning. He struggled to sit up but fell back again, screaming in pain.

"He's awake." Voices and faces he didn't recognize appeared before him.

"Let's move," another man's voice said.

He felt himself lifted up and then forward, up again, and then nothing. Doors slammed and sirens blared, but it sounded far away. Floating, the faces and voices faded. Drifting in and out of consciousness, his mind whisked him back into the past.

"Do you recall," Dr. Michael had asked, "how Sarah looked just before she told you this truth, this thing she said she hadn't been honest about?"

George stretched his legs and propped his feet up on the armrest of the sofa. He folded his hands across his chest and smiled. In a few hours, he'd escort his daughter to the father-daughter dance at her high school. Closing his eyes, the image of his daughter's face, so like his own, flitted through his mind. Elizabeth Grace was a beautiful person, a far better person than her father.

"George, are you listening?"

"Sorry," he said, opening his eyes. He sat up, still smiling. "I was thinking about my daughter. We're going out together tonight, just the two of us."

The therapist cocked his head to the side. "You seem happy at the prospect."

"I am. She asked me a month ago. We're having dinner first, then going to a dance at her school. She'll be dressed up." George smiled again, his heart swelling. "My little girl is growing up."

"Yes, children do that. They turn into adults rather quickly."

The patient turned his eyes toward his therapist. "You know, I've never asked you. Do you have any children?"

"No," Dr. Michael said, his mouth set in a thin line. "It's best if we don't discuss my personal life, George. Let's get back to Sarah."

"Okay. What was it you asked again?"

"Sarah said she hadn't been honest with you. How did she look right before she told you the truth?"

George leaned back on the sofa, no longer smiling. He picked at a loose thread on his pants. "It was a long time ago, I'm not sure I can remember."

"Try, please."

He pulled at the thread, twisting it between his fingers. "Sarah," he said, his voice soft. "I don't think she could look me in the eye." The thread broke and he let it flutter to the floor. "That's right. That's why I didn't believe her at first."

"At first. What does that mean?"

"I believed her later."

"Why?"

"Details. She gave me details. When. Where." George's voice cracked. "Who."

"I see. Could she still have been lying?"

"No. She knew too much. It had to be true." George seemed unsure, however. "But you think she might have been lying?"

Dr. Michael's tone was even. "I can't give you an answer, George. The truth, whatever that may be, is for you to discover."

"It was a long time ago," he said again.

"Think," the doctor said. George felt the heat of the doctor's gaze and shifted on the sofa. "Try to remember not just what she said but how she said it. Is it possible she was lying?"

George's eyes snapped open. Each breath brought stabbing pain.

A man's voice said, "Get him something now!"

He rolled his head to one side and glimpsed white walls, tubes, and shiny machinery. A hospital. He blinked. People in white jackets moved around him doing things, but said nothing to him. He slowed his breathing to the most tolerable level. There was a sedan and a truck. He remembered. The sedan had tried to run him off the road. The truck came toward him so fast. George had tried to avoid the truck, but there was nowhere to go. They'd crashed. So much noise and pain. He reached up touched his face, his fingers feeling the swollen cheeks and lips. He felt like someone had belted him with a mean right and followed with a serious left hook. He took another shallow breath.

"Must have been some wreck."

"Yeah, he was lucky."

George heard the voices and wanted to tell them it was no accident, but he couldn't speak, his lips fat and his mouth numb. His eyelids fluttered and he fell back in time again.

"It's not your baby," Sarah said, dark eyes focused on some distant point over his shoulders.

Was she kidding? After everything she'd put him through the past few weeks and the guilt he'd felt about his initial reaction, she had the nerve to use that as her way to end the relationship? He wanted to spit. "Don't give me that bullshit."

"I never told you it was your baby. I said I was pregnant." He said nothing, arms crossed. "It's not your baby," she repeated.

For several minutes, he couldn't look at her. "Lying is beneath you," he said when he could speak. "I don't know why you think I'm that stupid or why you think I'd believe that crap. I know I was a jerk, but I know you were faithful to me." He glared at her. "This is so unbelievable. You're a terrible liar."

She gasped. Tears mixed with frustration. "I'm not lying," she said, voice quivering.

"Yeah?" He took a step closer. "About which thing? Are you saying you just told me a lie or that you lied before? I refuse to believe the baby isn't mine. You're just trying to get me to hate you so I'll leave you alone."

Her cheeks were wet. "And will you? Leave me alone?"

They locked eyes and George knew he'd seen through her ruse. Was it her last attempt to push him away? Could he finally convince her now that he would stand by her no matter what? He took a chance. "No."

Someone squeezed his hand, pressing it hard and gripping as though they didn't want to let go. It was comforting as he drifted along, time shifting in his mind—past and present all lumped together. There were voices again—close by—he thought. The hand squeezed again. George tried to squeeze back, but no one seemed to notice. He felt so far away. Was that Mary Helen he heard? She sounded worried, her voice strained and thin. His lashes fluttered, eyes opening briefly. Mary Helen's face hovered close to his. She tried to smile, but her lips trembled. She said something he couldn't understand, picked up his hand, and kissed it. He drifted away again and thought, *Why did she look so old?*

Sarah wiped away her tears and raised her eyes to his. "It was Gordon," she said.

"What?" He laughed out loud. "Gordon? My roommate? Really, Sarah? You'll have to do better than that."

She looked past him up the drive. When her eyes slid back to his, her tone was harsh. "It's true. It was the weekend you went sailing with your dad. I went to your room with stuff I'd made for you—cookies and brownies. I wanted to surprise you. Gordon let me in and told me where to put everything. He gave me some paper to write you a note."

George remembered that weekend. He'd been looking forward to it, surprised his dad could get away and wanted to spend his free time with his son. Yet none of it went the way he thought it would. When they weren't sailing, his father had spent most of the time grilling George about his future, his career, and Mary Helen. Tired of the interrogation, he'd drunk a six-pack, much to the chagrin of his watchful dad. He remembered the weekend, but her story didn't sound right. There had been nothing for him when he returned to his room Sunday evening. No cookies. No note. And Gordon hadn't said anything, either.

"Good try. But you didn't leave anything, Sarah. You were never even there."

"He offered me a beer and I thought he was a nice guy, you know. He was your friend. So I took it and then he gave me another." She took a breath and pushed the dark hair off her face. "He sat a little closer to me on the bed and we started talking. I think I had another beer. Next thing I knew he pulled me onto his lap."

George's face flamed. He and Gordon had been roommates for three years. Gordon never had a steady girlfriend, preferring to drift from affair to affair. "The more the merrier" was his slogan. It occurred to George that Gordon had made comments about Sarah on more than one occasion.

"I made a joke about it and pushed him away. But he pulled me back, rubbing my arms and shoulders."

Every tendon in his neck pulsed. He balled his hands into fists. Gordon had come on to Sarah behind his back?

"He told me he wanted me and he knew I wanted him, too."

The vision of his roommate pawing Sarah sent waves of fury through the young man. He wanted to scream, to cry out, to throw something. "Are you trying to tell me," he said, his jaw clenched, "that while I was with my dad, Gordon attacked you?" Another, more horrendous thought, flooded his mind. "Oh my God, did he rape you?"

Chapter Forty-Two

MARTIN STOMPED AROUND the precinct, yelling at anyone and everyone, spit and toothpicks flying from his mouth. The news that Vandenberg was lying in a hospital, in no condition to be served with an arrest warrant for murder, had sent the captain into a tirade. As Cancini had suspected, Martin had used the analysis prepared by the precinct shrink to convince the D.A.'s office to issue the warrant in spite of a mostly circumstantial case. The pressure from the brass and the widow's lawyer had made him want the case solved yesterday. Cancini didn't like the decision, but the captain, not too subtly, reminded him he didn't make the call. His superior did. Still, it wasn't just the circumstantial evidence that didn't sit well with Cancini. It was the tapes, the timeline, and the unanswered questions. He'd lain awake half the night, ideas popping in and out of his head, some too far-fetched to be possible and others pure speculation. None of it proved anything and Martin wasn't the type to listen to theories, especially when he had an arrest warrant in hand. The warrant might be delayed a couple of days, but it would be served.

Heads down, Cancini and Smitty rechecked every piece of information. They pored over bank statements, receipts, insurance documents, and transcripts of interviews. Late in the day, Smitty tossed a phone log onto Cancini's desk.

"What's this?" he asked.

"That girl, Lauren Temple. What was your impression?"

"I don't know," he said with a sigh. His eyes itched, he was tired, and the knot between his shoulders had grown to the size of a baseball. "She was a smart-mouth, bratty."

"So, not the type to pay condolences."

Cancini snorted. "No, but we've been over this. Other than seeing her leave the Michael house, there's no connection between the two women. The maid had never seen the girl before. No one at Mrs. Michael's office recognized her, and Mrs. Michael didn't visit her husband's office so she couldn't have run into her there. We have no evidence they knew each other."

"Maybe. Maybe not. I've highlighted three calls made from the Michael house to the Stratford Grill in the last three months."

Cancini looked up. "Lauren Temple's restaurant." He scanned the phone record. The calls were made on weekdays between the hours of five and six P.M. when Dr. Michael would still have been at the office. He tapped his fingers against his desk. "Takeout?"

"Too far from the house and not convenient to either of the Michaels' offices."

"But not impossible?"

"No."

"Okay. Let's assume they did know each other before Dr. Michael died. That by itself is not suspicious and both women have alibis."

"Damn. I forgot." Smitty picked up another folder. "Funny though. Did you know Lauren Temple grew up in Boston?"

Cancini's fingers stopped moving. "You don't say?"

"I do say. Her boyfriend mentioned it. Said she only moved here a year ago, maybe less."

"Now that is funny." Cancini flipped through his notes until he found her interview. He had an address, work information, and age. She'd visited the doctor occasionally, but not regularly. The dates and times were listed in his notes. "A year ago?"

"Looks like it."

He scowled down at the pages in his hands. He didn't believe in coincidences. Had Mrs. Michael met the girl at the restaurant? Did they know they both hailed from Boston? He tossed the papers aside. Even if the women knew each other, it meant nothing. It didn't prove motive or opportunity. But that didn't stop him from wondering.

Smitty leaned in, his voice low. "You're not sold on Vandenberg?"

"Are you?"

"Well, Dr. Michael was pushing the guy pretty hard. He might've snapped." Smitty paused, then added, "But it would be better if we had the murder weapon or something that placed him at the crime scene."

"More evidence would be better." He heard Vandenberg's voice in his head, a sound he was having a harder and harder time forgetting. He didn't want to think about the tapes. "Still nothing on the girl?"

Smitty shook his head. "I checked all three counties near Vandenberg's river house. There were no death certificates or missing person reports listed with that name, but they're still looking."

Cancini frowned. It had been a long shot. Many of the rural counties hadn't yet gotten around to putting old cases on the computer system. And even if the files were located, it was possible her body had gone unidentified, a Jane Doe. He stood and swept several files into a bag. "I'm gonna call it a day."

For the second night in a row, the detective lay awake, tossing and turning. The king-sized bed he still slept in felt empty, his slight build stretched out on the large mattress. Hot, he threw off the covers and stared at the ceiling fan circling over his head, the whirling blades pushing the cool air down to his damp skin. His mind would not shut off and he couldn't stop thinking about Dr. Michael and what he was trying to accomplish with George. What if Vandenberg had confessed? What was in it for Michael? None of it made sense. What was he missing?

Sitting up, he flipped on a light. It wasn't just Dr. Michael. He knew he wouldn't rest until he found Sarah Winter. Vandenberg may have taken Sarah's life, but he couldn't have known she'd be erased from existence after she was gone. She deserved better than to end up a Jane Doe. His head ached. He got up and splashed cold water on his face. Staring into the mirror, his mind went back to Dr. Michael's timeline. He saw every moment, every second sketched out in detail. He blinked. Every moment except one. George had no idea when Mary Helen arrived on the scene. A large question mark had been penciled over her name. How long had she been there? And why?

He spread the files across the living room floor, picking out pages and laying them in a line. Two hours later he sat down, spent but relieved. He'd told Smitty he didn't believe in coincidences. He still didn't. He grabbed the phone and dialed his partner. He had more than a hunch now, more than an idea. Cancini talked, knowing how insane it sounded, even to him. Hanging up, he felt better. Maybe he could sleep after all.

He boarded the early-morning flight to Boston with less confidence than he would have liked. In the light of day, he worried the trip was a wild-goose chase. He'd bypassed the captain. If it panned out, he wouldn't get suspended. If it didn't, well, he guessed he deserved what he got. Smitty's buddy, Johnny, met him at Logan, two manila file folders in his hand.

Cancini scanned the first file, most of the information already in his notes. The second file was new, the primary reason he'd come to Boston. He read every word of the short report, some parts a second time, especially interested in the last few years of available information.

"That enough for ya?" Johnny asked.

It would do. "Yep. How'd you get it so fast?"

"I pulled a few strings."

"Thanks. You're a stand-up guy."

"Sure. Any friend of Smitty's is a friend of mine. D'ya need a ride?"

Cancini tossed the empty coffee cup in the trash and glanced around the airport. Men and women in suits hurried past the two cops, racing to catch their planes or collect their bags. Sighing, he thought about where he needed to go, and what he might need to do. For one brief moment he wished he were one of those people, stressed about some business meeting or spreadsheet or scheduled merger. But the image of a dead man lying on the floor popped into his head and the feeling passed. "I'm gonna grab a cab. Thanks anyway." He shook hands with the Boston cop.

He dialed Smitty. "I'm here."

"Did you get what you need?"

"Enough. Johnny's a good guy. I'll keep you posted."

"Hey, I talked to the boyfriend. You were right."

Cancini sighed. "Okay. See how far you can take it."

In the taxi, he pulled two photos from his pocket and placed them in the second file. He watched the traffic crawl by, his hands on his knees. He didn't know if he wanted to be right. Sometimes the truth hurt so much, wounded so deeply, some people never recovered. This could be one of those times. But he was a cop and no matter how gray life was, homicide was black and white. Dr. Michael was dead. Someone had to pay.

Chapter Forty-Three

MARY HELEN STAYED by his side. The children came and went when their mother allowed it. She joked that he looked as though he'd been in a prizefight—on the losing end—keeping things light for Wills and Elizabeth Grace. They stood next to the bed, confused by the sight of their injured dad. Mary Helen had done her best to prepare them, but the bandages and purple welts were terrifying to the teenagers. It broke his heart.

The police took his statement and she stayed. The doctors and nurses poked and prodded. Still, she stayed. He drifted off, drowsy with medication and exhausted by the pain. When he woke, the room was dark. He couldn't see her, but he knew she was there.

"Mary Helen?" he said through rubbery lips.

"Yes?" Her voice sounded soft and sweet in the cold hospital room.

He ached everywhere. The doctors had told him he'd cracked his ribs, broken his collarbone, and sprained his arm. His face had been badly bruised by the airbag. Even with the medication, the throbbing persisted, rising and falling with the timing of the doses. He took a deep breath, gritting his teeth. "I'm sorry."

Mary Helen picked up her chair and moved it closer to the bed. She took his hand and stroked the skin with her delicate fingers. He could feel her trembling. "You could have died, George." The fear in her voice stunned him. She began to weep and pressed his hand to her lips, kissing it over and over. "When I saw you, I was so scared."

He rolled to face her. She smiled through swollen eyes and tears. He didn't know what to say except to apologize again.

She shook her head and told him not to be silly. Slowly, awkwardly, they began to talk. They kept it simple, talking of the children, the house, nothing important. His fingers intertwined with hers and he didn't want to let go, but it was late. "I'll be back first thing, George. I promise," she said.

The truth of her words hit him then. He could have died. It was ironic, he realized. Only one week earlier, before Dr. Michael had been murdered, he wouldn't have cared whether he lived or died. He did now. Everything was different. He was different. All of it mattered now. Living, being with family, doing something with his life. Maybe Mary Helen wasn't to blame for everything between them. Maybe they had both made mistakes. It was probably too late for them—too much had happened—but he was glad she'd been with him, glad she was coming back.

He tried to fight the memories, tired of living in the past, eager to get on with the future. But Sarah's dark face, defiant and sad, forced its way into his mind.

"No, George, no one raped me. It wasn't like that."

Her tone irritated him. Was she saying she had slept with his roommate, gotten pregnant, and then told George the baby was his? Worse, she'd said it as calmly as though she were telling him his favorite TV show was on or the car needed gas. Where was her sense of decency? He could barely choke out the words. "How was it then, Sarah? Why don't you tell me?"

"You're mad."

"You're goddamn right I'm mad," he said, his hands clenched into hard fists. "I don't believe you." He took a step forward and her eyes widened. Shame flooded him and his shoulders slumped, anger forgotten. "I don't believe you," he said again. "It doesn't make sense."

She looked over his shoulder again. "Do I have to give you details, George? Just accept it and let me go."

He couldn't, and in his heart, he knew it was no longer about her. It was the baby. For weeks, he'd believed the child growing inside her was his. He knew he should be relieved she was trying to absolve him of that responsibility. She was letting him walk away with no strings attached, severing his connection to her and the baby. It was exactly what Mary Helen wanted. It's what his family would want if they knew. And it would be so easy. Too easy.

He took a deep breath. "I don't believe you, Sarah. This is my baby, and even if you don't want me anymore, too bad. I'm the father and I'm gonna be around, whether you like it or not."

Her face and chest flushed. "You have no say here, George. You haven't earned the right to tell me what I can and can't do with my baby. You're just a . . ." Her brows wrinkled as she searched for the words. "A spoiled, rich frat boy living on daddy's dime, playing around with the cocktail waitress." Her eyes blazed when he tried to interrupt. "Don't you dare tell me whose baby this is. It's mine. You got that? It's mine!"

"What about Gordon?" He knew he had her now, his heart skipping a beat.

"He doesn't know," she shot back, hands on her hips. "Don't act like you're so smart, George. Just because I haven't told him doesn't mean he's not the father. I just want to do this on my own."

"Give it up, Sarah."

"You asked for it, George. Just remember that someday. You asked for this." The fire in her eyes faded. "Gordon said he'd been attracted to me for a while, had even told you, and you hadn't said anything to him about it. He's a handsome guy and when he stood close to me, started kissing me, I didn't mind." George couldn't look at her, couldn't listen to her tell lies, spin such a sick story. "I was surprised how much I liked it. It was different than you. Gordon's a good kisser." A fresh wave of jealousy swept over him and he breathed heavily. "He took my clothes off slowly, telling me I was like an Amazon goddess. I remember he used those words. Amazon goddess. It made me think of that old Wonder Woman comic book. She was an Amazon, I think."

He put his hands over his ears to drown out her words, to stop it from happening. He didn't want to hear her anymore, but she kept talking, staring past him.

"I helped him undress, too. He's not as tall as you are and I could look him in the eye, but he pulled me over to the bed, telling me to lie down and stretch out."

He could taste the sickness creep into his mouth. Turning his head to the side, he threw up, hunched over, head hanging low.

She kept talking, her voice like acid on his skin. "He lay down next to me, touching me all over. I don't know what I was thinking at the time. I could say I was drunk and didn't know what I was doing, but that would be a lie. I knew. He wanted me to touch him." She paused then, taking a breath. With a sinking heart, he knew she wasn't lying. Sarah told him about Gordon, about the dark birthmark that stretched from his hip to his groin, the one a woman could only know about if she'd seen it. When she stopped speaking, he stood paralyzed. A heavy silence fell over them, and he could hear every breath she took. He'd believed in her, in them. The pounding in his head gathered strength and he wanted to punch her, wanted to hurt her as much as she'd hurt him, but he couldn't. He hated her in that moment, but he loved her still. He forced himself to look at her. She seemed different, older, less alive than when she'd arrived.

"I need to say good-bye now." She moved close to him and raised one hand. She touched a lock of hair and brushed it off his face. He stiffened with desire, fighting the urge to pull her to his chest. He swatted at her hand and pushed her away with more force than he'd intended. She tripped on the stones and fell backward, mouth and eyes wide in surprise. Her head smacked against the corner of the boathouse and she landed with a thud among the rocks, her long legs twisted beneath her body.

He rushed to her, dropping to his knees. "Oh my God, Sarah, are you all right?" He cradled her in his arms. Her head lolled back and he gasped. "Sarah? Sarah, say something." He pulled her legs from under her, talking all the while. "Sarah, c'mon, Sarah. Wake up." He felt the sticky warmth of her blood before he saw it and he held her close, stroking her back. She didn't move, didn't respond. He laid her gently on the ground, rocked back on his heels, and howled. He'd killed her. Sarah was dead and he'd killed her.

Chapter Forty-Four

CANCINI CLIMBED FROM the cab and raised a hand to block the sun. The Temple house, a white Colonial with a two-car garage, sat at the end of a quiet cul-de-sac. A dog barked somewhere in the distance and he glanced over his shoulder. He imagined children riding their bikes, tossing balls, and playing hide-and-seek among the bushes. On this day, everything was still, no screams or squeals ringing in his ear. He climbed the driveway and knocked on the front door. Silence. He peered in the front window and knocked again, louder.

"If you're looking for the Temples, they're not home," a voice called from next door. A gray-haired woman stood on her front stoop, a yellow-flowered housecoat wrapped tightly around her waist. She folded her arms over her thin chest. "They're in New York."

"Damn." He slapped the file against his leg. To her, he said, "Do you know when they'll be back?"

"Not till Sunday."

He didn't know if he had that long. Martin would have Vandenberg in custody as soon as he was able. There had to be another way. He crossed the lawn. "Maybe you can help me."

The lady clutched at the collar of her housecoat and took a step backward. "I'm not buying anything," she said.

"I'm not selling anything," he said, and held up his badge.

Her hand went to her throat. "Oh my. Is everything all right?"

"As far as I know," he said with a smile. "Do you have a few minutes to answer some questions?"

"What kind of questions?" She kept one hand on the door.

"How long the Temples have lived here, what kind of people they are, that sort of thing."

"I suppose it wouldn't hurt." She pushed her glasses up on her nose and peered at him with cloudy eyes. "You have a nice face, young man. Kind of a big nose, but nice. I was just about to make some tea." He followed her inside. "I'm Thelma Jenkins, but you can call me Thelma."

"Nice to meet you, Thelma. Mike Cancini." He walked through a narrow hall adorned with framed pictures, large and small. More pictures covered the refrigerator in her kitchen. The house smelled faintly of gardenias. "How well do you know the Temples?"

"Oh Lord, I've lived here since these houses were built. I know everyone. I'm an original owner, as they say." She talked while she filled the silver kettle. "Now, the Temples moved in later, bought the house from the Lancasters."

"Did they have a daughter when they moved in?"

"Oh yes. She was just a baby then. Cute little thing, too." She set the sugar and cream on the table. "Is this about her?"

"Sort of. I'm trying to get a background on her."

She sat down and placed a cool hand over his. "That poor dear. Is she in trouble?"

"That's what I'm trying to find out. It sounds as though you felt sorry for her. Weren't they a happy family?"

The teakettle whistled and she rose from the chair. She poured the hot water over tea bags and carried the cups to the table. "My children were older than Lauren. They didn't play together much, but no, I don't think 'happy' is the word I would use."

Cancini watched her dunk her tea bag and did the same. Steam curled up and warmed his face. "How would you describe the Temples?"

She pursed her lips. "Well, I think it was awful over there if you don't mind my saying so. Howard and Jean, those are Lauren's parents, aren't the most friendly of folks. The truth is, I always suspected something rather terrible was going on in that house."

"What do you mean?"

Thelma wagged her finger and clucked her tongue. "Broken bones is what I mean. One time it was her arm, then her ribs, even her jaw. There was always some bruise or other. I know children get hurt, but it was so often. That girl jumped every time they yelled her name to come in for dinner. I wanted to call the police, but my husband told me to stay out of it." She let out a breath. "I tried to be nice to her, gave her cookies, but I don't know how much it helped. Another neighbor told me the school was suspicious, too. They might have investigated. I'm not sure."

Cancini swallowed. He remembered the lump on the girl's collarbone. If there was any truth to Thelma's story, Lauren Temple's "parent issues" were worse than he suspected. "What about when she was older? Do you know if she told anyone?"

"I doubt it. She was terrified of them." She blew on her tea. "There was one time when I might have heard a fight in the driveway. Lauren was grown up then, maybe in high school. I heard her scream she hated them. Everyone in the neighborhood probably heard her. She said something like she wished she'd never been their daughter. I couldn't hear what Howard said back but it must have been something, because she fell to the ground and next thing I knew, she was crying like, well, I don't know what. Howard went in the house and shut the door." She leaned in and lowered her voice. "Asshole."

Cancini's lips twitched. "You didn't like Howard Temple."

"Correction. I don't like Howard Temple."

"And his wife?"

"I guess she's okay if he's not around."

He reached into his file and pulled out a photo. "Is this Lauren?"

She smiled, her voice soft. "Pretty girl, isn't she? She deserved better than them."

Cancini said nothing and pulled out a second photo, this one of Nora Michael. In the corporate photo he'd obtained, she wore a gray suit and silver earrings. Her hair, pinned up in a bun, emphasized the sculpted cheekbones and dark eyes. "Have you ever seen this woman?"

She leaned closer to the picture. "No, I've never seen her before."

"Would you mind looking again? Maybe she was a friend of the Temples? Maybe visited their home over the years?"

"No, I've never seen her," Thelma said again. "They don't have many friends."

He left the house, his steps heavier than when he'd arrived. Although no closer to proving a connection between Nora Michael and Lauren Temple, he'd learned more than he'd expected. He slid into the waiting taxi.

"Where to now, pal?"

Cancini rolled down the window and snapped a photo of the Temple house. It was picturesque, just the kind of house kids dreamed of growing up in. The only thing missing was a white picket fence. His pulse quickened and his fingers tightened on the file. He needed to know more. He needed to know it all. "Take me to Social Services."

Chapter Forty-Five

Cancini hung his brown leather jacket on a hook. He knotted his tie and slipped on a blue blazer. "Any stains?"

Smitty stepped back and appraised his partner. "Nope. You look good. Not used to seeing you so dressed up."

He rolled his eyes. "Is everyone here?"

"The Vandenbergs just arrived. I put them in the captain's office."

Cancini nodded and tucked his notebook into his jacket. "The widow?"

Smitty jerked a thumb toward the interview room. "In there, with her lawyer. He's pretty peeved, too."

"Good." The parties had been separated, just as he'd requested. "You ready?"

"As ready as I'll ever be, I guess." He raked his hand through his white-blond hair. "I've never worked anything like this before. This case is crazy."

Cancini clapped the young man on the back. Crazy sounded right. He'd fit most of the puzzle pieces together in Boston and the rest came together after his return. They'd worked through the night and the next day, sorting through the evidence, and planning the arrest of Dr. Michael's murderer. There were no more "what ifs." All the cards would be on the table, for better or for worse, and no player would be a winner. The stakes were just too high. "Martin okay?"

Smitty nodded.

Cancini's throat itched and his skin tingled. Gathering them here, in one place, could backfire. He swallowed some water. "Let's go."

The lawyer started in right away. "You have no right to keep us here. Mrs. Michael has been through enough. How dare you hold her here as though she were a suspect? Have you no compassion?" The man stood guard behind his client, hands pressed on her shoulders. Nora Michael stared straight ahead, her eyes sunken and impenetrable.

Cancini walked to the large pane of glass. He couldn't see the district attorney on the other side, but neither could the lawyer. "Mrs. Michael," he said, and swung around. "I've been thinking about our discussion the other day."

"What discussion?" The lawyer bent his head to hers. "Did you speak to the police without my knowledge, Nora? Please tell me you didn't do that."

Waiting to see what she would do, Cancini said nothing.

She shrugged. "It was nothing, Gerard. He asked me a couple of questions. That's all."

"Yes, that's all, Gerard." The lawyer's head shot up. "And your client failed to give me an answer." Her face remained placid, and Cancini wondered how much the lawyer knew about his client's private life. "Actually, I wasn't referring to that conversation as much as the one at Monty's."

The lawyer became agitated. "What's he talking about, Nora?"

She waved a hand in the air, brushing off the question. "I told you about this, Gerard. I spoke to him about a patient."

"Right. I knew about that." He eyed Cancini. "Did you find the patient?"

"Mrs. Michael told me she had spoken to her husband on the phone the night he was killed and he'd been upset about a patient. This patient, she didn't know the name, had lost his temper during his session that day. Also, she thought maybe the patient had a violent past." He shifted his attention to the widow. "I got to thinking, the way you were able to steer me toward one of his patients for the murder, I wondered if your husband talked to you about other patients. Maybe bounced things off you?"

"Of course not." Her skin turned pink. "I told you he didn't make a habit of discussing his cases with me. In fact, just the opposite."

"But you knew about this patient?"

"Yes, but only because this patient had shown violent tendencies and it made him nervous. And I did not steer you toward anyone. It just so happened something happened during their session that day."

"How long had you known about this patient?"

She threw up her hands. "I don't know. Like I told you, my husband was a little obsessed with this patient. He was worried so I guess he confided in his wife."

"He must have had other patients with severe emotional issues, even other violent patients, yet he never shared that information with you." Cancini cocked his head. "Did you ever wonder why he did now?"

"No. I just assumed he needed to talk. That's all," she said, the words clipped.

The lawyer spoke up. "Detective, why are we here?"

Cancini glanced at Smitty. His young partner stood near the door holding a thin manila file folder. He looked at the widow again. "I went to Boston the other day."

Nora's lips parted, then clamped shut. Even watching closely, he almost missed her split-second reaction and instant recovery. "I think of Boston as home, Detective. I hope you enjoyed your trip."

"Are you originally from Boston, Mrs. Michael?"

"No." She gave him a weak smile. "We moved a lot when I was a child. I'm from all over, I guess. Boston is where I've lived the longest."

"Fair enough. Would it be accurate to say you weren't eager to relocate to Washington then?"

"I suppose. Boston is my home."

"I guess you have a lot of friends and family there, don't you?"

The attorney pulled back the sleeve of his jacket and tapped his watch. "I've got other meetings, so can we please get to the point? Surely you didn't bring us here to talk about Mrs. Michael's friends or what town she's from."

Cancini forced a smile. "We brought you in because we thought you'd like to know we've got a suspect in custody."

The man blinked, then beamed at his client. "That's excellent news. Great news. Why didn't you say so in the first place?"

Nora Michael sat stone-faced. The lines around her mouth deepened. "Who is your suspect, Detective?"

"I brought you in to thank you personally, Mrs. Michael." He watched her face. Her lipsticked mouth opened, new understanding in her eyes. "You've been very helpful, especially the information about the patient." Her face paled. "You were right."

"So, it was one of Dr. Michael's patients," the lawyer said. He patted his client on the shoulder. "That's terrible."

"The patient you told us about was struggling. He and your husband had some sessions I can only describe as emotional and volatile. They did have another one of those episodes on the day your husband was killed." She dropped her head, breaking eye contact. "I must tell you, in a way, you provided the key to this case."

"Did you hear that, Nora?" The lawyer patted her again.

Cancini turned to the glass and then to Smitty. "Can you bring them in now?"

Her head came up, dark eyes brimming with tears.

The lawyer frowned. "Are you bringing the suspect in? This is highly unusual, isn't it?" He bent toward his client. "Nora, dear, are you sure you're up to this? Because if you're not . . ." He let the words trail off.

White-faced, she twisted her fingers, turning her wedding ring over and over. Cancini felt his muscles tighten. He moved back toward the viewing glass to see the door and the widow at the same time. The minutes passed and she lowered her head, shoulders shaking. Who was she crying for? The door opened and it was his turn to be surprised. Nora Michael, previously so cool and confident, wilted. Slumping over, she fainted.

Chapter Forty-Six

GEORGE'S BODY ACHED and he winced with every bump and turn in the road. Mary Helen sat close to him, her hand resting lightly on his leg. They passed Fredericksburg, and Quantico, and Springfield. Larry drove, making small talk occasionally, but mostly keeping quiet. No one spoke about the reason for their trip to D.C. No one spoke of Dr. Michael. Larry had prepped the pair as much as he could, but even he hadn't been told many details as to why they'd been summoned. George put on a brave face for Mary Helen, but he didn't think she was fooled. The closer they got to the capital, the less they talked, the silence among the three saying everything.

At the precinct, Larry did the talking. Face grim, he said, "You asked us to come in, Captain, and we have. Mr. Vandenberg has demonstrated his willingness to cooperate—more than once, I might add. So perhaps you could explain why we're here today."

Mary Helen squeezed his hand. She'd been doing that a lot since the accident. Unsure how to respond most of the time, he accepted the gesture without reciprocating. If she noticed, she never said.

"We appreciate you making the trip." The captain folded his hands, lacing his fingers together. "The reason we asked you here is we're hoping to clarify a few things about the night Dr. Michael was murdered." He squinted at George. "I don't think I have to tell you that things look a little suspicious that night. Your alibi, for one, Mr. Vandenberg, cannot be corroborated. You know that, of course?"

"Are you prepared to charge my client, Captain Martin?"

The captain flicked a toothpick in the trash and smiled. "I'd like to give your client a chance to explain a few inconsistencies in his story."

George's heart skipped a beat, the implication clear. They didn't believe him, and sitting there, he knew he couldn't withstand a polygraph. How could he tell the truth about his activities that night when he didn't know what the truth was?

"We'd like to do that, Captain," Larry said, nodding

"Good. Good." A new toothpick bobbed along with the captain's words. "Why don't we start with when you left the club? You told one of my detectives you went straight home, guessing you arrived back at your apartment no later than ten-thirty. Is that what you said?"

George cleared his throat. "I did say that, but I don't know if it's true or not."

The toothpick stopped moving. George felt the heat of the captain's scrutiny. "You don't know if it's true? Either you went home or you didn't, Mr. Vandenberg. There's no in between."

"Actually, Captain, my client is telling you the truth when he says—"

Martin held one hand up in the air. "I'd like to hear what your client has to say for himself."

Mary Helen squeezed his hand again, but did not utter a word.

It was odd, he thought. He couldn't remember a time when she hadn't taken over and spoken for him. Stranger still, he almost missed her sure-handed approach. On his own, he felt shaky but answered as honestly as he could. "I don't know if it's true, because I don't remember. I blacked out."

The captain's face hardened. "That's convenient, isn't it?"

George winced. "I had a lot to drink at the club. I remember leaving and I remember waking up the next morning. That's it."

The captain chewed on his toothpick until it fell out of his mouth in a pile of mush and spit. "All right, let's say I believe you." He reached behind him and placed a videotape on the desk. "We have a surveillance tape that shows you in a convenience store just before midnight, nearly two hours after you left your club. That's a lot of time. Plenty of time, in fact, to drive to Dr. Michael's office and back."

George's fingers and hands went cold. His breath quickened.

"Being at a store isn't a crime," Larry said. "If you have something that places him near the doctor's building, we'd like to hear it. Mr. Vandenberg is being truthful. He cannot explain his whereabouts or actions. We are in the dark as much as you are."

"Actually, I'd like to ask you another question, Mr. Vandenberg."

He licked his lips. "I'll try."

"We searched your apartment a few days ago. Were you aware of that?" George nodded. "You have a set of knives in a butcher block—some steak knives and larger ones. Is that right?"

He nodded again. His tongue felt too large in his mouth and he couldn't speak.

"One was missing. The same size and brand as the one used to kill Dr. Michael."

Mary Helen's free hand came to her mouth, stifling a small cry.

George's stomach rolled, the familiar nausea back. "I didn't know that." The magnitude of this news, hearing it in front of his wife and lawyer, stunned him. "I don't think I knew it was missing," he said, almost to himself. The tape. The knife. The blackout. A wave of hopelessness washed over him. They were going to arrest him for a murder he didn't believe he could have committed and certainly didn't remember.

"Captain, this is all terribly interesting, but it sounds circumstantial to me." George looked at Larry with admiration and gratitude. "I'll ask you again. Are you planning to arrest my client?"

He wouldn't let Larry or Mary Helen down. This wasn't their fight. His fear ebbed and he squeezed his wife's hand. He would meet his fate head-on, whatever that fate might be.

A knock on the door broke the tension. George recognized the tall blond detective. "It's time," the man said.

Martin came to his feet. "If you'll follow me."

"Why?" Larry held an arm in front of George and Mary Helen. "Where are we going?"

The captain waved them on. "It won't be long now. Things will be made clear in a few minutes."

The group followed the captain to a large interview room. Cancini stood in the back of the room. At the table, George saw a man and a woman. The lady sat with her head bowed, her hands clasped in front of her. The man stood with his hands on her shoulders. He looked at Cancini again. Why was he here? Who were these people? He followed Cancini's gaze back to the man and woman. She raised her head. He sucked in his breath and stumbled. She looked older and sadder, but as beautiful as ever. "Sarah."

Chapter Forty-Seven

CONFUSION REIGNED. THE man with Sarah screamed for a doctor and then water. Larry demanded to know what was going on. George, wide-eyed, wobbled on his feet and leaned against the wall. He mouthed her name again, but no sound came out. Someone rushed in with water just as she appeared to be coming around. The man with Sarah shielded her from view and bent close to her ear. Who was he? George took a step forward and then another. How could it be Sarah after all this time? How could she be alive? Hadn't he been mourning her death for more than twenty years? He stopped in his tracks, a new thought coming to him. Maybe it wasn't Sarah at all.

The woman lifted her head and pushed the man away. George stepped closer. She came to her feet. Close now, no more than ten feet apart, the two of them stared at each other. Dumbfounded, George felt the years slip away. His heart fluttered and his palms sweat. Sarah, older and more sophisticated, but still her. He'd know her anywhere.

"It's you," he said. "I can't believe it."

"George." She brushed a stray hair off her face. "It's been a long time."

He shivered when she spoke, and he forgot about the others in the room. "I thought you were dead."

She half smiled. "I know. I'm sorry about that. It had to be that way."

His heart leaped again. A million thoughts and feelings flooded his mind, but none more than joy. He was so glad to see her alive, the embodiment of his greatest fantasy standing before him, not dead but alive. "What are you doing here?"

She opened her mouth, then seemed to lose whatever courage she'd gathered up to that point. Tears filled her eyes and she shook her head.

Cancini moved between them. "This woman you know as Sarah," he said, "is Dr. Michael's widow, Nora Michael."

"What?" Sarah didn't move, didn't deny the detective's words. "What?" George swayed on his feet. Larry caught him by the arm and guided him to a chair.

Sarah's voice trembled and tears ran down her face. "I'm so sorry. I didn't know it was you. Oh my God, how could he not have told me?" She collapsed again.

George watched the man pat her back and speak in her ear. His arm and shoulder throbbed, but he ignored the pain. She was alive. That alone was miraculous, the most wonderful thing he could imagine, but the rest George didn't understand. Sarah was married to Dr. Michael? His therapist? Told her what? Seconds ticked by and no one said anything. Blood rushed to his head and he bent over. Dr. Michael had known. He'd listened to George pour his heart out and he'd known all along. Why did he let George suffer? It was sick!

An anger bubbled up in him and his jaw hardened. Sarah hadn't died. She'd lived and married. A new thought brought him to his feet and his head rotated toward his wife. She huddled against the wall near the door.

"How could you not tell me? How could you let me think I'd killed her?" he screamed, oblivious to the eyes watching him. "I was your husband, for God's sake! You knew how I'd suffered. You knew I couldn't forget. And you never stopped reminding me, either, always bringing it up and how you always had to save me from myself. It was all a lie. Everything was such a lie!"

"No." Mascara trailed down her cheeks, "It wasn't like that. It was for your own good and—"

"Stop lying!"

She shrank away but didn't back down. "I know you won't believe me, but I was trying to save you from yourself. I loved you." She took a shaky breath. "I thought I didn't anymore, but I was wrong. I still love you."

He laughed a high-pitched laugh, a tinny, crazy sound that died in his throat. "You've got to be kidding me." Wild-eyed, he pointed at Mary Helen. "Did y'all hear that? My wife loves me! She let me think I could kill someone, let me spend my whole life hating myself, never let me forget what a loser I was. But guess what? She ruined my life because she loves me. Yes! She loves me!" His fists clenched and unclenched. Sweat dotted his forehead and he wanted to punch something—anything—but instead stood motionless, breathing in and out.

"It's true." Sarah wiped her eyes and swallowed hard. "Mary Helen is telling the truth. She did love you."

George spun around to face her. "How . . . how can you defend her?"

Sarah drew herself up to her full height. "Because it was my idea."

The words were enough. George's fury faded. He fell back to his chair, shaking. A deathly silence filled the room. George, head in his hands, couldn't look at either woman. Was she defending Mary Helen?

Sarah's voice wobbled. "I'd like to explain, but I wonder if I might have some more water first?"

Cancini had a pitcher placed on the table.

George considered walking out. What could she possible have to explain? It would only be more lies. How could they do it? And how could Mary Helen claim it was out of love? All these years, all the blame, all the time wasted.

"You wouldn't let me go, George. Not easily, anyway. It's no excuse, I know, but that's how it started." Sarah blew her nose and drank another sip of water. Pale and tear-streaked, her beautiful face looked ravaged and old. "Mary Helen came to see me a few days before I came to the boathouse. She wanted me to break up with you, begged me to let you go. I told her not to worry. I wasn't stupid, George. Our worlds were too different. I couldn't take your family or your future from you. You couldn't see the hold they had on you, always complaining about your dad, how he wouldn't leave you alone. But to me, it sounded like heaven. My parents were gone and even when they were alive, they didn't care about my brother and me. But it was more than that." She paused and glanced at Mary Helen. "I loved you and I knew you loved me, but it wasn't enough. I knew if we'd stayed together, you would have ended up resenting me until you'd wonder what you saw in me in the first place. I didn't think I could cut it in your world. Call me a coward if you want." She stopped, her words ringing in the silence that followed.

"You thought you knew everything, but you were wrong." His words sounded bitter to his ears and he took a breath. "I never would have resented you. I loved you too much. I had faith in us. It was you who didn't."

She held his gaze. "Maybe. It doesn't matter. I had made up my mind and Mary Helen promised to help me financially if I left town."

"What?" He jumped to his feet, his face hot. "You gave Sarah money to leave?"

Mary Helen didn't answer, but she didn't have to. The slope of her shoulders and her plaintive expression told him it was true. His pulse raced. His wife had bribed his girlfriend to leave him. Disgust and long-suppressed resentment hit him and he lunged at her. Cancini stepped in front of him, and the blond detective caught him from behind.

Larry stepped in. "George. That's enough. You have got to calm down." The lawyer shot a look at Mary Helen, eyebrows raised. Pale, she nodded once. "Okay. Let's figure this out." They sat down together, George breathing hard.

Cancini cleared his throat. "I think we all need to calm down a little." When no one said anything, he went to Sarah. "Mrs. Michael, I think the best thing would be for you to explain to everyone what happened at the boathouse and why you let Mr. Vandenberg think you were dead all these years. A lot has happened since then and in light of your husband's murder, I think you owe him that."

Her gaze shifted from the detective to George. "Yes, I guess you're right."

Chapter Forty-Eight

"I THINK I was unconscious after I fell. I don't know how long. My head hurt so badly when I woke up. There was blood on my face and in my hair." Her voice was so low, they leaned forward to hear. "George, you were gone when I woke up. Only Mary Helen was still there. I told her I broke up with you, but I knew you'd be stubborn. You wouldn't listen." Mrs. Michael sighed, her face drawn and tense. Her words were jumbled, skipping around in time. "All of it had taken a lot longer than I'd expected and I knew Mary Helen was going to show up soon. So I had to go to the backup plan."

Vandenberg's head came up. "Gordon?"

"Yes." She blushed, unable to meet his eyes. She took a deep breath, focusing on Cancini instead. "I told him this story about how I'd slept with his roommate. At first, I could tell he didn't believe me but then, later, he did. I used some gossip from one of the waitresses where I worked. Some personal stuff. That did the trick." Nora Michael took a breath. "I shouldn't have done it, though. He was pretty mad, not that I blamed him. It was a rotten thing to do, but he hadn't left me any choice."

"So you fought about the roommate?" Cancini asked.

"Right. And then I tried to leave."

"That's when he pushed you and you fell?" Cancini had heard the story on the tapes, but that was George's story. This one belonged to her.

"Yes. Mary Helen was supposed to get there after I was gone to comfort him, but I was still there when she pulled up. She saw everything. He didn't even know she was there."

Cancini remembered the detailed timeline prepared by Dr. Michael. Sarah had been looking over George's shoulder when she told her story, not because she couldn't face him as George had assumed, but because she'd been expecting Mary Helen all along. Had Dr. Michael been trying to help George discover the truth on his own?

"Mary Helen helped me to my feet and got me cleaned up. That's when I cooked up the plan. She told me George thought he'd killed me, and I decided it was for the best. It was easier that way and I could leave town knowing he wouldn't follow me. I wanted to start over. I wanted my brother to be able to start over and get all the chances he'd never been able to have with our parents." Nora Michael looked at Mary Helen. "The money she offered was everything to us. It wasn't a lot, but we had enough to move, change our names, and start college. If it weren't for her, neither of us would have gotten as far as we did."

George's lips curled. "You took a bribe."

"You're wrong. I was grateful, don't you see? I was going to leave anyway and she knew that. I didn't leave because of the money. Mary Helen and I weren't friends, but we understood each other. She helped me."

His face fell and his shoulders slumped. "But why? Maybe I was a jerk but I would have gotten the hint eventually. Why this way?"

She bit her lip and turned her head away. "My husband was preoccupied with you, George. He told me about a man who'd committed an act he regretted, who was depressed and angry, that he hadn't been able to help. He told me he thought you should come forward and confess." Her voice cracked. "I didn't know it was you. I wouldn't have told them about you if I'd known. I swear."

Cancini watched as both Vandenbergs recognized the irony. The lie they'd shared had come full circle.

A sob escaped Mary Helen's lips. "It's my fault," she said. Her gaze slid to Cancini. "You knew, didn't you? You knew I'd been to see Dr. Michael." Cancini gave a quick nod. Dr. Michael had given it away on one of his session tapes, referring to Mrs. Vandenberg's diminutive size and hinting at the impossibility of her moving Sarah after she was assumed to be dead. He couldn't have known that without meeting Mary Helen. Again, the therapist had tried to help George see the truth without betraying Nora, but the patient's self-loathing had made that impossible. "It's my fault. George didn't confess because I knew then he'd find out the truth. Maybe not at first, but eventually. I was so afraid," she said, the words difficult to understand between sobs. "I didn't want to lose everything. I didn't want him to know. I didn't want him to hate me." She couldn't look at her husband, her head in her hands.

Cancini watched the emotions play on Vandenberg's face. Disbelief, anger, sadness, but mostly confusion.

"Why didn't Dr. Michael just tell me the truth? Why keep pushing the confession when he knew my wife was pushing me not to? He knew the stress was making everything worse. I kept getting madder and madder at him. Why didn't he just tell me?"

"He couldn't," Cancini said and cast a quick look at the widow. "There were ethics involved and he couldn't betray things he'd learned from his patient."

"What do you mean? What patient?"

"I think he means me," Nora admitted after a moment. "I was one of my husband's first patients. My brother introduced me to him. They were friends in med school, both studying psychiatry. I was having a hard time dealing with everything and what had happened, so he thought I should talk to someone. That someone was Edmund. A couple of years after I'd stopped going to therapy, we ran into each other and started dating, got married. It felt so natural and safe. But it doesn't matter, everything I told Edmund before was privileged. He couldn't tell you."

Stunned, George's face was blank. "Oh."

"Your husband must have loved you, Mrs. Michael," the detective said, "to keep your secret for so long."

Her lower lip trembled. "I suppose he did."

Cancini's eyes swept the room, his job not yet finished. There was still a little guesswork to do, although after his trip to Boston, he had filled in most of the blanks.

"Mrs. Michael, the day of your husband's death, Mr. Vandenberg argued with your husband. That night, at a party, he had too much to drink. He left the party early, around ten, originally claiming he went straight home. However, a surveillance tape has come into our possession that places him in an all-night convenience store just before twelve. The coroner estimates that your husband was murdered between nine and twelve. Mr. Vandenberg has no alibi for most of that time." He studied each of the players, gauging their reactions. Mary Helen listened to every detail, eyes wide. Her husband, however, sat slumped again, resignation on his face. Mrs. Michael looked past him at the large pane of glass, her face unreadable.

"Mr. Vandenberg owns a set of cooking knives. One is missing, the same brand and size that was used to murder your husband. The coroner has also been able to give us a partial description of your husband's assailant, including approximate height and strength. Mr. Vandenberg fits that description." The detective paused. "In addition, Mr. Vandenberg voluntarily allowed us access to his sessions with your husband. They were all recorded on tape." Mrs. Michael's eyes met his, then dropped away again. "After listening to most of the tapes, we learned that Mr. Vandenberg did have a temper, had a history of blackouts, and was under tremendous pressure from your husband, at times expressing deep anger. Our precinct psychologist agreed with this assessment and the district attorney felt we had enough evidence to arrest Mr. Vandenberg."

Larry started to say something, seemed to think better of it, and closed his mouth. Mary Helen sobbed openly.

"Dr. Michael knew the truth about Mr. Vandenberg and wanted him to confess, knowing if the truth were exposed, his patient might discover he wasn't actually guilty of anything. I couldn't understand at first why Dr. Michael was pushing so hard until my partner pointed out to me that the patient's case had become almost personal to the therapist. I think he began to see Mr. Vandenberg as more than a patient, as someone to whom the truth was owed. I kept asking myself, *What was in it for him?* Reading through Dr. Michael's notes, it occurred to me that he felt a responsibility that went beyond doctor-patient. Against his will, he'd become a party to the lie, but professional ethics kept his hands tied. Yet I think he did everything he could to steer Mr. Vandenberg in the right direction." Cancini walked toward the widow and placed his hands on the table. "He would no more betray George than he would betray you, Mrs. Michael."

She blinked, saying nothing.

"Tell me about your relationship with your husband, Mrs. Michael."

Her lawyer placed a protective arm around her shoulder. "I don't think this is necessary, Detective."

Cancini shrugged. "What I'm getting at is my question from the other day, Mrs. Michael. Who did you call three times on the night your husband was murdered?" Every head turned in her direction. Mrs. Michael slumped down low in her chair, her lower lip quivering. "As I said, I went to Boston the other day. Is it possible you have another secret, Mrs. Michael, one even your husband didn't know about?"

Chapter Forty-Nine

A HUSH FELL over the room. All eyes on her, Mrs. Michael pressed her lips together and shook her head.

Cancini stepped back. "You can't answer, Mrs. Michael, or you won't?" Behind him, Vandenberg breathed heavily. "Who did you call that night? We know the phone is in your name, but not in your possession. Why can't you tell us?"

"The lady chooses not to answer," Gerard said. She mouthed a thank-you to her lawyer.

Cancini shrugged. "Then I'll tell you a story and you can listen." Keeping his voice soft, he spoke to the widow as though she were the only one in the room. "Although you moved to Washington, you've maintained your Boston ties. In fact, you still have a bank account at a local branch there, a bank account in your name only and one I'm pretty sure your husband didn't know anything about. Not only that, you've been making cash withdrawals from that account even after you moved, having the money wired to you at your office, never at home." She looked down at her hands, twisting and twisting her fingers. "So, one has to wonder what all that cash was for? Naturally, we checked out all the usual possibilities. Alcohol? Drugs? Gambling? Nothing we could find. Then we discovered you have two cell phones on your personal account, but the second phone doesn't belong to your husband or to you. An affair maybe?" Nora's face reddened. "Mrs. Michael?" Cancini asked, but she turned away. He shrugged again. "You called your second cell phone three times on the night your husband was stabbed to death. Three times."

Nora's lawyer's lips tightened. "Detective, harassing my client is unnecessary. Can we get to the point, please?"

"I'm glad you asked," he said, his eyes sweeping over the man. "The rest of the story goes something like this." He looked again at the widow. "Mrs. Michael, feel free to correct me at any time, but I'm reminded you brought me a piece of evidence, a threatening note that couldn't be substantiated or traced. You claimed there was a connection between your brother's hit-and-run and your husband's murder. You successfully distracted more than one of my detectives, but there was no phantom killer targeting psychiatrists. Your brother's death was an accident, fully investigated and corroborated by witnesses." The widow flinched. "Then you came to me with the story about the violent patient and told me your husband was anxious and uptight, maybe even scared." Vandenberg's chin dropped and Mary Helen stifled another sob. Cancini continued, "This part was true but still only meant to distract me. This I understood, but what I couldn't know at the time was the reason." Cancini paused. "Tell me when I'm way off base."

"Enough." The lawyer took Nora by the elbow and pulled her to her feet. "Detective, I don't see what any of this has to do with Dr. Michael's murder. So what if Mrs. Michael used to be Sarah Somebody? So what if she keeps a bank account in Boston and takes out some cash? So what if she made some phone calls the night her husband was murdered? She gave you the note and information in good conscience. Mrs. Michael has been more than cooperative with you and this office." He glared at Vandenberg. "We know who killed Dr. Michael. Why don't you arrest him now and stop putting Mrs. Michael through this torture?"

Cancini smiled thinly. "Perhaps Mrs. Michael would like to tell us why all this is relevant. Maybe she would like to explain what she did with the money and why she didn't want to move away from Boston and why she's made so many trips back." He waited, but still she said nothing. "No? Well, then, I'll tell you what I think. Mrs. Michael has a lot of secrets and she has been hiding something for a very long time." He paused again. "Actually, someone, for a long time."

"No. No." She clung to Gerard, eyes begging. "Please don't."

Cancini had to look away. His job wasn't finished. "If Mrs. Michael won't tell us, maybe Mrs. Vandenberg can."

Mary Helen's blond head snapped up. "Me? How? I didn't know she was Dr. Michael's wife. I didn't even know she lived in Boston."

Cancini pulled a notebook from his jacket pocket and flipped a few pages. "Mrs. Vandenberg, in January you took out one thousand dollars in money orders. In February, two thousand. By March, it was up to three. Shall I go on?"

White as a sheet, Mary Helen swayed. Vandenberg and the lawyers gaped at her, but no one with more interest than Nora Michael.

"At first," Cancini said, "I thought maybe there was some conspiracy between the two of you, some passing of money I couldn't understand. Why the cash withdrawals? I just didn't get it." He glanced at Mrs. Michael. "The second cell phone bothered me. Why call that phone three times that night? Who was on the other end of that phone? I was missing a key piece of evidence, but I just couldn't put my finger on it. Then it came to me. Boston. There was someone else in Boston." He looked from one woman to the other. "I think both of you know who I'm talking about."

"Please," Mrs. Michael begged. "Please, don't."

For a brief moment he felt sorry for her. Then he remembered she'd allowed this to happen. All this could be traced back to her and the secrets she was so determined to keep. Her reasons didn't matter now. He was a homicide detective and there was no room for absolution or forgiveness or gray areas. The guilty had to be punished. That's the way it had to be. He swallowed the lump in his throat. "It's too late for that, Mrs. Michael. Your husband is dead and I think you need to tell the truth, the whole truth."

Gerard moved in front of Mrs. Michael. "I'm advising my client to keep quiet at this time, at least until after we've been able to discuss these matters in private."

Cancini ignored the attorney, speaking softly. "It's over, Mrs. Michael. We've already picked her up. She's in custody."

Her legs gave out and she landed in a heap. The wail started low, a mournful moan that grew louder and louder. "No, no, no," she repeated over and over, holding her arms close to her stomach, her body shaking with sobs. Mary Helen went to her and crouched down. She reached out a hand and rubbed her back in soothing circles.

George sprang to his feet. "What in God's name is going on? Why is she so upset?" He whirled in his wife's direction. His voice was strained, thin with fear. "Tell me, please. Who was picked up? Who are we talking about?"

Cancini opened his mouth to speak, but Mary Helen stopped him. She took Sarah's hand and squeezed. Tears ran down her face, too, but she held her husband's gaze. "I'm so sorry, George. I had no idea it would end up this way." She took a deep breath. "It's your daughter, George. Yours and Sarah's."

Chapter Fifty

Vandenberg doubled over as though he'd had the wind knocked out of him. His breath was ragged and his hands shook. Cancini took a step toward him, then backed away.

A pained expression crossed Mary Helen's face. "She came to see me several months ago. She wanted money. God forgive me, I gave it to her."

Still bent over, he raised his eyes to his wife's. "Blackmail? My daughter was blackmailing you? Why?"

Mary Helen's voice wavered and she glanced at Nora. Mrs. Michael nodded. "To keep the secret, but I think it was more than that. She wanted me to know what she thought of me."

"That's what the money orders were for? Blackmail money?" Vandenberg found his voice, his tone hard, bordering on cruel. "You paid her, kept me from my own daughter. It wasn't enough that you and Sarah deceived me about the accident. You hid my daughter from me!" He whipped around to Cancini "Why did you pick her up? When can I see her?"

Cancini put his notebook back in his pocket and took Vandenberg by the arm. He led the man back to his chair. He pulled up a chair beside him. "You can see her later, Mr. Vandenberg, but right now she's being processed." He paused. "We arrested her for the murder of Dr. Michael."

"What? No, she couldn't have. She wouldn't have . . ." His voice trailed off. He pulled his broken arm in close and took deep breaths. "Why would she kill him?"

"She won't say. In fact, she won't speak at all without a lawyer. But I've got a feeling about it, Mr. Vandenberg. And I think Mrs. Michael might have a pretty good idea, too. You could call it revenge."

Vandenberg's mouth hung open. "Revenge? Against who? Dr. Michael?"

"No." Cancini hesitated. How much more could the man take? "Against you. You and Mrs. Michael."

"Why?"

There was no sound in the room other than Nora Michael's sobs. The detective looked over at the large pane of glass. Captain Martin and the D.A. watched on the other side. They had their murderer. He was sure of that. Lauren Temple's alibi had cracked once her boyfriend was threatened with a polygraph. Her adoptive parents, once located, were also cooperative, even telling the detective exactly when the girl had discovered her birth mother. The county social worker had filled him in on most of the rest. Smitty's search of the girl's apartment had turned up a key to Dr. Michael's office. She'd conned the spare out of her mother, making a copy weeks earlier at a local hardware store. As an occasional patient of Dr. Michael's, she learned the layout of the office. She studied his schedule, right down to knowing he'd work late with his wife out of town. Only Nora had been a problem. The daughter she'd given up needed her mother to suffer, insisting Nora call her at scheduled times that night, hinting at what she had done. They'd discovered the second cell phone in the girl's car.

Vandenberg made it easy for the girl to frame him. Lauren had taken a part-time job with the same cleaning company that serviced several apartment buildings in D.C. It wouldn't have been hard for the girl to pocket the knife while on the job. She'd quit the cleaning service three weeks earlier. The night of the murder, Vandenberg left his club and drove to the convenience mart. Based on the time lapse, Cancini suspected Vandenberg had passed out in the store lot. Lauren Temple already knew her father's habits and haunts. After murdering Dr. Michael, she'd driven to the club, then followed him to the convenience mart. The detective suspected she'd been planning to plant the glasses on him, but that effort must have failed. Buying the convenience mart tape and sending it to the police proved to be just as useful. Although the police hadn't recovered the glasses, they had motive and opportunity.

Framing her father hadn't been enough. During his search, Smitty found a receipt for a rental car, a dark sedan, on the day Vandenberg was run off the road. Cancini didn't want to speculate on her motive, preferring to believe she wanted to scare him, not kill him. If that was her intention, he guessed it worked.

Vandenberg looked over at Smitty. "I know who she is, don't I? It's the girl I saw that day, the one you said was one of Dr. Michael's patients." Smitty nodded. "I thought she looked so like my Elizabeth Grace." He swung around. "What's her name?"

Cancini's eyes stung. Damn. "Lauren Temple."

Vandenberg lips moved, mouthing her name in silence. Then,

"I still don't understand why she would do all this? Why would she kill Dr. Michael?"

"Because we hurt her. I hurt her." Mrs. Michael stood now. Mary Helen stayed close by her side. "I gave her up for adoption. I thought it was the best thing to do at the time, but it was a terrible mistake. Terrible." She took a deep breath. "Her childhood was, well, it wasn't good. Her parents were awful, awful people."

His brows creased. "How? Why?"

"She told me they beat her every day, used her, treated her like a dog." Her voice grew stronger. "When she got older, they told her she was adopted. It was a double blow to her. She believed it wasn't just the Temples who didn't want her, but her real parents, too. Not long after that, she found me through the adoption agency, approached me for the first time. I was thrilled, so happy. I had never stopped thinking about her from the day she was born. Edmund and I didn't have any children. He didn't think he had the time for them and after everything he'd done for me, I couldn't force them on him. I knew he wouldn't change his mind." The luminous eyes were sad, old beyond their years. "I had given her up before we met, and somehow, it became my secret, my special secret. I suppose that hurt her even more. And she . . ." The woman hesitated. "She wasn't well by then. Angry all the time. They'd done that to her. Taken this innocent child and turned her into a bitter young girl. Demanding. She'd sometimes erupt into uncontrollable rages. It was my fault though—all my fault. We both knew it. I should have kept her. I wanted to make her better, show her I cared. I wanted her to know I would do anything for her. I didn't know how much I would love her until it was too late." Her voice cracked again. "But somehow, no matter what I did, it wasn't enough."

"But you must have told her about me. She knew enough to go to Mary Helen," George said, face troubled. "Why my wife and not me? Why did she want so much money?"

"Because I made the mistake of telling her about us and our affair and you thinking I was dead—all of it. I was trying to explain why I'd given her up for adoption, explain how I'd tried to do what was right for everyone, and it all came out. The lies. The money. She thought we were all despicable. God knows she was right. I think she thought the least she could do was get her share of money out of it." There was a brief pause. "She told me once she'd tracked you down and that she was glad I'd run away. Please forgive me, George, but she said you were a worthless drunk and she hated you even more than she hated me. There was so much anger in her." She covered her mouth with her hands. Her shoulders rocked with quiet sobs.

A quiet fell over the room. Cancini glanced again at the glass behind him. The D.A. was waiting, and no doubt Martin had already chewed through a dozen toothpicks. Maybe he'd even scheduled the press. If he did, Cancini decided he would be sorely disappointed. "I think now would be a good time to take a few minutes. Smitty, could you bring in some coffee and some more water?"

During the break, Mary Helen sat with Mrs. Michael and her lawyer. Larry sipped water and tried to talk to his client. Vandenberg waved him away. He refused coffee and water, head bowed low. Hands in his lap, his body remained eerily still.

Fifteen minutes later, Cancini broke the spell. "Mrs. Michael, your daughter was the reason you didn't want to move to Washington. Is that right?"

"Yes. I stayed in Boston as long as I could and went back

whenever I could," she said, her tone flat. "I gave her money even though I knew it could never make up for what I'd done. She needed me full-time. She needed a mother, but I didn't know how at first. When she came to Washington, she became a patient of Edmund's. She'd brag about it to me, imitating him, saying things to hurt me. I let her, believing I deserved it. But I wanted to keep Edmund out of it. Even after everything, she seemed to be getting worse. Her anger got more irrational and she sometimes made threats. I tried to stop it. I wanted to get her help, but she refused. I was letting her down again, but I didn't know what else to do. I started to think she hated me as much as the Temples. Maybe more." She clasped her hands together. "Please understand. It's not her fault. It's mine. I'm the reason this happened."

Cancini disagreed. "She killed a man, Mrs. Michael. You didn't do that, did you?"

Her wet eyes were wide. "Not in the way you mean." Her lawyer shook his head, but she ignored him. "I did kill him though—in every other way. I lied to him. I lied to my daughter. I lied to George. Don't you see? It was me in the end. Not her."

"You tried to protect her," Vandenberg said, his voice tinged with admiration. "Even now. You guessed what she'd done and you protected her anyway."

"I had to. She's my daughter, my only child. Didn't she deserve that at least? You don't know how damaged she is, how hurt she's been." Her hands still clenched, she searched for the words. "I thought I could save her, that I could change her somehow with love and support." Her eyes slid back to Cancini. "You think I did the wrong thing, but you don't understand. You don't know what it's been like for her." Her hand waved in the direction of the door. "This place will not help her. This is not the answer. She deserves a chance."

"She's right." Vandenberg had come to his feet.

"I'm sorry. It doesn't work that way." He understood the horrors of the young lady's childhood, probably better than anyone in the room, but they were wrong. Lauren Temple had taken a man's life and that was a crime. His job had been to find her and arrest her. The rest was not up to him. This had gone on long enough. They had motive and opportunity, unknowingly confirmed by Mrs. Michael. Lauren Temple had stuck a knife in the back of her mother's husband in a calculated and cold-blooded plan of revenge. He had his answers.

He looked around and saw a roomful of broken people. They'd all suffered and now, with the young woman in custody, it would not get easier. He nodded at the glass. "I think that's it then. Thank you all for coming in. Mrs. Michael, we can have a car take you home if you'd like."

Tears streaked her face. "I'd like to see her if I could."

"I'm sorry. Like I said earlier, she's being processed. We can call you later." She collapsed against Mary Helen. "Mrs. Vandenberg, you and your husband can go back to Richmond. It's over."

"No," George said, voice loud. "I'm not going anywhere."

"But you can't see her yet, Mr. Vandenberg."

"You don't understand." He held out his hands, wrists pressed together. "You've arrested the wrong person. I confess to the murder of Dr. Michael." Six pairs of eyes swung around.

Mary Helen gasped. "No, George, you can't. Please, you can't."

Cancini raised his chin to the ceiling. He didn't know why, but he wasn't surprised. He'd heard the tapes. The man had already lived a life under a cloud of guilt. Now, just when he could be free of it all, he confessed to a crime he didn't commit. More insane, he'd done it for a daughter he'd never even met. The detective sighed. "We know you didn't do it, Mr. Vandenberg."

"Actually, Detective, you don't know anything."

Cancini raised an eyebrow. He knew now why Vandenberg had refused coffee, refused to speak with his attorney. It wasn't the shock. He'd been thinking, planning. "Tell me, Mr. Vandenberg."

"Not one thing you've said adds up to proof that will hold up in court. I'm guilty, not my daughter. If you go through with the arrest of my daughter, I will hire the best lawyer in town, and she will never tell you anything. Everything you've said is based on guesswork. None of it will convince a jury. She'll go free and you will have accomplished nothing. And I will skewer you in the press by telling everyone I confessed to the murder and you let me go." His tone challenged anyone in the room to deny him. When he spoke again, his words were softer, final. "You said so yourself, Detective. I have no alibi. I was angry with Dr. Michael. It was my knife that killed him. I'm the logical suspect. I confess to the murder. You have to let her go."

Cancini opened his mouth to protest, but came up with nothing. His eyes locked on Vandenberg's. Cancini understood, but he didn't like it. "That's not how the legal system operates, Mr. Vandenberg. We have your daughter in custody. The D.A. issued a warrant."

"Well, have him issue a new one. You have the wrong person in custody." The man raised his hands again. "I'm guilty."

Cancini glanced at Smitty. His partner shook his head. Damn. Vandenberg was right. The case against Lauren Temple was solid, but a confession from Vandenberg would make it difficult and throw reasonable doubt into the case. They couldn't prove the girl ever used the key and they couldn't prove she'd stolen the knife.

Without the glasses, it could go either way. He studied the man in front of him. Vandenberg might have been physically battered, but the strength in his face said something else. He didn't doubt the man's conviction, but that didn't make it right. Then again, neither was it wrong. Guilt and innocence had become intertwined, two sides of the same coin. Father Joe's words came back to him. *A man's worth cannot be defined solely by his goodness, but also by his desire to battle that in him which is not good.* Vandenberg knew something about that battle, but what he was suggesting went against everything the detective believed. Could Cancini just sweep what the girl did under the rug? Damn. If only Vandenberg had held his temper in check that day. If only he'd come forward in the beginning, everything might have been different. After that, the lie got bigger and more twisted, until it manifested itself in the form of murder. An innocent child had been damaged in ways that most people couldn't comprehend. Another innocent man, Dr. Michael, had paid the price. Nora Michael had lost her husband. There was plenty of guilt to go around.

Cancini cleared his throat. Maybe the girl could be saved and maybe she couldn't. For today only, for this one moment, guilt didn't feel black and white. It was an illness, a disease that had infected too many already. His head pounded with the knowledge that he was liable to have his ass strung up and handed back to him for weeks. He took a deep breath and allowed himself one more glance at the glass.

"Mr. Vandenberg, you are under arrest for the murder of Dr. Edmund Michael. Are you ready to make a statement?"

Epilogue

THE ORANGE JUMPSUIT hung loose on his slim frame and the prison-issued shoes cut into his feet. He didn't care. Clothing and other material things were irrelevant to him now. George hurried after the guard and burst into the visitors' room. There she was, on the other side of the glass. Her eyes followed him until he sat across from her, both of them picking up the phones hanging near their tables.

"Hello, Sarah." His heart pitter-pattered at the sight of her, but not the way it had in his youth, racing with lust and blind love. Now his love was more complicated. Partly based on sweet and distant memories and partly tainted with the truth and harsh reality of the present, it was mostly made up of a mutual love and dedication to their one and only daughter.

"You look good, George," she said. He smiled at the lie. His hair had turned gray and the lines had deepened around his mouth and eyes. The weight loss wasn't a bad thing but unfortunately, it was more a function of bad food than good health. Prison life was a challenge for George, but he kept that to himself. "Lauren sends her love."

"When is she getting out?" he asked. Using her husband's connections, Sarah had placed their daughter in an overseas facility. The battle with Lauren had been uphill, but in light of her father's sacrifice and his willingness to save her life, she'd relented.

"Next month. You won't believe how well she's doing in spite of everything. Her prognosis is better, and the doctor says she can move in with me and might be able to get a job soon. The anger is better, too, mostly gone; the medication helps."

A tear came to his eye. He'd seen her only once after his confession, had marveled at the sight of her, a willowy, darker version of his Elizabeth Grace. Having admitted guilt in the murder, George had waived his right to a jury trial and chosen to be sentenced immediately. Lauren had attended the sentencing with Sarah, standing in the back, apart from Mary Helen and his other children. His two families, neither of which was perfect and neither of which was whole.

"Will she need the medication forever?"

Sarah's hair hung past her shoulders, long and lustrous, as it did in her younger days. "Probably, but they don't know for sure. She's still having a hard time with the guilt. I think when she gets back to the States and can see you, it might help. She needs to see that you're okay."

A pinched look of concern crossed his face. "What do the doctors say about her seeing me? Are you sure it wouldn't upset her too much?"

"It might, but she's in a better place now. Let's wait and see what's best when she gets out." Sarah hesitated and placed a hand against the glass. He raised his hand to meet hers. "I'd like her to know you. It would be good for you both."

The former lovers sat a moment longer, each cradling the phone, saying nothing. So much was still unsaid, yet ultimately unnecessary. She broke the silence. "How are things with Mary Helen?"

"Better. The same. I'm not sure she'll ever forgive me completely, but at least she understands now."

"Wills and Elizabeth Grace?"

The thought of them made him smile. Oddly, his relationship with them was better than it had ever been. Not at first, but to his great surprise, he discovered he mattered more than he'd thought. He wrote them every day, knew all the details of their lives, was an attentive listener, and loved them without bounds. Yet it was hard on them, knowing their father couldn't come home. There were occasional flashes of resentment, but they were becoming less frequent. "Okay, I guess. As well as can be expected." Sighing, George put his head against the glass. He hated prison. He wished it could be different. But he'd had no choice. Sarah had understood and so had Mary Helen, to a lesser degree. She just didn't want to accept it.

He admired the beautiful woman on the other side of the glass. There had been so many mistakes, so much sadness and heartbreak. He'd tried to rectify it, tried to give everyone a chance, the kind of chance he'd never given himself. Maybe he hadn't actually murdered Dr. Michael, but he might as well have. The night he pushed Sarah with such force and anger, he had changed all their lives. He'd set things in motion, culminating in his own daughter's rage and hate. Cancini had offered him a chance to change his mind and rescind his confession, but George had refused.

With a grim expression, the detective had let it go. He'd clapped George on the back and wished him luck, a vague understanding in his hazel eyes. George had taken responsibility for his actions. Even then, George recognized the guilt would never be gone. Too much had happened.

When their time was up, Sarah rose, her hand dropping back to her side. He nodded and she smiled, tears dotting her lashes. He left the visitors' room and returned to his tiny cell with its hard floor and lumpy bed. It was a lonely and solitary life. But Dr. Michael had been right about one thing. Coming forward, the act of confession, was good for the soul, the highest form of redemption. George Vandenberg, convict for life, was at peace.

Acknowledgments

A GUILTY MIND is a story that's been swimming around in my brain for close to a decade. Although I left it more than once, distracted by the real world and other projects, I kept coming back to it, drawn to the concepts of guilt and consequences. After so many years, it is an honor to share George's story and to introduce readers to my favorite detective. Thank you to all who have found and read *A Guilty Mind*.

So many people helped turn this story into the first Cancini mystery and for that, I will always be grateful. Thank you to Chloe Moffett, my talented editor at HarperCollins, for inviting me into the Witness Impulse family. Thank you also for finding my work and making the editing process so easy and enjoyable. Thank you to my wonderful agent, Rebecca Scherer at Jane Rotrosen, for your support and your enthusiasm. It is truly appreciated.

In addition to my editor and agent, this book would not have been possible without the support of a long list of friends and family. At the beginning, my local book club selected an early (and very rough) draft of *A Guilty Mind* as their "book of the month." As with any good book critique group, their questions were pointed and their constructive criticism spot-on. Although I can never thank that group enough, a special thank-you goes out to Kate Hamson and Maria Gravely for spearheading the distribution. Thank you also to Roberta Sachs, Julie Ehlers, Lisa Wood, Beth Rendon, and Louise Ingold for reading additional drafts, vetting characters, and parsing plot revisions. Thank you all!

Also unfailing in their support were Mary Mitchell, Ginger Glenn, Virginia Glenn, and Ann Horowitz—forever willing to spend hours discussing the progress of my novels (over wine and great food, of course) and always encouraging me to stay in the game. Thank you, ladies!

Thank you to all the Freeman moms (you know who you are!) that not only lifted me up but leaped into action to help celebrate this first book. Thank you, Paula Holm, for your generosity and kind spirit.

I am also indebted to another early editor, Anne Victory, and to one of my favorite artists, Guy Crittenden, for providing me a visual landscape. Thank you to my parents, Don and Nancy, and to my late mother-in-law, Shirley, who passed away before she could see this story published. I'd also like to give a big shout-out to my sister and brothers, extended family, and amazing friends— truly the best group of readers and critics any writer could hope to have.

Most importantly, thank you to my wonderful husband and four beautiful children. Thank you for my detective gifts, my nickname, and my personalized calendar. Without your encouragement and humor, I might have abandoned the process altogether.

If you enjoyed
A Guilty Mind,
keep reading for a sneak peek at

Stay of Execution,

the next exhilarating Detective Cancini Mystery
from K. L. Murphy

Chapter One

Shadows danced along the cinder-block walls. A light shone through the tiny window in the door, then moved past as the guard made his rounds. The prisoner lay still while the steps faded, then rolled to a sitting position, rusty bedsprings squeaking under his weight. His head jerked up toward the door. He waited before standing, bare feet hitting the cold, concrete floor.

In a few days, a week, it would all be over. No more guards. No more looking at the same walls twenty-three hours a day. No more crap food. No more of this godforsaken hellhole. He would go home, where he belonged.

On the far wall, a steel container served as his toilet. The stench of old piss stung his nose, but for once, he didn't mind. How quickly things had changed. Maybe he should've been surprised, but he wasn't. Hell, he'd been expecting it for a long time. Some would say he was lucky, might even call his release a miracle. Shit. Maybe it was a miracle. After all, it wasn't every day a man on death row got handed his walking papers. Not that he cared much about cheating death. So what if he wouldn't be executed tomorrow, or next month, or next year? He would still die eventually. Everyone does.

He knew how it would go. The lawyers would show up in their tailored suits and Italian shoes, all smug with their accomplishment. There'd be backslapping, and people he'd never seen before asking what he needed. No one had done that in a long damn time. He ran a hand over his heavy beard. They'd have clothes in his size, a suit and a tie. A barber would give him a haircut and shave. They'd clean him up. It was part of the deal.

He understood his role. His lawyers had shown him the newspapers. The governor himself had weighed in. None of the lawyers could understand why he wanted to go back home. His family was dead. He had no friends. Yet his return would not go unnoticed. There would be a press conference and cameras. It was reason enough.

In the semidarkness, he lay shirtless on his cot. A bead of sweat dripped from his temple to his ear. He'd have to be on his best behavior. Everything he said and did would be watched. Reporters would follow him for a story. The injustice, they'd say. The outrage. An innocent man had suffered, and now his ordeal was over. But they didn't know anything about injustice. They didn't know anything about him. He'd been inside for a long time, and the years had not passed quickly. He had unfinished business now, scores to settle. Everything was about to change.

Chapter Two

Detective Mike Cancini sat up with a start. For the third time in a week, he'd dozed off in the hard hospital chair. He shifted to look at the old man lying in the bed. The rise and fall of his father's sunken chest kept time with his snores. Tubes ran from his arms to the green lights on the monitor. His pulse was steady and his blood pressure read normal.

The television cast a soft light across the room. Cancini stood, stretching his stiff limbs. He used the remote to click to the nightly news. His eyes went back to the old man. His father looked so pale. What little hair remained was snow-white and combed back. Dark bruises dotted the thin skin of his arms where doctors and nurses had poked and prodded. If it weren't for the snoring, Cancini would wonder. He shook away the thoughts. His father had always been stronger than he looked. Strong and stubborn.

"In a surprise move today," a TV reporter said, "the governor has granted a writ of innocence to Leo Spradlin, the man once known as the Coed Killer."

Cancini's head whipped around. He moved closer to the screen.

"Mr. Spradlin, currently housed in solitary at Red Onion State Prison, was convicted of the rapes and murders of five women, all students at Blue Hill College. Sentenced more than twenty years ago, Mr. Spradlin was scheduled for execution later this month." Behind the reporter, a camera panned the dreary prison campus, the highest security facility in Virginia. "A statement from the governor's office and the attorney general indicated that new DNA evidence exonerates Spradlin."

Cancini's temple throbbed. A headshot of Spradlin appeared in the corner of the screen. The man's hair was longish now, not short the way he wore it back then. A heavy beard covered his chiseled face, but his pale blue eyes were the same, clear and cold as a winter night.

"Lawyers working for the newly innocent man had this to say."

The picture switched to an attorney in a gray suit. "Leo Spradlin is a grateful man tonight." The lawyer stood on the steps of the state capitol, microphones shoved under his chin. "He is particularly grateful to the governor for hearing his case. As many of you have already heard, DNA evidence that had previously been used to help convict Mr. Spradlin has been reexamined using more current technology. That same evidence now proves beyond a shadow of a doubt that Mr. Spradlin is not the Coed Killer. Mr. Spradlin is also immensely grateful to the Freedom and Justice Group and men like Dan Whitmore." He paused, nodding at the short, squat man standing to his right. "Finally, he would like me to thank all the friends and family who stood by him through this long ordeal and for their strong faith in him."

"What friends? What family?" Cancini muttered. His long fingers tightened on the remote. No one had stood by the man. Spradlin had alienated anyone and everyone who might once have cared for him. Not just during the original trial. Through count-less appeals and hearings, no one ever appeared on Spradlin's behalf. Cancini should know. He'd never missed a single one.

The reporter returned to the screen. She nodded. "The governor's office also issued the following statement: 'In an effort to right this terrible miscarriage of justice, Mr. Spradlin will be granted a full pardon along with his writ of innocence and will be released within a matter of days.' "

A heat rose in Cancini. He'd heard rumblings the DNA evidence was getting another look, but he hadn't given it much thought. It was true some of the evidence in the murder case had been circumstantial, but the DNA evidence—such as it was at the time—had been convincing. The jury had deliberated less than two hours. What had changed?

The newswoman shuffled papers. When she spun to the left, the camera followed. "And on Wall Street today, the Dow Jones took a tumble. Stockholders were warned to brace for another market correction."

Cancini hit the mute button, shaking his head. The sheets ruffled behind him. He squared his shoulders, meeting his father's gaze.

"What does it mean? Is it true?" His father sounded tired, his words barely audible.

The detective swallowed. "How long have you been awake?"

"Long enough. Thought that was your case."

Cancini winced. It wasn't a question. He put the remote back on the nightstand, then tucked the blankets under the old man's spindly arms. His father's hands, blue with puffy veins, lay flat on the bed.

"Well?"

Cancini didn't answer, unable to wrap his head around the reversal. He rubbed the stubble on his chin. How could a man as guilty as Spradlin suddenly be innocent? That case had made his career, started him on the road as a homicide detective. Did that mean everything was built on a lie? If it was, he knew what his father would think. His son was a failure.

"I don't know anything, Dad. I only knew they were looking into old evidence. Not this."

"You said he was guilty. He went to jail."

"He went to jail because a jury convicted him. They thought he was guilty. We all thought he was guilty." He grabbed his jacket and glanced once more at the monitors. Everything appeared normal. "I've gotta go." He started toward the door. "I'll try to come by tomorrow night."

"Michael?"

"Yes, Dad?"

The old man's eyes, still sharp, glowed like shiny coins at the bottom of a murky fountain. "Did you make a mistake?"

The detective swallowed his resentment. His father wouldn't be the only one to ask. Had he made a mistake? The governor seemed to think so. But if Spradlin was innocent, who was guilty? After the arrest, the murders and rapes had stopped. Coincidence? Cancini didn't know if he could accept that.

"I don't know, Dad. I'm not sure."

"Then get sure."

Chapter Three

Julia Manning looked over tortoiseshell readers and peered at the digital clock. After midnight again. She shifted in the worn leather chair, pulling her legs to her chest and resting her head on her knees. It would be another sleepless night. She had no one to coax her to bed, no one to pull her close during the night. She lifted her chin. Damn him.

Holed up in her office, she felt the emptiness of the large house echo throughout the halls. She'd carved out a workspace from the smallest room, barely larger than a closet, but she loved it anyway. Behind her, a wall of shelves overflowed with books and papers. Her collection of knickknacks and pictures from childhood hung on the walls and cluttered the battered desk. It was a mess, but it was hers.

"How can you stand it in here?" Jack had asked one day, leaning in the doorway. His eyes had swept across the room to the furniture crammed in corners and the stacks of old magazines. "Doesn't it make you claustrophobic?"

"No," she'd answered honestly. It didn't and never had. Although the space was small, the window overlooking the backyard made it feel larger, and the light that shone through all day made it bright and warm. "It's comfortable."

Jack had not seemed convinced. "When Marta comes next time, you should have her clean in here." He'd waved a hand toward the junk spilling from the bookcase and said, "It smells." He'd left quickly, as though the foul odor he'd detected might follow. At the time, she'd laughed. Curled up now, she was no longer amused. Then again, blame comes in all shapes and sizes. Laying it all on Jack would be too easy. She couldn't deny she'd begun to spend more time in her office. It hadn't happened all at once, but they had drifted away from each other. Still, she wasn't the one who'd brought other people into it.

Blinking back tears, she picked up the oversized manila envelope perched on the corner of her desk. It was heavy in her hands, thick with the background research she'd requested. A story of this magnitude came with expectations and a whopping amount of history. Julia rifled through her desk for an empty spiral notebook. She pushed up her glasses and studied the first several pages, photocopies of old newspaper articles.

Little Springs Gazette
November 8

Late yesterday, the body of a young woman was found at the edge of the Thompson River. Three hunters, guests of the Powhatan Lodge, discovered the woman's remains. The deceased has been identified as Cheryl Fornak, a sopho-more at Blue Hill Christian College.

Julia skimmed the remainder of the article. She picked up her tea, sipping the lukewarm liquid. "Cheryl Fornak," she said out loud. She'd had a friend named Cheryl in college. They'd been close for a while, even sharing an apartment the first few months after graduation. They'd drifted apart when Cheryl got engaged and followed her fiancé to Texas. In her notebook, Julia wrote the number one, and next to it, the girl's name, her age, and the date of her murder. On a separate line, she wrote down the names of the police chief, the town, and the college.

She flipped through the next few pages. After the autopsy, the case had been classified as a rape and murder. Days and weeks had passed with little progress in the investigation when a second girl was found.

Little Springs Gazette
December 5

Early yesterday morning, the body of a second young woman was found nearly ten miles outside Little Springs. A truck driver headed to Blue Hill Christian College spotted the woman, identified as Theresa Daniels, lying on the shoulder of 81 South. The police and a college spokesman confirmed that the young woman was a student at the school, a senior biology major. Authorities revealed that the death would be listed as a homicide. The autopsy is expected to begin as early as today.

It has been almost one month since the body of Blue Hill Christian College sophomore Cheryl Fornak was discovered on the banks of the Thompson River. Dozens of students and local residents have been interviewed in connection with the case. However, the investigation has stalled, and the police have declined to name any suspects in Fornak's rape and murder. Police would not make a statement regarding any connection between the two deaths.

A spokesman for Blue Hill issued this statement, "We are stunned by both murders. Nothing like this has ever happened in the history of our school or in the history of this town. Our highest priority is to protect our students. In light of the second murder, we have instituted a curfew and all school buildings will be locked down by campus security at eleven P.M. each evening. Where it is possible, the faculty will reschedule evening classes."

Manny Fulton, the mayor of Little Springs, attended a town meeting at the high school last night and addressed the murders. "Chief Hobson and the rest of the men are doing their best to find out what has happened to these young women. The best thing we can do is cooperate in any way possible and help them do their jobs so we can all sleep better at night."

Julia shifted in her chair and finished her tea. Her notes were a jumble of names and dates. She drew a line connecting the names of the dead girls, adding the words, "one month." Julia returned to the articles. A third young woman was found just before Christmas break that year.

Little Springs Gazette
December 7

Shocking the town and Blue Hill Christian College, a third victim was found in the early hours of the morning by campus security. The body of Marilyn Trammel, a freshman, was spotted in a Dumpster behind the campus center. Onlookers who saw the naked body pulled from the trash bin reported seeing dark welts and dried blood. Police would not elaborate on the extent of her injuries, only indicating that the woman had probably been dead less than six hours. This murder comes forty-eight hours after the discovery of the slain Theresa Daniels and a month after that of Cheryl Fornak. Although all three victims were students at Blue Hill, there does not appear to be a connection among the three women. They did not share classes, dormitories, or sororities. One source admits that police are stumped. When asked if each of the victims had been raped and how each was murdered, the police spokesman would not comment.

Michael Hudgins, dean of student affairs, announced the immediate cancellation of all classes and exams. "In light of recent events and the ongoing investigation, we are suspending exams until after winter break. Campus will officially close at five P.M. tomorrow, and all students are expected to vacate college housing."

Julia tapped the notebook with her pen. Only two days between the second and third murders and the first body to be found on campus. The first two girls were found miles from Blue Hill.

The third was clearly a departure. Was the killer growing bolder or more reckless?

Julia rifled through the next set of articles. Although there were no murders over the Christmas break, there was also no apparent progress in solving the first three cases. The lack of an arrest was bad for the town and worse for the college. Some students—mostly girls—had applied for deferrals, opting not to return for the spring semester. The town had invoked a curfew of ten P.M. and had brought in additional police from neighboring towns. Still, the killer remained at large.

Julia dropped the pages in her lap, thinking about the dead girls from Blue Hill. No doubt their parents thought they were sending their teenage daughters away to a safe place, a college with strong Christian principles and no city crime, a place where they could grow up and get an education. But Cheryl Fornak, Theresa Daniels, and Marilyn Trammel didn't get to grow up. Head bowed, Julia continued to read. Within days of the students' return, another girl was found, and then another. Five college girls. All raped. All dead. Shivering in the air-conditioning, Julia rubbed her arms.

In an unprecedented move, the college had announced the immediate suspension of the semester. She read the statement from old papers.

The safety of our young women and all of our students is at the forefront of this decision. We cannot, in good conscience, ask the students to remain on campus until this situation has been resolved.

The FBI had been brought in after the fourth murder, spearheading the interviews with every male student enrolled at the college.

With a serial rapist and murderer on the loose, the Little Springs town council was forced to invoke "sunset" curfews. The media dubbed the murderer the Coed Killer, a name that stuck. Rumors of vendettas against the college and the town spread like wildfire. Fights broke out among locals as suspicions ran high. Businesses suffered and still, no suspects.

Julia circled the dates of all the murders. The timeline was curious. Had the killer had second thoughts after the first? Why the long gap and then increasingly smaller ones? Over the break, they'd stopped. Did that suggest the killer was also a student? After Christmas, he hadn't waited long to strike again and then again. After the semester was suspended, the murders appeared to stop. Then the police arrested Leo Spradlin.

Julia sifted through the stack of research for pictures of the victims. She placed the photos in a row. Five girls smiling at the camera, all young, all pretty. There was nothing obvious linking them, no common physical traits that she could see. According to the articles, they had different majors and different friends. Yet they'd all known Spradlin—a one-time student at the school—a fact he'd never denied. She set the pictures aside and picked up Spradlin's mug shot. He was young, barely older than college-age himself. Attractive, with dark hair, he had a strong chin and a straight nose. It wasn't hard to see how a young woman might have wanted to be alone with him. She squinted at the black and white photo that was more school portrait than mug shot. His hair was combed and he was neatly dressed. He looked directly into the camera. She held the picture closer, trying to read his expression, but saw nothing. No fear. No anger. No remorse.

Now he would be a free man. His impending release had already made a big splash across Virginia. It was a story that promised to get even bigger, fueling the death penalty debate and causing increased speculation about the governor's political agenda. The release was one thing, the aftermath another. If Spradlin wasn't the Coed Killer, who was? No newspaper could resist this story. The *Washington Herald* was no exception.

Julia turned the page in the notebook and wrote a list of questions. Rereading the short list, Julia hoped she knew what she was doing. She was not the first choice among the staff, and she knew it. Conroy was the star reporter at the paper, and he wouldn't miss this story for the world. But Jack owed her. If he wasn't going to be a great husband, the least he could do was help her rebuild the career she'd let slip from her grasp.

Now that she had the story, she had to do something with it. She picked up the picture of Spradlin again. He'd spent two decades in prison for crimes he didn't commit. Was he bitter? Angry? What would that do to a man? She shook her head, stacking the pages and sliding them back into the large envelope. Spradlin was going back to Little Springs after his release. His lawyers had announced he would hold a press conference the day of his homecoming. The town would be flooded with press, publicity-seekers, and gawkers.

Julia knew a story like this attracted all kinds. She also knew most stories die after a few days. And that was precisely her strategy. She would attend the press conference like the others and position herself for an interview. But when the others were gone, scurrying after the next headline, she would stay. She was in it for the long haul. She was in it for the story of her life.

Chapter Four

THE NIGHT WRAPPED around him like a soft blanket, comforting and soothing. He lay on top of the covers, his body still, letting the darkness seep into his thoughts, his dreams. During the day, he pushed it away, but at night, he embraced it. Eyes wide, he stared at the bare ceiling. After a while, he could see the girls again. He breathed in, nostrils flaring. The memories were all he had.

They'd fought like hell. In vain, of course, but back then, even he hadn't understood his strength or the depth of his needs. The first one, Cheryl, had been especially difficult. He thought most often of her. Swinging her arms and kicking her legs, she'd tried desperately to fight him off, but was the first to learn he was not to be underestimated. What she couldn't have known was that the fear in her eyes only fueled his desire. With each girl, his hunger grew. Their screams and their tears gave him a rush that made him forget everything but the ecstasy of the moment. When they closed their eyes to shut him out, he would jerk their heads, forcing them to watch, to see him as he really was. Since that first night, he'd fallen asleep replaying those beautiful images.

He smiled, his loins hot. It had been such a long fucking time, but now it would be different. The release was big news, and the homecoming was fast approaching. He'd been told there would be press, regional and national. A story of this magnitude was bound to stir controversy. He didn't give a shit. The words "guilt" and "innocence" were thrown around, but few understood how they worked, how closely they were intertwined. One could not exist without the other.

He closed his eyes, holding on to the image of Cheryl. He'd left her in the woods, buried under leaves and sticks, her white skin smeared with mud from the river, her blond hair spread out like a fan around her twisted head. Even dead, her eyes had looked back at him, round and gaping. Nothing could ever erase that beautiful picture. Nothing. And now he'd been given a gift. The Coed Killer would be back.

About the Author

K. L. MURPHY was born in Key West, Florida, the eldest of four children in a military family. She has worked as a freelance writer for several regional publications in Virginia, and is the author of *A Guilty Mind* and *Stay of Execution*. She lives in Richmond, Virginia, with her husband, four children, and two very large, very hairy dogs. She is currently working on her next novel, *The Last Sin*. To learn more about the Detective Cancini Mystery series or future projects, visit www.kellielarsenmurphy.com.

Discover great authors, exclusive offers, and more at hc.com.